BETH GREEN by Nicci Rae

PROLOGUE

You know, I Googled myself the other day for the first time since it happ
first few hits were almost identical, all starting with 'Will Thorn, Con Man', as though that
were my job title like Post Man or, as once was the case, Platform Assistant. Hard to
get rid of that sort of thing though and I suppose it would probably bother me if I could
be bothered to think about it for too long. To be honest, I mostly try not to think about it
at all - the press have long since got bored and moved on to more interesting stories
involving celebrities, their partners and, quite often, their nannies and I'm no longer in
touch with anyone from back then. That's really no great loss. The great thing is that I
no longer have any desire to defend myself or to try to convince anybody of anything
and, quite honestly, I'm tired of talking about it. I'm also tired of thinking about it and so
I've decided to write it down and then put it behind me and get on with my life, such as it
is. So, I have decided that this is the last time I'll talk about what happened. About
Beth.

CHAPTER 1

'Are we gonna get blown up Mister?' There was a kind of eagerness in the American
kid's voice and I had to bite and swallow the response that would have left the kid in
tears.....and lost me my job. It wasn't the kid's fault that I was in a foul mood - this was
the third time in just over a week that the sodding alarm had gone off and, this time, only
four minutes before I was due to clock off.
'Course not son, this is just a precaution because some silly sausage has left their
suitcase on the platform. I do need you and your Mum to follow that man with the
yellow vest though as we need to get everyone out as quick as possible.' With some
reluctance, the little boy and his mother did as they were told and I watched as they
joined the mass of people being herded up the stairs and out into the street. Silly
sausage indeed, I thought as I gathered up the last of the strays and directed them
toward the stairs; no doubt some tourist from a gentler country had, yet again, left their
luggage on a platform or in a corridor while they trawled the station for somebody to tell
them how to get to Oxford Circus. I always wanted to tell them not to bother - to forget
the headache-inducing crowds of shoppers on Oxford Street and to, instead, head off
to the breathtaking views on Hampstead Heath or Greenwich but they wouldn't listen; I
was just the platform guy, just there to help them get from A to B and then to be
forgotten. Mostly my job is dull, hours of standing on platforms directing harassed and

angry people to the correct platform, station, or life, rarely expecting - or getting - any thanks. Weekends are the best when there's a steady but manageable flow of human beings to take care of but weekday mornings can be hell; trying to manage a solid wall of bodies while running the tannoy to ask passengers to please, for the love of Mary, Joseph and baby Jesus, let the other passengers off first - and never mind the gap of about three inches that you're sure you can squeeze into. Still, that's only a couple of hours and then things go back to a bit of a saner pace for the rest of the day. Then came the terrorist attacks and, all of a sudden, every bag or rucksack without a human being attached to it is suspect; leading to cases, like this one, where we would have to evacuate the station and wait for the emergency services to determine that the bag contained nothing more offensive than a Princess Diana commemorative plate. As I ushered the last of the stragglers to the exit, I could still hear the American boy whining loudly and I had a brief moment of sympathy for the mother for whom the whining was no doubt a constant soundtrack to her life. The trick to an evacuation is to encourage passengers to move quickly without causing panic and I had become quite adept at it, if I do say so myself and so, within ten minutes, myself and my colleagues had a couple of hundred disgruntled and cold people standing on the pavement outside the station. Leaving the others in charge of leading the passengers to the evacuation point (a fancy name for the bit just inside the gates of Bethnal Green Gardens across the road), I trotted back down the stairs and into the station to check that everybody was out before the emergency services arrived. Most folk are fairly obedient in these situations but, every now and then, you will get somebody who has decided for themselves that it's just a false alarm and will gleefully take the opportunity to get a prime position on the platform for when their train finally arrives. Crossing the ticket area over to the escalator leading down to the Central Line, all that was on my mind was getting the all clear from the emergency services, getting all the passengers back into the station (easier than getting them out as the more impatient among them would have headed off to find a bus or taxi) and then clocking off and meeting Shandy in The Bethnal Green Star. Personally, I would have been happier in the Salmon And Ball on the corner of Cambridge Heath Road where the beer was cheaper and the punters were mostly normal blokes like myself but Shandy preferred the Star with it's trendy decor and prices to match. She'd even been talking lately about wanting us to go into town for a show and cocktails in Covent Garden. A show and cocktails in Covent Garden! I dunno where she gets this stuff from but I'll be honest, I could do without it. Walking quickly down Platform one toward the connecting corridor to Platform two, something caught my eye and I froze for a moment, alarmed, before realising that it was just a reflection of myself in one of the convex mirrors - a slightly pissed off looking thirty eight year old bloke whose dark brown hair needed cutting and I thought for about the millionth time that it was definitely time to think about looking for another job. Platform one was clear, as was Platform two and I quickly cleared the rest of the station before going back up and out to join everybody else at the evacuation point, exiting the station just as the "bomb squad" came hurtling in. As I had predicted, the group of commuters shivering in the park had lost several members in my absence and I assured them again that everything was no doubt fine and we'd be getting them on their way again in no time at all. Most of them didn't look convinced, having obviously travelled on the London Underground before, but that wasn't my problem and I left them to their muttering and wandered over to my colleague, Andy Lowe, who was having a crafty ciggie behind the tall bit of the memorial.

'Bloody waste of time,' Andy muttered as I approached and I nodded,

'Yeah, I did a walk through of the whole station and didn't see any bags or anything lying around. Imagine this won't take long,' I said with a nod in the direction of the station entrance that the police guys had just disappeared into.

'Shame,' Andy said miserably, 'If there was a bomb, I might get the rest of the day off, I'm on til seven then back at six tomorrow.' I shrugged sympathetically, knowing full well that the reason Andy was annoyed was that TFL's regulations meant that he wouldn't be able to have a few drinks when he finished.

'Nothing to look forward to,' he said as though reading my mind, 'but crap telly and an early night.' He fished another cigarette out of his packet and lit it from the butt of the one he already had, 'You and Shandy still coming for a curry on Saturday?' I nodded,

'Yep, that's a definite, Shandy's Mums having Adele for the night.' I hoped. Lately Shandy's Mum had been getting a bit tetchy about her going out too much and I always worried that it was about me, even though Shandy said it wasn't - I wanted to ask her and Adele to move in with me but that plan would be well and truly scuppered if I didn't have her Mum on board.

'You asked her to move in yet?' Andy asked, doing his spooky mind-reading thing again and I shook my head,

'Not yet, building up to it you know?' He sniffed and examined the glowing end of his fag,

'Better man than me, taking on another bloke's kid and that,' he said and I laughed.

'Doesn't bother me - and it's not like I can ask her to leave Adele behind is it?' The thought had crossed my mind though. I'll admit that the prospect of playing Dad did make me more than a little bit nervous - I was already anticipating the inevitable 'You're not my Dad' tantrums whenever I told the stubborn four year old to do something that she didn't want to and the thought wasn't a happy one. Before I could brood further on my impending parenthood there was a clatter of equipment and heavy duty boots from across the road and the emergency guys re-emerged from the station and headed for their truck parked across the road, except for their leader who we watched approach our Manager.

'All clear,' he grunted in a heavy Scottish accent, 'I'll put my report through but you can go back in.'

'Thanks,'Jim called but our action hero was already turning away and heading toward the truck so he gestured to Andy and myself to make a start and, feeling magnanimous, I turned to Andy and said, 'You finish your ciggie mate, I'll do another walk through then call you to give you the nod to get them all back in.'

'Thanks Will, you're a star and,' he shuffled awkwardly, 'like, no offence meant about Adele and all that.'

'None taken,' I grinned, grateful that he hadn't been able to read my mind that last time, and I headed back toward the station, checking my phone as I went. I had a text from Shandy asking what time to meet at the pub and I hurriedly fired off a reply as I trotted once again into the station. 'Are we gonna get blown up Mister?' The American kid's words returned to me as I walked briskly across the ticket area and I glanced around uneasily, the rogue thought that the bomb squad might have missed something running through my mind. Although I shook the thought off easily enough, I couldn't help but wonder what would happen if that were the case and the bomb chose that precise moment to go off - as the sole victim, would I be the hero who put his passengers safety before his own or, the idiot who had the bad luck to be the one to do a final walk-through? Don't get me wrong, I had absolutely no desire to be a hero - I was an entirely ordinary bloke living an entirely ordinary life and that suited me just fine; no excitement means no drama and I was certainly happy enough with that! Quickly clearing platform one, I moved through the corridor to platform two, my eyes sweeping the platform and then the track where the only activity was a rat who, startled by my presence, ducked under one of the rails and disappeared. Satisfied that all was as it should be, I was about to radio Andy to tell him to start bringing the passengers back in when I heard it; a sound that would have been drowned on a normal day by the hubub of the crowd on the platform - or on a day like this by the clatter of the bomb squad's boots and equipment - but there, in the silence of an empty platform in an empty station, I heard it. Having seen the empty platform with my own eyes, my brain immediately tried to dismiss the sound as the hum of the wind struggling it's way through the tunnel or the distress of the rat as it fled its perceived danger but these assurances were shot down as I recognised the sound for what it was - the whimper of a frightened child.

CHAPTER 2

For a moment, I froze. 'What the hell?' I hadn't realised that I'd said it out loud until I heard a tiny gasp in response and immediately my inertia lifted 'Hello?' The word echoed in the empty space but I still heard the second gasp when it came and I looked around, frantically trying to get a bead on where the noise was coming from. 'Where are you?' I called softly, well aware that yelling was likely to frighten whoever it was even more and prod them back into silence. 'It's OK,' I added, 'I'm not going to hurt you.' I was standing around the middle of the platform near the Help Station and I suddenly felt a mad urge to press the button and demand assistance even though I knew that there would be nobody on the other end as they were all standing across the road in the cold so, instead, I began to walk quietly toward the end of the platform from where the next train would emerge - whenever that might be. Impossible as it was, and despite the evidence in front of my eyes, there was somebody here and I slowed as I approached the mouth of the tunnel. I'll be honest; as I made my way past the tube map and a poster advertising something starring Cate Blanchett, my main thought was that somebody was going to get it in the neck for this and I was really really hoping that it wasn't going to be me. My second thought was that I was going to have to revise the ETA that I had just texted to Shandy. 'Where are you?' I called a second or two before the question became unnecessary and I picked up my pace as I spotted the huddled figure crammed onto the narrow ledge just inside the mouth of the tunnel. 'I'm not going to hurt you,' I repeated as I approached, 'but we need to get you out of there, it's not safe.' By now, I was inches away and my heart sank as I watched the figure recoil and move a little further into the tunnel along the ledge. 'No no, can you move toward me, this way?' I asked, already knowing the answer; the child was petrified and the only way he or she was coming out of the tunnel was if I went in after them. I had just stepped onto the ledge when my radio gave a squawk and I heard Andy enquiring as to just what the fuck was taking so long, causing the child to squeal and shift further still along the ledge. 'Sorry, sorry,' I whispered urgently, 'I'm turning it off OK, it's just us here alright?' I took an experimental step along the ledge which felt perilously narrow underneath my size twelves but, to my relief, the child stayed put. 'That's the way,' I soothed, 'we'll soon have you out of this nasty dark tunnel, won't we eh?' I took another step and still the kid didn't move so I took another at which point he or she slid down the wall into a sitting position, skinny legs dangling over the track. When I'd I re-entered the station, I had almost been able to taste my first beer of the evening but now my mouth was full of the metallic taste of fear, for myself and for this kid who had somehow managed to dodge the attention of all of the station staff and the emergency services. 'Nearly there,' I said in an absurdly jolly voice, 'soon have you out of here.' Covering the last few inches between us, I reached out, balancing precariously on the ledge and awkwardly scooped the child up, all the while expecting him or her to start fighting and tip us both over on to the track but it was like carrying a rag doll, limp and as light as a feather. Shuffling backwards, I moved slowly, all the while crooning nonsense words to the child in my arms. 'Not far now," I said, still using the insane children's TV presenter voice, 'I bet your Mum's going frantic by now, eh? She's gonna be very happy to see you!' Because, of course, that is exactly what I thought was going to be the case - I would take the kid back upstairs and out of the station where she would be reunited with the mother who, being a slightly sillier sausage than the imaginary careless tourists, had left on the platform not a tattered old case but a different kind of baggage altogether. There would follow that peculiar mixture of anger and relief that only a very scared parent can express and then the rest of the of the impatient passengers would be shepherded back into the station and it would all be over barring the paperwork. Except, a little voice in my head, piped up, there hadn't been any distraught parents outside in the evac zone had there? - No mother wailing that the precious fruit of her loins was missing and no angry father who, having taken his eye off the ball, was taking his guilt out on the station staff. Of course there was another explanation - had to be. As I've said, I don't know that much about parenting but I do know that people don't lose their kids and just go "That's a pain, I'll have to cancel it and get another one". No, there'd be tears and police and panicked talk of abduction and of the sort of blokes whose bits should have been chopped off at birth. 'That's it,' I said, placing the girl finally, safely, onto the platform, 'We're gonna get you back to your Mum now, can you remember where she was?' The girl just stared at me and I hunkered down so that our faces were level, 'Can you tell me where you saw your Mum?' When the kid still continued to gaze at me I started to wonder if she was foreign - God knows most people in London these days are - and I stared back at her helplessly, taking in her straggly muck-stained blonde hair and tatty dress that looked like it was once a perky pink thing with a dropped waist but which now clung damp and grimy to her tiny frame. I guessed that she was about Adele's age, maybe a year or so more but the huge blue eyes staring out of her filthy face made her seem older. I reached out to take her hand and she flinched before, seemingly, remembering that I was one of the good guys - or claimed to be at least, and she tentatively moved toward me and took my hand, all the while never taking her eyes from my face. I tried again to wheedle some information out of her as I began to lead her along the platform toward the exit corridor, 'Do you speak English, sweetheart? Can you understand what I'm saying?' Nothing. 'Is there anything you want to ask me?'

'What the fuck are you up to Will?' The disembodied voice belonged not to the possibly foreign, possibly mute, possibly just plain ignorant child but to Andy who, it seemed, had decided to come and find out what was taking so long and the girl pressed herself into the side of my leg at the sound of his none too dulcet tones,

'It's OK,' I said, looking down at the top of her head, 'that's just Andy, he'll help us find your Mum and then we can get you cleaned up.'

'You having a wank on company time or something mate?' I cringed as the girl stared fearfully towards the middle corridor and the direction of Andy's voice, 'We've got trains backed up to Holborn Will, we need to get all these punters back into the station pronto or we're gonna have a ton of......Holy Fuck!' Andy had finally traversed the corridor which now spilled him out onto the platform and he was standing at the entrance staring at me and the kid with his mouth open.

'Firstly,' I said quietly, 'I'm not actually on company time as my shift finished about twelve minutes ago and, secondly,' I cocked my head toward the girl, 'we've got a slightly bigger problem than trains "held at a red signal" at Holborn.'

'Where the bloody hell's she come from?' Andy spluttered and I shrugged,

'That's what I've been trying to find out - in more ways than one; I found her just inside the tunnel and she hasn't said a word since.'

'Hello Love!' Andy said in a weird, high pitched voice which I suppose was his version of my Kid's TV Presenter Voice and I briefly wondered if mine sounded as ridiculous as his did, 'What's your name then?' The girl glanced at him briefly and then recommenced her efforts to graft herself onto my right thigh and I nudged her gently forward toward the exit corridor - we needed to get her back to her Mum or Dad who were, demonstrably, not lurking on Platform one (or anywhere else the traitorous voice in my head added) so there was no reason to prolong the misery of the passengers any more than necessary.

'So who is she?' Andy asked as we trudged through the corridor that led to the escalator,

'I don't know.'

'How come The A Team didn't see her when they were crashing about down here?' he asked as we made our painstaking way up the temporarily stilled escalator,

'I don't know.'

'So,' he persisted, slightly out of breath and I made a mental note to tell him, for maybe the millionth time, to cut back on the fags, 'do we even know that she's got a Mum or Dad waiting for her?' I stopped at the top of the escalator, slightly out of breath myself, 'Andy, mate, do you remember the bit where I mentioned that the kid hasn't said a bloody word since I found her in the tunnel? I don't know the answers to any of that but she's got to have a Mum or Dad cos kids just do have those things and the sooner we find hers, the sooner I can get out of here and into the pub.'

'I was just saying,' Andy continued, sounding slightly hurt, 'that nobody out there in the evac zone was going on about being light a kid or two - bit weird, no?' It was the same thought that I'd had only minutes before and hearing it coming from somebody else made me feel uneasy for reasons I couldn't explain; maybe it was just that hearing my own thoughts repeated back to me made them real or maybe just because it was so damn weird but, whatever the reason, the tiled walls of the station seemed to close in on me as we arrived at the main concourse and then made our way outside where a light but cold rain had started to fall on the passengers still crowded miserably together across the road. At the sight of all those people, the kid froze and grabbed onto my leg with the hand that wasn't holding mine and I smiled down at her, 'Don't worry love, we'll go and find your Mum now, it's gonna be alright.' Of course, at the the time I didn't know if that was true or not, it was just something you said, or assumed. Hoped.

CHAPTER 3

'What? You've got a kid? What are you on about Will?' I was standing outside the Station Manager's office, talking to Shandy on my mobile as I tried to dodge the frenzied influx of passengers eager to entomb themselves once more in the network of underground tunnels beneath us.

'No, well, it's complicated,' I said hurriedly, 'I can't explain now but I don't think I'm gonna be able to make it to the pub or, at least, not for another hour or so.'

'Sorry mate,' I turned awkwardly and glared daggers at the back of the bloke who had just run over my foot with his wheelie suitcase and swore under my breath,

'What? Will, are you still at the station?' Dragging my attention back to an increasingly pissed-off sounding Shandy, I grunted,

'Yeah, that's what I've been saying. Look, I dunno what time I'm gonna get out of here but I'll give you a buzz when I'm on my way.' She wasn't happy and I knew just exactly how she felt - after all, I was the one stuck in this mess and I wasn't exactly ecstatic about the idea of another (unpaid) hour in the place but I knew I'd end up apologising anyway - to Shandy and to her Mum who had no doubt had to shelve her plans to suck up the best part of a bottle of Cabernet whilst watching X Factor in order to spend quality time with her grand-daughter. I pushed open the door to the manager's office and went back inside. The Manager, Jim, was standing with his back to the window and the kid was sitting in his tatty TFL-issue chair, swinging her legs and staring at the phone on his desk. After bringing the girl outside, Andy and I had polled the impatient passengers in the evac zone but nobody remembered seeing or hearing anyone who had lost a kid and, to be honest, we were lucky to get a shrug and a 'no, sorry,' from most of them as their body language screamed irritation at the fact that we were further delaying their journey to work, home or the pub by selfishly trying to reunite some kid with its parent. Having exhausted the other options, Jim had reluctantly phoned the police who were now hunkered down in front of the little girl who was no chattier than she had been down in the tunnel.

'There's nothing to be scared of love,' the female officer said for the second time, 'we just need you to tell us your name so that we can find your mummy for you - I bet she's missing you!' If the girl heard her, she wasn't letting on as she continued to stare at the phone which was plastic, ordinary and probably a hot-bed of bacteria from the spit of everyone who had used it to find out why a train was delayed, why a passenger's umbrella wasn't in Lost Property and why the hell it's so difficult to get uniforms delivered on time. 'I know what,' the officer continued gamely, 'Let's play a game - I'll say some names and you tell me if I guess it right. Are you Abigail?' No response from the kid. 'No? Course not, I'm Abigail! Are you Agnes? Alice? Alexandra?' She didn't look like an Abigail, was my first thought as I glanced at the officer's sturdy build and sensible short haircut. My second was that I really hoped that I wasn't still there by the time she got to Zoe. As the police woman continued reciting names at the unresponsive child, her colleague, John, turned to me with a sigh, 'Sorry to make you go over this again Mr Thorn, but could you run through for me once more, just exactly what happened from the moment this bomb scare went off?'

'It wasn't really a bomb scare,' I sighed, 'just an evacuation alarm, they happen.....well, never mind.' I ran through what I remembered from the alarm going off to the point where I brought the mostly inert kid upstairs into the station and then here to Jim's office. It seemed pretty pointless but I assumed that the officer was hoping to glimpse a clue to the situation from my clueless description and so I did my best to remember as many details as possible. By the time I'd finished, Abigail "call me Abby" had reached Deborah and the kid still hadn't so much as looked at her, let alone responded with a name, address and postcode and I could see my simple dream of a couple of pints of Stella and a couple of hours with Shandy retreating further into the distance. Andy had been sent to go through the station and surroundings again just in case the distraught parent had maybe taken time out to grab a coffee or get a key cut before returning to their search but, as I glanced at the girl's image on the security monitor I realised miserably that, in my head, I was already seeing her on TV on the evening news. The police officers had cleaned her up as best they could in the station toilets and she was now wearing a TFL shirt that was ludicrously large on her but better than the grimy and tattered dress that she'd been wearing when I found her. Having had a bit of a wash, I could now see that her hair was that fine, pale blonde that only little kids have and I remember thinking that, in a few years time, it would fade to a much more ordinary shade. As Abigail continued throwing names at the kid, I was shifting awkwardly from foot to foot, wondering what the etiquette was for extracting myself from the equation - it wasn't that I didn't care about the girl; I did, or at least, I felt sorry for her but, other than the fact that I was the one who found her, it was really none of my business and, having told the officers everything I could, I just didn't see what could be gained by my hanging around.

'So,' I began tentatively, interrupting Abby's flow around about the Elizabeth mark, 'Do you still, you know, need me here?' Abby paused in her mad litany of names - which I think was a relief to all of us, including the kid - and glanced at her colleague before looking back to me,

'Oh, sorry Mr Thorn, no, you can go. Do we have your contact details just in case?' I thought I sensed disapproval in her tone but that could just have been a vague sense of guilt at my eagerness to split the scene.

'Yes, I gave them to John here, my mobile's on there if you need to get hold of me for anything.' I turned and pushed the door release button and it was just as I was reaching for the door handle that we discovered that the kid wasn't foreign and most definitely was not mute. As I grabbed for the door, a big part of me was already walking down Bethnal Green Road, busily working out how to redeem myself with Shandy and so I didn't really register the girl's voice until I felt a hand grab the leg of my trousers, painfully grabbing a chunk of flesh at the same time. I belatedly realised that the first word she'd yelled was 'No,' and I stopped in my tracks and turned round. Her little face was twisted in genuine anguish and I let go of the door and stepped away from it with the kid still clutching my pants, her eyes never leaving mine as I let her "lead" me back to my original position. Once I was stood roughly where I had been a few seconds before, she seemed to calm down a bit and I suppressed a sigh - if the kid was gonna kick off every time I tried to leave, this was going to be a very long night; and one that would no doubt find me single at the end of it. Again, it wasn't that I didn't care but she wasn't my kid - I was already apprehensive about becoming pseudo-parent to Shandy's daughter and I really didn't need any further complications in my life. I know how selfish that sounds but, as I said, all I really wanted was a quiet life which, when you think about it, isn't really that much to ask for, is it? Once she realised that I wasn't going to leave (yet), not-Alice and not-Deborah shuffled back to her chair and sat down before staring once again at the phone and Officer Abby resumed her name game seeing as how it had been working so well before.

'How long does it normally take?' I interrupted and Abby gave me a questioning look, 'You know, to find out who a kid belongs to?' I thought it was a reasonable question but the way the two officers exchanged a glance told me I could be wrong - it had happened before.

'Why? Got a hot date have you?' Abby asked and I wondered if Andy had been teaching her his freaky mind-reading trick as the man himself slipped quietly into the room and stood by the door, looking from Abby to myself and then back again like a spectator at a tennis match and I regretted forgetting to bring the champagne and strawberries.

'Well, sort of,' I admitted, 'but that wasn't why I was asking, I was just thinking about the kid.' It sounded insincere even to my own ears and I wished I hadn't asked but wishes don't un-break dishes as my Nanna used to say. As though to prove that I wasn't desperate to rush off (even though I was, in fact, desperate to rush off), I moved closer to the kid and it was then that I saw that it wasn't the phone that she was staring at but a few photographs of the station taken from outside and from the steps. The pictures had been taken a few days before for use in some kind of article for the TFL website and, as well as a couple of moody shots showing the Bethnal Green London Underground roundel there was a cheesy image of Jim standing on the station steps grinning inanely and it was this picture that seemed to be holding the girl captivated. Without knowing that I was going to do it, I reached over and gently pushed the photograph of Jim to the side of the desk and the girl's eyes followed - and the same when I pushed it back again.

'That's Jim,' I said needlessly, 'he's just here!' I beckoned Jim over to the desk where he stood looking awkward but the girl never took her eyes off the photograph. 'Look,' I tried again, pointing first to Jim and then to the picture, although the kid had surely seen a photograph before, 'It's Jim here - and in the photo!' Instead of acknowledging my brilliant observation, the girl simply pulled the picture closer to herself, letting it droop over the edge of the desk so that only the top of Jim's bald head and the station steps were visible and, as she gazed at the picture, she whispered something to herself. My spirits lifted as I realised that she was talking and I moved closer, 'What was that, sweetheart, can you speak up a bit?' Without looking at me, she again whispered something that sounded like pop cushion and, frustrated, I shook my head, 'Once more love?'

'Stop pushing,'

'What do you.......' Suddenly, the girl swung toward me, eyes streaming and spit flying from her mouth as she yelled 'Stop pushing, Stop pushing STOP PUSHING!!'

'Pack it in!', Jim hissed, sounding distressed, 'she wants us to stop bugging her!'

'STOP PUSHING!' the girl screamed, now clutching the photograph so tightly that her tiny fingernails punched through it,

'Can't we stop now?' Jim wheedled, 'we're upsetting her.'

'No!' Andy's voice was hoarse and, as he inched toward the desk, he was paler than I'd ever seen him - and I'd seen him through a good few Jager bomb hangovers since I'd known him.

'Andy, you alright, what.........' Ignoring me, he crouched down beside the girl's chair and jabbed a finger at the photograph she was holding,

'She's not looking at Jim, see?' he said in a voice that I barely recognised, 'she's looking at the steps.' He glanced up at me, '*Those* steps!'

CHAPTER 4

'Let's all just calm down shall we?' Officer John had started to look like he was wishing that he'd been called out to the latest domestic in Tower Hamlets or possibly a nice little pile up on the A1209 as he stood and raised a hand. The girl had gone quiet again but, to be honest, I didn't think that was down to John's command; it was more like her little outburst had exhausted her and she needed to regroup. Of course I knew what Andy was getting at - we all did; you don't work in a station like ours without hearing your fair share of ghost stories and urban myths but I was tired and more than a bit keen to be anywhere but that bloody office. All those annoying safety posters tell us that a little patience won't hurt us but, I'll be honest, I wasn't really feeling that particular virtue just then.

'Really not helping Andy,' I snapped into the temporary silence of the room, 'I suppose if we were a bit further West and she was holding a suitcase, you'd decide she was Paddington sodding Bear!' There was a squawk from Officer Abby's radio and I was expecting the kid to freak out again like she did when mine went off but she didn't even flinch, whatever storm that had just visited, had passed for the moment. In the quiet of the room, we heard the voice on the other end of the radio spout a load of codey sounding things that the officers seemed to understand although they sounded like gobbledygook to me - of course we have our own codes on the Underground but ours are a little bit more basic - such as 'Assistance needed on platform one regarding customer concern', meaning "pissed up wide boy moonwalking a bit too close to the yellow line for anybody's comfort" and so on. The next words from Abby's radio were, however, a lot less ambiguous and we all held our breath as we heard the words 'Child reported missing from the City View Hotel.' The City View is a flea pit above a chip shop just a few doors down from the station - not quite the Ritz, it's used most frequently for the kind of liaisons that pay by the half hour and I glanced at the girl with pity, wondering if she was the unfortunate offspring of one of the ladies of the night, evening or afternoon who did business there. Forgive me if that sounds harsh - my Nana always used to say that only God can judge but, quite frankly, he wasn't around and he most definitely hadn't just pulled a nine til six with unpaid overtime.

Still, this was hopeful, and I remember thinking that I might make it to the Star after all (not that I had a one-track mind or anything but you try standing on a draughty platform for eight hours and you'll understand my eagerness to get away). I could see my relief mirrored in Jim and Andy's faces as Officer John responded to his radio with more insensible code words and then asked for a description of the missing kid. As we all waited with breath that was more than a little bit bated, I guessed that we had our explanation - there was no moaning parent in the evac zone because the parent in question was currently engaged in a different kind of moaning altogether and soon the girl would be child services problem and we could all get back to our evening, or what was left of it. I had no idea what would happen to the kid once the authorities stepped in but I hazarded a guess that it would probably be an improvement on the hotel whose view of the City included the Bethnal Green Library, a bunch of council flats and maybe, on a clear day, a vague outline of the Shard. I'd been in there once, helping a bewildered tourist carry her bags and, I'm no snob but, I'd rather sleep on a bench in

Bethnal Green Gardens than in that place. Having cheered up considerably since the interruption by the police radio, I once again started mentally preparing to make good my escape and so it was a crushing disappointment when the radio squawked again and we heard the faceless police dispatcher describe the missing kid as twelve, black and male. Unless this was some kind of clever police code, our gal wasn't the kid missing from the East End's version of the Bates Motel and I sighed and yawned at the same time, earning myself a pointed look from Officer Abby. I'm ashamed to say that, at that point, I had very little sympathy for either the missing black boy or our own Jane Doe - and the fact that I was starting to think about her as '*Our* Jane Doe' only served to compound my misery. With a sigh, Officer Abby informed the radio that it was a negative on visual identification and spouted some more codey stuff which turned out to be a request for the CPS to attend our little party. Throughout all of this, the kid had stayed quiet and still, ignoring the colouring book that Jim had magicked up from somewhere and even ignoring the photograph that had so fascinated her only minutes before.

'OK if we wait in here until Child Protection gets here?' Officer John asked and Jim shrugged,

'Be my guest, any idea how long they might be?'

'Hard to say, no more than an hour probably but,' the Officer's face brightened as he spotted Jim's mini kettle in a little corner nook, 'in the meantime, a cup of tea would be lovely!'

'No problem,' Jim said and flicked a hand from the kettle to Andy who looked like he couldn't decide whether he was miffed at being elected tea lady or pleased to be delaying his return to the platform chaos that always follows an evacuation. Having not moved for the best part of five minutes, the kid now swivelled in her chair to watch as Andy began clattering about with cups and spoons and I thought it was probably a nice change from staring at the picture of Jim as she even laughed as Andy tentatively sniffed at the contents of the little plastic bottle of milk before making a 'good enough' face and sloshing it into the waiting cups. Evidently the milk was fresh enough for tea for the police officers but not for the kid to drink as Andy then began to rummage around inside the little fridge before finally emerging with one of those kids juice boxes and handing it to the girl who looked at it like she'd never seen one before. 'So', I began hesitantly, 'what will happen to her once, you know, the child protection people get here?'

'Well, there's a process,' Officer Abby said, her expression suggesting that the process was not filled with fun things and happy endings, 'but, ultimately, if we can't find any family or allocated care-giver, she'll most probably end up in the foster system unless somebody comes forward to apply for temporary custody but,' she added hastily as she saw the girl glance in her direction, 'I'm sure that's not going to happen as I'm sure that we'll find this little one's Mum sooner rather than later.' Despite the two sures in one sentence, her face said that she was anything but and I felt a stab of sympathy for the girl - even having a mum who does business on her back in The City View would be better than having none at all and I wondered what sort of woman would leave a little kid to wander round the East End by herself. My Nan always said that being a mother was the best job in the world but this girl's Mum would clearly not agree.

'Anyway,' Andy chipped in as he handed out equally chipped mugs of tea, 'She's cute, somebody'll probably adopt her won't they?' and then 'What?' as I gave him a warning look, 'I was just saying!' If the girl understood what was being said, she didn't seem overly alarmed by it as her attention had returned to her juice box and she stared, fascinated, at the little straw attached to the carton before yanking it off and turning it over in her tiny hands. Impossible as it was, she didn't seem to know quite what to make of it and so, after a minute or so, I gently took it out of her hand, unwrapped it and stabbed the pointy end of the straw into the hole in the carton, at which point she started sucking eagerly - and noisily - at the contents.

'Like the officer says,' I said glaring at Andy, 'We'll find her Mum soon and she'll be off home.' Andy shrugged and slurped his tea and I picked up my own mug which had been in Jim's office more years than I care to remember and would probably still be there long after I'd left - even if that happy day was my retirement! It was a nasty old thing, stained and chipped but the girl stared at it, her juice box forgotten as she reached out a hand to touch the picture on the yellowed ceramic,

'Careful, that's hot,' I warned but she didn't seem to hear me as her little finger traced the photograph, a look of puzzled wonder on her face and she looked up at me questioningly as she whispered almost to herself,

'Old. So old!' I glanced down at the mug in my hand and couldn't help but agree,

'It certainly is!' I said, gently moving her hand away from the hot cup, 'maybe Father Christmas'll bring me a new one next month eh?' I suppose I was hoping that the mention of Santa might prod her into talking some more - all kids get excited about Christmas don't they? But it was like she didn't hear me as, again, she reached out to touch the mug, repeating,

'So old?' but this time it was a question and I glanced down again at the cup and then, helplessly, at the two police officers as I realised that she wasn't referring to the mug itself but to the photograph on it; a photograph of the Queen taken specially for the Jubilee in 1977.

CHAPTER 5

Over the years, the mug had become a bit of a standing joke at the station - Given to me by my Nana when I was a kid, it was handed over with the solemn reverence of a treasured heirloom, the one item that she could seemingly spare from her not insubstantial collection of Royal memorabilia and tat. After she passed, most of her stuff was packed away into my parents loft, probably never to be looked at again but the mug had travelled with me to Uni and then here to the station where it had survived fourteen years of indifferent washing and clumsy handling. The picture on the mug was one that I'm sure you're familiar with - a photo of Her Maj when her hair was still dark (although the style hasn't changed much), with her crown and expensive stick - at the time it was reproduced on any number of cups, plates, t.shirts and, of course stamps, and it was impossible for me to believe that the kid hadn't seen it before but that was certainly the impression that she was giving as she continued to stare at the mug in my hand.

'So old. Why?' Although the kid was nothing to do with me, I didn't like to see her upset and so, if I'd known what Andy was about to do I would have stopped him but, by the time I realised what he was up to it was too late - as the girl continued to focus on the cup, Andy took a ten pound note out of his pocket and slid it onto the table in front of the girl. For a moment, it was as though she didn't even notice it - or Andy - but then she dragged her attention away from my cup and glanced at the note, indifferently at first but then a frown creased her features as she picked it up and pulled it closer to her face to inspect it. God knows I don't see enough of them myself but, I couldn't for the life of me see what was so fascinating about the note that, these days, would barely buy you a pint and a bag of chips. Still the kid stared intently at it for what seemed like ages before slowly dragging her eyes back to my cup and then back to the note which had on it a picture of Old Betty taken in her usual pose but this time sometime in her fifties.

'Lies.' the kid whispered, still looking back and forth between the two Queens, 'So old. Not true.'

'What do you mean...?' I began and then stopped as the girl's gaze swivelled in my direction,

'LIES!' Suddenly and shockingly, she tore the note in half, stuffing it inside my still full cup before knocking that out of my hand where it fell to the floor and broke into three thick pieces. Sorry Nana. For a moment there was complete silence in the room as the tea that was still steaming spread and then sank into the cheap carpet that was already stiff from all of the cups of tea, takeaways and fizzy drinks that had been spilt on it previously (house-keeping's a fairly low priority in a job where you spend your days trying to stop passengers from killing each other and, on occasion, themselves - nothing says delay better than a punter chucking themselves in front of a rush hour train).

'Shit,' I muttered as I grabbed a manky old tea-towel from the sink and attempted to damage-control the mess but the kid was oblivious as she sat, fists clenched and eyes closed as though to block out whatever it was that had upset her. God help me, it was about then that I remember wishing that Child Services would bloody hurry up - the kid was clearly unhinged and, although I was fairly sure by that point that my evening was beyond salvaging, I could still look forward to a couple of cans in front of the telly, if nothing else. As though summoned by my thought processes, there was a squawk from my radio then, after a couple of seconds of static, I heard,

'Will, there's someone to see you at the ticket office.' I frowned at the radio, confused as to why the authorities would be asking for me rather than the police officers then I pushed the button and spoke into the mouthpiece, glancing at the officers as I did,

'Thanks Sharon, if it's Child Services, they can just come straight through to Jim's office.' There was a pause followed by another squawk and then,

'I dunno what you're on about Will but it's a woman and she asked for you.' As it was clear that Sharon was not going to be escorting our guest to the office any time soon, I glanced apologetically at the two police officers before standing, noticing as I did that there was an uncomfortable damp patch on my trousers from where the tea had splashed, and I headed for the door, confident that there was a chance that this day was finally coming to an end. I'd got no further than a step or two before the girl was out of her seat, a wordless shriek of outrage issuing from her as she saw that I meant to leave the room but I continued toward the door, working on the assumption that she would either accept the situation or the officers would step in and distract her. Neither of those things happened and the kid's protest increased in volume with every inch closer to the door I got until her piercing shrieks could, I discovered later, be heard not just outside of the office but throughout the entire ticket area.

'Maybe it would be best if you stayed here for the moment, Mr Thorn,' Abigail said without a trace of sarcasm and I pulled a face,

'You think?' I had, of course, reached this startling conclusion all by myself and it did nothing to improve my mood - an hour ago, I had been minutes away from a couple of cold ones followed by maybe a bit of hot stuff with Shandy and now, through no fault of my own, I was stuck in a damp office with cold wet tea stuck to one leg and a small child stuck to the other. With a sigh, I led the kid back to her chair once more whilst hitting the button on my radio that would allow me to communicate again with the lovely Sharon.

'Sharon, I'm not going to be able to come through to the ticket office just now, we've got a bit of a situation here.'

'Well, she said she wants to see you,' came the slightly petulant reply and I bit back a sarky comment before replying,

'I know, you said, but I'm kind of stuck here for the moment. Can you bring whoever it is through to Jim's office for me?' There was a pause while Sharon considered my audacious request and then,

'No, we're too short-staffed as Andy's gone AWOL as well.'

'He's not AWOL, he's in here too,' I replied, deciding to ignore her implication that I, too, was AWOL - I was starting to get a headache and decided that explaining, once again, that I was now off duty would sound perilously close to whining.

'Thanks Sharon,' I muttered before putting the radio down onto the table with a clunk. I glanced at Andy who was eyeing the mess on the floor and, in particular, his torn and sodden ten pound note, 'Serves you right,' I snapped at him and he shrugged,

'S'Ok, I might be able to salvage it.' As though to prove this, he reached down and delicately picked up the soggy mess and placed the pieces on the radiator, presumably in order to dry them before attempting to stick them back together. Bit stupid but the kid seemed intrigued as she watched him and, at that point, I was grateful for anything that took her attention away from me for a minute or two. There was a chirp as Officer John's phone received a text and I glanced at him hopefully, ready to be told that the cavalry, or in this case, Child Services, were on their way but he shook his head apologetically after quickly reading the message,

'The wife,' he explained sounding slightly embarrassed whilst simultaneously managing to wedge in a "women eh?" tone earning himself a dirty look from his colleague. Before he could elaborate and, maybe throw in a mother-in-law joke for good measure, I started again toward the door, confident that, if my visitor was who I thought it was, she wouldn't be going away any time soon.

CHAPTER 6

I first met Shandia 'Shandy' Washington about two years ago but we'd only been going out for about a year or so. The first time I saw her - or the first time that I remember seeing her - was a filthy September day when I was on the early shift. It had been raining for about a week solid without the slightest sign of let-up and the station floors were a constant hazard with puddles and slicks of mucky water covering practically every inch of the place. Despite the plastic signs warning people about the wet floors, we still had at least a dozen passengers a day going arse over tit as they ignored the warnings in their rush to catch the seven oh three, or the seven oh six or the seven oh what the hell ! On that particular morning, I had just run through the station with a dry mop in an attempt to keep the carnage to a minimum when I saw her. Hurrying down the steps of the station into the concourse, her face was set in an expression of determination, her focus on the board advertising our daily specials such as the seven oh nine to Ealing Broadway until all of a sudden, she caught a wet patch that I had missed and her expression changed to shock as her foot shot out from beneath her. With reflexes that I'd never possessed before - or since, for that matter, I had covered the short distance between us and grabbed her round the waist before her other foot could join in the fun and tip her onto the filthy floor. She didn't even spill her coffee.

After that, I noticed her all the time; hard not to really as, every time she came through the station she would point her dazzling smile in my direction with a little wave.

Despite the smiles and waves and the occasional cheeky comment, it still took me about a year to ask her out and then another month or so before she told me about Adele but by then it was too late; I was hooked. With skin the colour of an extra-shot latte and mad corkscrew curls, she oozed exotic sophistication - until, that is, she opened her mouth and let forth an accent that was pure Tower Hamlets with the dirtiest laugh that I had ever heard. When she told me, over a cheeky Nandos, that she had a daughter the floodgates were opened and I got to hear the whole sordid story. Having left school with quite a bit better than average GCSEs, she had delayed college for a few years to help look after her Dad, a fruit and veg man with cancer who has since moved on to that great produce stall in the sky. By the time she made it to college, it was Hackney Community College rather than the hallowed grounds of Oxford, Cambridge or even Loughborough that she had always dreamed of and, at the age of twenty four, she was a realist, deciding to study something that might, reasonably, lead to a half decent job rather than the political courses that her sixteen year old self had had her heart set on. She ended up on a teacher training course. Although it may not have been the escape that she'd dreamed of, she'd thrown herself into her studies, buoyed by the passionate encouragement of her tutor, a married forty year old whose passions, it turned out, were based on something a little more base than an interest in Shandia's education. Within a few months, Shandy was expecting - and expecting nothing from her tutor; which was lucky for her as that was exactly what she got. Panicked by the thought of losing both his job and his wife and kids, the tutor, one Alistair Knox, applied and got a transfer to the University of Westminster in Harrow and deftly moved his family to the far end of the Metropolitan Line, effectively removing himself from the line of Shandy's fire and any responsibility towards Adele. Unwilling to drag herself, and her reputation, through the courts, Shandy quietly continued with her studies for as long as she was able, picking them up again after Adele was born, and forced herself, as far as was possible, to forget all about Alistair Knox and his unorthodox curriculum just like he'd managed to forget about them. These days, Shandy was working part time as a teaching assistant in Bonner Primary School, primarily because she could walk there from her Mum's place which was a flat in one of the squat little blocks across the park by the library and would, I'd already figured out, be just a reasonably short bus ride from my place in Hackney. I never kidded myself that I'd 'saved' Shandia - nothing quite that gallant - but I did hope that our relationship would offer a kind of stability that had been missing from her life and get her away from her Mum whose constant disappointment with life tended to rub off on both Shandy and Adele. In the short time that we'd been together, Shandy's Mum had taken great pleasure in savaging every aspect of my shortcomings from my 'ordinary' job to the fact that I was still renting a flat at thirty eight but I persevered in the hope that I might grow on her - at times though I worried that I was using the wrong kind of fertiliser as that growth could be described, at best, as slow.

Now that I look back on it, I suppose our relationship was a little uneven - whether it was an inheritance of her mother's discontent or just being ground down by life as a single mother, Shandy could be difficult to please and appease and I spent a lot of our time together tying myself in knots trying to keep her happy - to make sure that I didn't break any of the ever-evolving rules; like that particular day when I had failed to meet her at the appointed place at the appointed time and so, there she was at the station, to no doubt find out why this particular directive had been breached.

I sighed and glanced at the kid who was still, for the time being, quiet and calm, placidly toying with the straw that was sticking out of her juice carton. Although I didn't have kids, I still couldn't fathom how someone could just throw theirs away like so much rubbish. A few weeks back, I'd been sent to work the night shift at Tottenham Court Road station as they were short staffed and, on the tube home, late that night, I'd found myself sitting opposite a young lad with Down's Syndrome who was on his own. He offered me one of his sweets and we chatted for a while - he was a really sweet kid and I remember thinking that if I had a kid, especially a vulnerable one, there's no way I'd let him travel on his own late at night - really makes you wonder what his parents were thinking!

Once again I stood and took an experimental step toward the door which seemed to go alright and so I took another, at which point all hell broke loose. All of a sudden, the juice carton that had seemed so harmless only a moment ago was detonated against the office wall with a force that I would have thought impossible for such a little kid and, once more, she was on her feet and by my side, once more clutching onto me as though her life depended on it. Taking a deep breath, I looked toward the police officers, not quite able to believe my own words as I said,

'Look, there's someone out there that I have to see - just for a minute - but I don't want things kicking off in here. Can I, you know,' I jerked my head toward the girl, 'take her with me?' Although a frown immediately creased Abby's forehead, I could have sworn that I saw John smirk as he said,

'I don't see why not,' and then, as Abby chucked a disapproving glance at him, 'I'll come along and keep an eye on things, just to keep everything above board.' Great. I wasn't always sure what it took to make Shandy happy but I was fairly certain that turning up for a quiet chat with a little kid and a police officer in tow wasn't on the list. I'd been sighing so much in the last hour or so that I was in danger of hyperventilating but I couldn't suppress one more as I picked the kid up and opened the door that would lead our merry gang out into the station concourse.

CHAPTER 7

As it turned out, just like on the first day that I met her, that last time that I saw Shandy, the floor of the station was once again mucky and hazardous from wet footprints that had been schlepped into the station and then smeared about by more careless feet. Fresh out of the rain with a face like thunder, she was waiting by the little information booth in the ticket area. As I've said, normally my first instinct with Shandy was to appease; to do whatever it took to get us back to a happy place but, that day, as I watched her face darken further as we approached, I got angry.

'I said I'd call you when I got a chance,' I said quietly as Shandy silently took in the scene in front of her, 'You couldn't have just waited, could you?' We were already gathering curious looks from the passengers around us and why wouldn't we? A Platform Assistant, a Policeman, a little kid and a stunning but furious looking woman - I would have stared too.

'What the fuck have you done, Will?' Shandy hissed, and that's when I lost it. For a moment I thought I would choke on all the responses that I wanted to make but had to hold back because I was in my workplace. And in the presence of a small child. And a policeman.

'That's it?' I finally hissed back, 'That's the first thing you ask me - what have I done?' I registered the look of shock on her face and was glad, maybe it was time that I stuck up for myself. She opened her mouth to reply but I was already turning away, taking the kid with me as she was still clinging to my hand. 'I said I'll call you,' I repeated, 'and I might - or not; I'll see how I feel.' If I'd known what would happen in the next few weeks, maybe I would have tried harder to smooth things over with Shandy as it might have been nice to have her support rather than reading her bitter comments in the press but, at that moment, I was concerned only with getting away before I said something that I may or may not regret. I took a step toward the increasingly uncomfortable looking Officer and tried for another before I realised that the kid had turned back toward Shandy and was holding her ground which was, quite frankly, pretty impressive considering that I had about eight stone on her. 'Come on hon,' I muttered impatiently but it was as though she didn't hear me as she continued to gaze at my soon to be ex-girlfriend.

'Are you sad because you lost your little girl?' The kid asked softly and Shandy turned her furious glare on her,

'What did you say?'

'I saw you,' the girl answered immediately, 'with your little girl. I liked her ribbons.'

'What is she on about Will, where did she see us?'

'Don't ask me,' I shrugged and Shandy turned her attention again to the girl,

'When? When did you see me and my little girl?'

'I liked her ribbons. Lucy Locket lost her pocket, Kitty Fisher found it. Not a penny was there in it, Only ribbon round it.'

'What's that meant to……'

'Stop it, Shandy,' I said helplessly, and then again to the girl, 'Come on, let's get back to the office and your juice shall we?' Although the increasingly uncomfortable looking officer looked like he was down with this plan, the kid showed no sign of moving as she continued to stare at Shandy and I wondered if I was going to have to pick her up and carry her back to the office.

'I asked where you saw us,' Shandy persisted in a nagging tone, 'Who are you? Were you following us?'

'Don't be stupid,' I snapped, 'she's just a kid, and one who's lost, she probably just saw someone who looked like you.'

'I saw you,' the girl insisted softly, 'on the steps when you fell with your little girl.' For a long moment it was as though all of the air had been sucked out of the station and I realised that I was struggling to breathe as panic made me grip the kid's hand so tightly that there would be little bruises left.

'What...I didn't….' As Shandy struggled to form a sentence, the spell was broken and, this time, I was able to pull the kid away and lead her back toward Jim's office.

'Don't you walk away from me Will, I want to know what's going on.' Ignoring her, I carried on walking, flanked on one side by the six foot tall Policeman and the two foot tall kid on the other, aware of but unable to care about the curious and disapproving looks we were getting, although later it would strike me that, from the outside, it must have looked like I was taking a woman's kid off her but then, that's the problem with seeing things from the outside - you make assumptions without knowing how things look to those on the inside and, at that moment, things couldn't really have looked much worse. As we got back inside the office and closed the door, I let out a shaky sigh and then forced a smile, unwilling to admit even to myself how much that little exchange had unnerved me.

'She wasn't a nice lady,' the kid said, still staring in the vague direction of where we'd left Shandy and I saw Andy try - and fail - to hide a smirk,

'The lovely Shandy was it?' He asked and I snapped,

'Not now Andy.'

'Bit pissed off was she?' He persisted and I sighed,

'Yeah a bit. I think the kid rattled her a bit, thought she knew her but she probably just mistook her for someone else.'

'Well, that's not enough to have turned you a whiter shade of pale,' he continued, 'there's more to it than that isn't there?'

'The kid told the lady that she'd seen her and her little girl when they fell on the steps.' Officer John interjected helpfully and I suppressed a groan - not only was Andy like a dog with a bone but, when it came to this particular subject, the bone was filled with rump steak and sausages.

'She what......' Andy began and Jim turned to snap at him,

'Andy, any particular reason you're still here?'

'Just trying to help,' Andy said sulkily but, mercifully, got to his feet and headed for the door

'I did see her,' the girl said, staring at me with an intensity that made the hairs on the back of my neck stand up, 'She fell and it was all her fault and now she's sad because she lost her little girl.'

'She didn't lose her,' I said gently, 'Her name's Adele - she's about your age and she's just fine!'

'My mother, and your mother, went over the way; said my mother, to your mother,"It's chop-a-nose day."

'Well, that clears that up!' Andy quipped and I ignored him as I watched Officer Abby surreptitiously look at her watch - it seemed I wasn't the only one looking forward to the arrival of the cavalry and, again, I felt a pang of sympathy for the kid who was probably coping admirably under the circumstances.

'What's chop your nose day hon?' I asked, feeling more than a bit uneasy, 'it doesn't sound very nice!'

'It's probably one of those kid-parent things,' Andy sniffed, 'You know, like when you pretend to steal a kid's nose but it's really just your thumb?'

'Actually,' Jim interjected, 'what she just said is from an old kid's rhyme - chop-a-nose-day was a bit like "heads, shoulders, knees and toes" meant to teach your kid about biology,' he shrugged, 'haven't heard that for a while though - not too popular with kids these days, now they've all got ipads and what have you.'

'Bit before my time that,' I muttered absently before realising what I'd just said and I felt that sense of unease again as I glanced back at the kid - part of me wanted desperately to know who she was and how she managed to end up wedged into a tunnel in Bethnal Green tube station and the other, bigger, part of me wanted to run like hell and get as far away from her as I could.

'How did you do it?' I turned and frowned at the girl who seemed to be staring a fixed point beyond the grimy window where only a vague suggestion of the station concourse could be seen.

'What do you mean?' I asked, 'How did we do what hon?' She didn't look at me, or anybody else, her gaze still fixed as a little smile played at the corner of her mouth,

'Make the office go away,' she replied simply, the hint of a smile suggesting that we were somehow playing a bit of a joke on her, 'How did you make the ticket office go away and make all the machines?'

'The...?' I began but Jim interrupted in a voice that was somehow tense and weary at the same time as he said,

'The ticket office. That was replaced by ticket machines in 2013'. For a moment the silence was so absolute that it was possible to believe that the world had entirely vanished and then, in a voice that wasn't quite steady, Andy said,

'So, tell us Will,'

'Tell you what?' I asked, not taking my eyes off the girl,

'Tell us what your Nana would have to say about this shit!'

CHAPTER 8

March 3rd 1943.

Another rainy day in Bethnal Green - Sometimes it seemed to Lillian as though there was nothing else but, on that particular day, the weather was the last thing on her mind as she rushed along the Cambridge Heath Road toward her bus stop. She had just finished her shift at the hospital and was rushing to get home to babysit for her sister's little girl while Helen went off to work at the pub. With relief, she'd just spotted the bus turning the corner toward her when the siren went off and she swore under her breath; Helen would lose a night's pay if she didn't show up to look after Ronnie but the rules were clear - when the sirens go off, you seek shelter; and you do it fast. For a moment, she was torn until she realised that the decision wasn't hers to make anyway; the bus would be going nowhere until they were given the all clear and so she turned and hurried back down the road toward Bethnal Green Junction station which was a temporary designated air raid shelter for the area. By the time she got there, with all the passengers from the temporarily halted bus hot on her heels, there were already a couple of hundred people making their way into the station with more coming from all directions. Twice, her heels skidded on the wet and slippery tarmac as she ran to take her place in the queue of people at the entrance to the steps and the siren seemed to get louder and louder as she waited but, thankfully, she didn't hear any aeroplanes. Yet. After what seemed like an age, she was inside out of the rain and moving onto the steps that led down into the station, barely moving as the sheer volume of people made any movement beyond a slow shuffle impossible, and then it happened. Ahead of and below her, she saw the dark-skinned woman from the shop - she didn't know her name, only knew her to say hello to really but here she was, just below her on the steps and she was carrying a little girl. Whether it was someone just being too impatient or the steps were slippy from the rain, Lillian couldn't tell but she gasped as she watched the shop woman trip and then fall downwards, her arms wrapped around her as she tried to protect the child she was holding but it was too late. Clutching onto the wall at the top of the steps, Lillian could only watch in horror as people - not one or two but twenty, thirty at a time - fell over the stricken woman and tried to get up again, only to be trampled by those who, in turn, had fallen over them. Faster and faster they came until the stairs were buried beneath a seething mass of bodies, some of whom were yelling, some of whom were screaming and others who were ominously, horribly silent.

'Go back!' She screamed as more newcomers shoved past her and headed down the steps, 'Stop pushing! Go back!' But they weren't listening - all they heard were the sirens, the ones warning them that the Germans were on their way with their planes and their bombs and she knew it was hopeless. Spotting a gap, she climbed her way back up and out, hands clutching at her feet from the dark until, finally, she was back outside the entrance from which point she would be able to run to find a policeman. Before she went, she took one last look back into the stairwell at the frenzy of human beings fighting and falling down there in the dark. By the following day, one hundred and seventy three of them would be in a make-shift morgue over at the church.

CHAPTER 9

They say that all's fair in love and war but, of course, that's just simply not true - how can it be? No idea who came up with that pearl of wisdom but if they really believed that there's anything fair about innocent people - innocent children - dying horrible, lonely deaths then, quite frankly, I don't want to know either. Of course I wasn't there - wasn't even a twinkle in my Dad's eye by then as the old folks used to say but you don't live in the East End without hearing the stories over and over or without knowing someone whose Gran was there or whose Uncle wasn't there because he missed the bus. Since the memorial was built a few years back, the one hundred and seventy three people who perished that day have been properly honoured and remembered and the steady stream of visitors paying their respects at the memorial never fails to move me. One lady I spoke to had come all the way from America just to pay her respects to a Grandmother she had never met. New York she was from; Manhattan to be precise and I couldn't help but wonder what she thought of our little corner of London. 'It's a place,' she had replied, 'just like any other.' I remember thinking that I couldn't decide whether that was comforting or depressing. It's a peculiar thing, the memorial - It's called The Stairway To Heaven and was designed by Harry Pattticas and Jens Borstlemann - it consists of a long white piece of stone that lies along the ground and then raises into the air, topped by a triangular sculpture which looks like, well, a stairway I suppose. It was unveiled complete with permanent, plastic flowers and Barbara 'one of our own' Windsor was enlisted for the ceremony. I wasn't there but I'm told it was very tasteful; I had to work so, that day, I honoured the dead by keeping as many of the living underground as possible.   As Jim had mentioned, that solemn occasion very nearly coincided with the ticket office at our station being closed (despite much public clamouring and hollering) and being replaced by those ticket machines that you now see in most stations - a process which was meant to speed up the process of processing hundreds of people at rush hour but tends to do the very opposite as people wait impatiently for some bewildered tourist to stand there randomly stabbing at the screen hoping for answers. What Jim - and Andy - were, of course, getting at was that there was no way that the kid could remember the station in it's pre-machine days; the estimation was that she was five at the most which meant that she would have only been a baby when the transformation took place and, yet, she continued to stare at us with that little smile that suggested that we were trying to play a little trick on her. Peering through the grimy office window, I couldn't make out Shandy's outline among the throngs of people milling around and I imagined that, the moment, we were out of sight, she had stomped out of the station back to her mother's house where my name would be taken in vain for the next couple of hours - or until the wine ran out - and I found that, curiously, I didn't much care. Andy had finally slunk off to Platform one, Jim was checking his emails, the officers were texting and the kid was doodling in her colouring book and, for a few blessed moments, silence reigned.

'She must have seen pictures of course,' Officer John said, breaking the all too brief peace, 'No other explanation. Plenty of pictures about after the memorial and all that, pretty hard not to see any of them.' That made sense, I remember thinking at the time - For a brief few moments, during the anniversary, Bethnal Green had become famous and there had been lots of photographs in the media and online, most featuring Babs 'Eastenders' Windsor but a lot were also of Bethnal Green Gardens and the station. It made sense but it didn't feel right.

'My Granddad had a friend who died that day,' John continued and I laughed softly - anybody who grows up in the East End knows somebody who knew - or claimed to have known - somebody who died that day. My Nana didn't like to talk about it but she did tell me that she was working at the hospital that day and Granddad was off to war but both of them had lost people, although she never seemed to feel the need to 'claim' the disaster as so many do.

'Mine too,' I said dismissively, not especially wanting to hear about John's Grand-dad's long lost friend or the gory details of his demise - John's Grand-dad was, apparently, still around to tell the tale whereas mine was buried in a field somewhere in France along with too many others, their headstones identical apart from the names. Unconcerned by this talk of death, the kid carried on doodling, the tip of her tongue poking out in concentration and I was itching to see what it was she was drawing but held back as, for the moment, she was calm and I was really hoping she'd stay that way until Child Services finally turned up.   As though summoned by that thought, there was a knock at the door and Jim opened it to reveal a woman who looked to be in her forties wearing a lot of beads and a harassed expression. Stepping into the room, the woman introduced herself as Judith and flashed her ID at Jim before making a beeline for the kid.

'Hello there,' she said brightly, 'My name's Judith.' The girl responded by ignoring her entirely although the scratching sound of her pencil increased as she continued with her drawing and Judith turned to the police officers and asked 'What's the girl's name?'

'Your guess is as good as ours,' John shrugged and a crease appeared between Judith's eyes as she turned to glance at the girl,

'She doesn't talk?'

'She can talk!' I butted in, feeling defensive on the kid's behalf for some reason and Officer Abby sighed,

'She can speak - and has been doing so but not really communicating.' When Judith didn't respond, Officer John added,

'She's been saying some stuff - rhymes and things but nothing helpful. We haven't been able to get a name out of her yet.'

'I'm sure you can tell us your name can't you?' Judith said as she returned to where the girl was sitting at the desk, 'I bet a pretty girl like you has got a lovely name!' She could bet all she wanted, I thought as, again the kid responded only by pressing harder on her pencil which seemed to be in danger of snapping at any moment. Although she still didn't look at the woman, a frown appeared on the girl's face and then deepened as, with much clacking of beads, Judith hunkered down so that her face was level with the seated girl.

'Do you think you can tell me your name so that we can find your Mummy or Daddy?' Nothing from the kid but more pencil scratching. 'Can you tell me where you live then?' Still no answer but I saw that the girl was now holding her pencil so tightly that her knuckles were white and the frown was deepening further.

'I think you're upsetting her,' I ventured, trying to avoid another meltdown and Judith stood up, her knees popping as she glared at me.

'I'm sorry, you are.....?'

'Will Thorn,' I offered, 'I'm the one that found the kid in the tunnel.'

'In the tunnel?' I sighed, hoping that I wasn't going to have to go through the whole bloody story again but, thankfully, Officer Abby jumped in with,

'Mr Thorn was checking the station during an evacuation and he found the girl hiding in one of the train tunnels. He brought her here and called the police - and then we called you and now, here we all are.' She stood and dusted off her trousers, 'Which means that, I think we're done here so we'll be on our way.' The two police officers made their way to the door without the slightest bit of interest from the kid - it seemed that I was the only one who wasn't allowed to leave - stopping only for Officer John to offer his slightly feeble hope that the kid would be ok and then they were gone. Once the officers had left, Judith's manner became brisk as she took a look around the office and asked if the child had had anything with her,

'No, nothing,' I replied, she was wearing a dress but it was filthy so we cleaned her up and put her in that shirt. She didn't have a bag or anything like that with her.'

'No doll or teddy?' I shook my head,

'Nothing.'

'Right then,' she said, 'We'd best be on our way then, traffic was horrendous on the way here.' She glanced at the girl who was still scribbling furiously at her drawing,

'Do you have a carrier or something that we can put her colouring book and pencils in?' I opened the cupboard under the sink and pulled out a Tesco bag and handed it to her

'Come along now,' she said to the girl, 'we're going to go for a little ride in my car. That'll be nice won't it?' The kid didn't seem to agree as she just carried on with her picture and I could see that Judith's bright smile was beginning to look a little tense. 'Here we are, we can take your book with us, shall we put it in this bag?'

When there was no response from the girl, Judith reached out a hand to take the drawing and then let out a shocked scream. It had happened so fast that it took my confused mind a few seconds to catch up and it was only when I took a couple of steps closer and saw the pencil protruding for a moment from the woman's hand before coming loose and falling to the floor with a lead-snapping clatter that I realised what had happened. Judith managed to paste her benign smile back on impressively quickly but not before I'd spotted the flash of anger that crossed her face and I quickly moved toward the kid, some instinct making me protective despite all of my deep misgivings and it was then that I saw what it was that she had been drawing.

CHAPTER 10

'I don't understand…..' Judith spluttered, her expression a mixture of shock and confusion, but I did. Or, at least, I thought I did. The girl was no artist but there was no mistaking what it was that she had been so busily working on. As though fearing recriminations for the pencil stabbing incident, the kid had leapt from her chair and was now cringing behind me and so I took the opportunity to grab the drawing for a closer look. The outline of the drawing was a rough copy of the photograph that she'd been entranced by earlier; a view of the entrance and the steps leading down into the station except that, in her picture, instead of Jim's grinning figure and bald head, the steps were a teeming mass of bodies, crudely drawn with mouths so wide open that they dominated the faces that could be seen.

'What is this love?' Judith demanded, snatching the drawing from my hand and the girl cringed further behind me, pressing herself between my legs and Judith gave me a sharp glance as though I had, somehow, forced the kid into making this slightly inappropriate but totally innocent move, rather than it being a consequence of her fear of this strange and increasingly irritated woman. Judith glanced again at the drawing before shoving it roughly into the carrier bag and shovelling the pencils in after it, 'Well, never mind, we really must be going now.' She reached for the girl who responded by shuffling further still away from her and she sighed. 'Mr Thorn, I'm going to have to get this girl outside and into my car - I really don't want to have to call for back-up but, if this continues, I'm not going to be left with any choice.'

'Easier said than done,' Jim chipped in with an expression that suggested that he too had had just about enough of this woman, 'Get all the back-up you want - to remove one tiny little kid - but you'll find that if you try to take her anywhere without Will, she'll start screaming bloody murder.'

'Yes, I'm sure,' Judith shot back, 'That's what children do when they're upset - as adults, it's our job to rise above that.' She took a plaster from her handbag and slapped it onto her hand where the girl had pencil-stabbed her although, quite frankly, it seemed like a bit of unnecessary theatre as it wasn't even bleeding and then, with her other hand, she reached for the girl again. 'Come along now love without any fuss and maybe we'll find a McDonalds on the way.' The kid didn't look impressed as she simply gripped the back of my leg tighter and I could see that Judith's patience which, thin to begin with, was about to snap and I sighed - the last thing I wanted was for her to phone a couple of goons to come and man-handle the kid into her car like some kind of government-approved abduction.

'Look,' I said, 'What about if I come with you - just to the car. I think she'll come along easily enough with me and then,' I shrugged, 'once she's in the car, it's up to you.' The woman looked from me to the girl and then sighed as she came to a decision and she hoisted her over-sized hand-bag onto her shoulder as she said, in a tight voice, 'Well, I suppose that makes sense.' She glanced at her watch and I found myself echoing Officer Abby's words as I said,

'Got a hot date or something?' Her furious glance was the only response she felt I warranted as she headed for the door and so, reluctantly taking the kid's hand I followed, stopping only to advise Jim that I would be off myself as soon as this business was taken care of. As famous last words go, those would come back to haunt me for quite some time. Following Judith through the busy station, the kid seemed placid enough and, having advised Judith that it would be best to avoid the steps, our little merry gang made it out of the station without incident and I made the mistake of allowing myself a few moments of optimism as we made our way to Potter Street where Judith had parked her car. For some reason (maybe it was the beads) I had expected her to be driving one of those old yellow Citroens or something and so I was surprised to see that the carriage of choice for Child Service employees these days was a sleek metallic grey Lexus.

'Very green,' I muttered and Judith shot me a prim look as she remarked,

'We all have to do our bit, Mr Thorn.' It struck me that having to drive a rather nice and almost brand new car wasn't really the height of self-sacrifice but I decided to keep that bit to myself in the interests of finally bringing this day to an end. Judith opened the door to her environmentally sound status symbol with a beep and a click and pulled open the back door,

'Here we go, love,' she said brightly, 'let's pop you inside and get your seatbelt on shall we? Tempus fugit!' I wasn't sure what it was that led her to believe that the kid understood Latin but it soon became clear that, whatever language she chose, the girl had no intention of placidly getting into the car as she pressed herself further against me. The rain had started again, just spitting at first but gathering momentum and irritation began to show on Judith's face so I took the kid's hand in an attempt to gently steer her toward the car door and, at first she came easily enough, taking one step then another and placing her little hand on the door,

'That's the way,' I said, unconsciously matching Judith's bright tone, 'in you go!'. She turned to look inside the car before glancing back at me and I can only assume that something in my body language alerted her to the fact that I wouldn't be following her into the car and she suddenly twisted away from the vehicle and lunged toward the road, only the fact that I was still holding onto her hand stopping her from running straight into the path of a souped up teen-mobile with music blaring from it's open windows. I'd lived in the East End my entire life and never really given it much thought but, at that moment, I looked around me, seeing as if for the first time, the grimy council estates and shops full of tat. The worn-down people shuffling down the street laden with shopping from cut-price stores and those prowling the streets looking to score drugs, a fight or sex. Although I can't say for sure, that may well have been the moment that the idea of escape first came to me, although it would be several more weeks before I would put the idea into action. I tried again to gently prod the kid toward the car without much hope of success - which worked out well as I wasn't then disappointed when she let out a piercing shriek and dug her heels into the wet pavement as the rain darkened her hair a couple of shades as it plastered it to her forehead.

'Mr Thorn?' Judith snapped and I glared at her, slowly counting to ten in my head to avoid snapping back (it had never worked for me before but I was working on the basis that it's always possible that there's a first time for everything). Ignoring the woman's increasingly impatient stare, I gave myself a moment, knowing that what I was about to do was likely to change life as I knew it, at least for the immediate future but my resolve grew as I looked at the woman's pinched face which was devoid of anything that could fairly be called compassion.

'Wait a minute,' I said unsurely, 'about what Officer Abby said before.'

'And what,' Judith snapped, biting off each word, 'exactly did Officer Abby say before?' She shook her head, 'Mr Thorn, can we at least talk about this in the car, I'm getting soaked.' And for me that was it - the fact that her issue was in the fact that her no doubt expensive silk blouse was getting soaked rather than concern for the little kid who was standing there shivering in nothing but a flimsy London Underground shirt, was the moment when, for better or worse, my decision was made.

'Don't let me keep you,' I said wearily as I turned on my heel, bringing the kid with me,

'But we won't be coming with you.' I heard the slam of the car door followed by the double beep of the lock being re-activated and then the sound of Judith's heels clacking along the pavement behind me, all of which I registered but as though from a distance as my mind whirled at the ramifications of what I was about to do.

'Mr Thorn, you can't do this, there are rules. I will call for back up and take the child forcibly, is that what you want?' Of course that's not what I wanted - the kid had been through more than enough without that, which was precisely why I was launching into this fool's errand in the first place. I sighed and slowed my pace, allowing Judith to catch up,

'What did you mean?' she asked after taking a moment to catch her breath, 'about what the Officer said.' I stopped walking and the girl immediately stopped too, coming to heel like an obedient dog and a middle aged woman in a suit swore at us as she had to swerve around the sudden roadblock that the three of us made.

'She said that the kid would go into foster care unless her parents were found or,' I took a deep breath, 'somebody else applies for temporary custody.' Judith blinked at me, her round face full of suspicion,

'And, what? You're saying that you feel that you're qualified to apply?'

'Qualified?' I asked, honestly perplexed, 'what qualifications do you need?'

'Do you have children Mr Thorn?' she sneered and I shook my head,

'No, do you?' She reeled back as though she'd been slapped and I felt a vicious stab of satisfaction at my sordid little victory as she composed herself.

'That's hardly the point. I am a qualified social worker and child services representative - I have several years experience of dealing with children like this one.'

'Dealing with?' I snapped, 'dealing with how? By getting them off your hands as quickly as possible and into foster care? That's your job isn't it?'

'It's a lot more complicated than that as I'm sure you realise.' Her tone softened as she looked at me, 'are you really sure you want to start this Mr Thorn? If this is just the heat of the moment and there's a chance that you'll change your mind once you've thought about it then you're really not being fair to this little girl.' Well, I knew that - none of this was fair; it wasn't fair that my buggered evening was shaping up to something a bit more serious when all I wanted from life was a couple of pints and some time with

Shandy and, it wasn't fair that this kid, who should have been tucked up in bed somewhere with a Mum and Dad watching telly in the other room was standing in the middle of the street shivering while two virtual strangers argued about her fate. It probably wasn't even fair that Judith's seemingly straight-forward job for the evening was turning into a major headache but, as priorities went, her inconvenience was at the bottom of the list as far as I was concerned. Judith's words weren't lost on me though - I understood that the decision that I was making was maybe the biggest one that I'd ever made and that, once made, there would be no going back and I was already getting a headache from the numerous questions that would have to be addressed, probably even before that night was over and yet, still, I turned to her and said,

'I'm not going to change my mind, but, you were right about one thing - we really do need to get out of this rain.'

CHAPTER 11

'No.' It was a word that I was starting to get accustomed to. No, you cannot have custody of a child, No, we won't make this easy for you, No, we can't offer you any help now that you have temporary custody and now, No, I won't wash my face.....or eat my dinner........or go to bed at a reasonable time. Another favourite over the past few days had been "Why". Why would a single thirty-something bloke suddenly decide to take in a little kid - the many things implied in that particular question would keep me awake for many a night to come, the instant assumption that motives always always had to be bad, sinister or selfish. Much to Judith's annoyance, the harried and over-worked Child Services Department had, eventually, decided that I would be granted temporary custody of the child, to be reviewed on a monthly basis. I won't bore you with all the details of the all the paperwork and all of the interviews and meetings which left me simultaneously weary and terrified but, suffice to say that I felt that, should I ever decide to commit a major crime, I was now fully prepared to mount my own defence. After my humble abode had been inspected thoroughly for God only knows what and then approved, I was allowed to bring Beth to what was to be her temporary home. Beth; that's what we called her - despite the fact that she had, sporadically, begun to talk to me, she still hadn't been able, or willing, to supply her name and so she had become Beth Green, named after the station that I found her in. It had started as a little joke and then had somehow stuck and she began to respond to the name as though she expected nothing different. I had taken some time off work - just a couple of weeks I told Jim, just until things settled down. I suppose the vague 'things' I was referring to came down to either Beth's parents being found and a reunion organised, or, the resolution of a more suitable alternative arrangement. As it turned out, I would never again put on the uniform of a TFL employee - just one more thing that I would discover that I really didn't much care about one way or another. It was about nine o'clock on the Sunday morning when I brought Beth to my flat for the first time. After spending the last day or so surrounded by various officials, it felt strange when, suddenly, it was just the two of us. Having not been offered a lift, I'd taken her home on the bus which went fine after an initial wobble when I realised that I didn't even know if she needed an Oyster card or not - just one of a million things that I would discover that I didn't know over the next couple of weeks. When I showed Beth to her bedroom which, although not decorated as such (not wanting to count my chickens and all that), had at least been painted in preparation for Adele's arrival, she had simply nodded as though, again, it was no more or less than she expected.

'We'll go shopping later,' I told her, 'get you some stuff.' She looked at me questioningly and I smiled, 'you know, some clothes and shoes and maybe some dolls and things.' I had been making a mental list of the things that she would need, even just for a couple of weeks and now I decided to put the list into writing. Grabbing a pad and pen (how very old school of me), I planted Beth in an arm-chair and turned on the TV, flicking through the channels until I found something that would be suitable for a kid to watch. Dismissing an old Western, a documentary about the latest teen killer and a soap omnibus, I lingered for a moment on Channel 10. Although it was a Sunday, one of the week-day morning presenters, Tiffany somebody or other, was gushing about having found her long-lost brother; I vaguely remembered that she'd been in the news recently regarding some reality programme about a black couple that had gone horribly wrong and I watched for a minute or two before remembering that I was supposed to be looking for something for Beth to watch. After a few more tries, I found something that appeared to centre around a talking pig and left that on while I set about making my shopping list. As I listed jeans and pyjamas, jigsaws and jumpers, Beth watched the TV, a small frown on her face as though she were concentrating hard and I smiled,

'Do you like Peppa Pig?' She glanced at me briefly then returned, unsmiling, to the program. Well, at least it was keeping her occupied, I thought, understanding why, right or wrong, so many parents use it as a kind of babysitter. When it comes to shopping for myself, I'm an internet man all the way but I decided that, after a late breakfast, I'd take Beth into town and we'd make a bit of a day of it and grab a late lunch once we'd finished with the shopping. I quickly made us both some toast and scrambled egg which Beth ate without comment or expression and, once finished, I rinsed our plates and then realised that I could do with a rinse myself but I hesitated, unsure as to whether it was OK to leave her on her own but, in the end, as her attention was still fixed firmly on Peppa and her mates, I hurried upstairs to take a quick shower. As I hurriedly pulled on jeans and a sweatshirt, I had a brief urge to call Shandy - it would have been nice to have brought her and Adele along on our little shopping expedition; the company of someone her own age might have been good for Beth and, more importantly, Shandy would know where to go and what to buy but I resisted. We'd spoken briefly on the phone the night before last, a terse and uncomfortable conversation, as you can probably imagine, and she'd made it perfectly clear that, while Beth was in my life she wouldn't be.

'I accepted your child without a moment's hesitation,' I told her and there was a pause before she replied,

'Yes, Will, but she's not yours. Beth is not your child.' As though I didn't know that. As though I didn't know that it was, as the social services put it, "irregular" for somebody like me to do what I was doing. As though it was much more acceptable and reasonable to cheat and lie and avoid any responsibility like the Alistair Knoxs of this world and the millions like him who do everything in their power to shun the children that they had created. Walking back into the living room, I had time to register the fact that the television volume had been turned up to the point that Peppa and her pals' voices had progressed from an annoying squeak to a nerve-damaging shriek and then I stopped dead as I took in the scene in front of me. Beth was still sitting where I had left her but the remote control for the telly which I had left on the coffee table was now on the floor and shattered to pieces. At first I thought that the room was covered in some weird kind of confetti then, as I picked one of the pieces up from the floor, I realised that it was a strip from the week old Metro that had been perched on the edge of the coffee table - the purple pop star, Prince, had died the week before and I recognised the piece of paper in my hand as part of the photograph of him that had dominated the front page that day. He'd been something like the 30th celebrity to pop his clogs in only four short months - 2016 was shaping up to be a really good year for the newspaper boys and girls. 'What's going on Beth?' I asked as I moved around the room, picking up shredded pieces of newspaper and it was then that I noticed that she was holding a page of the paper, the only page, by the looks of it, that was still whole and I moved closer to see what it was that she was looking at. Half of the page was taken up by an advert for PC World featuring a lion and I wondered if it was the animal that had gripped Beth's attention but, as I got closer, I realised that it was the other story that she was looking at - something about a drug tunnel in the States and, in particular, the main photograph that accompanied it which was of some bloke, his face blurred, sitting inside a narrow and crumbling stone tunnel. As I registered what it was she was looking at, I realised that there were tears rolling down her face and I put an awkward hand on her shoulder - I still wasn't used to this strange new relationship and was desperately unsure about what kind of level of physical contact was required or desired on Beth's part. 'It's OK,' I said, gesturing at the man in the photograph, 'He's alright, he's not stuck or anything.' She shook her head as the tears continued to fall and, for a moment, I was at a loss, baffled by her apparent compassion toward this Mexican drug smuggler who she had never met and who (I fervently hoped) she never would. 'What is it hon?' I asked, 'Can you tell me why you're so upset?' I knew that Adele cried quite often but usually because she'd hurt herself or wanted something that she couldn't have (if we all continued this behaviour into adulthood, the entire world would probably now be under-water and we would have all developed fins), but not usually through any kind of sympathy or empathy for others and so I tried again; 'Do you not feel well?' Again, she shook her head but at least now the tears had stopped.

'Trapped.' She said and again, I tried to reassure her,

'No hon, he's not trapped. It says here,' I pointed to the text underneath the picture, 'he's just digging, that's all. Doing a job.' Well he was. Of sorts.

'Trapped.' Beth repeated, 'Buried. All gone.' With a shiver, I realised that we were no longer talking about the drug smuggler.

'Who, Beth? Who's trapped?' She looked at me then with an expression filled with more sorrow than should ever be seen on the face of a child as she whispered,

'All of us.'

CHAPTER 12

I fell asleep on the beach yesterday. I'd been walking along it like I do most days when I'm not working; not walking to get somewhere but just walking for the sake of it. A lot of people talk about wanting time to think but, for me it's the opposite, most of the time I work quite hard at not thinking about anything at all other than work, food and the practical bits of my day to day existence. I'd been walking for about an hour and I was tired so I sat down in the shade of the old pier and, before I knew it, I'd closed my eyes and sleep had taken me. I dreamt that I was back in the East End, still in the little flat that I called home for the best part of ten years and Beth was there with me but she was all grown up, pretty and competent looking with shoulder-length blonde hair and the same blue eyes that I remembered. Although she didn't say a word during the whole dream, at least not that I remembered, I felt like we were communicating and, when she stood and walked toward the door, I followed, some implicit understanding that this would be the case meaning that she didn't once turn to check that I was still with her. She opened the front door to reveal not the ordinary Hackney street that had always been on the other side of it but a tidy tree-lined avenue with new looking old cars parked outside a handful of the houses. I blinked and saw that Beth was now pushing an old-fashioned pram, a small smile playing at her lips as she peeked inside and then, another blink and, this time, as well as the pram, there was a little girl of about five holding onto Beth's hand. At the time, I was confused - the dream-me I mean - but still I followed, watching as the pram disappeared to be replaced by a little boy holding onto Beth's other hand and I watched as the children grew, as Beth's hair shortened and turned grey. We reached a small park with a well-kept playground and Beth sat down, in her lap one of the grand-children that had appeared during our short journey, a chubby baby girl with hair the exact same colour that Beth's had been when I first found her. A man of about sixty appeared and approached the ever-growing family, handing out ice-creams and kicking a ball about with one of the boys and then, suddenly, they were gone - all of them but Beth and I realised that the unknown park was fading and now we were back in Bethnal Green Gardens. This last time, I was unable to follow as Beth stood and walked toward the memorial, turning to give me one last smile before fading and then vanishing. Although the dream-me hadn't understood, the awake-me did and I spent the rest of the day indoors, filled with a dark sorrow as I understood what dream-Beth was doing - that she was showing me all that had been taken from her.

CHAPTER 13

As suddenly as it had appeared, Beth's sadness vanished, the way it does with kids, and she resumed watching the TV as though nothing had happened. I wanted to understand what had upset her as I wanted to know how to protect her - and my living room - from it in the future but, for the time being, I was just grateful that it had passed and I remembered that I'd been planning a shopping trip. As I attempted to get Beth ready for our expedition, dressing her in the scruffy but clean clothes that the authorities had provided, I felt weary with the weight of everything that I didn't know about children and, this child in particular. To the point that even a simple trip to the shops to get provisions seemed like a potential minefield and so I did what any self-respecting bloke in that position would do. I called my Mum. For the past ten years, craving a bit of peace and quiet, Mum and Dad had been living away from the bustle of Hackney in a leafy suburb of Stratford and so, after a brief explanation, I arranged to meet Mum outside the Costa Coffee at the Westfield Stratford shopping centre. Grateful that Mum had, for the time being, very uncharacteristically kept her questions to a minimum, I buckled Beth into her shoes and turned off the television, happy for the respite from whatever hellish creature it was that had replaced Peppa Pig. After the short walk to Hackney Central station, we jumped onto an overground line train which was empty save for a handful of hungover looking people either just on their way home or on their way out for a hair of the dog and Beth watched them curiously but without any noticeable alarm as I bit back a swear word at the realisation that I'd left my shopping list behind after all that. When we emerged from Stratford station, the rain had finally stopped and the sun was making a valiant attempt to come out. The shopping centre was Sunday-busy; lots of people milling about but without the frenzied energy of a Saturday and we quickly made our way to the Costa, noticing, as we approached that Mum was already there waiting. Her expression was hard to read as I kissed her hello and introduced her to Beth and her first words were,

'So, Shandy couldn't come along to help then?' I pulled a face,

'Didn't ask,' and then, when there was no response, 'Not sure where things are with us at the moment, to be honest.' I thought I saw a brief smile appear and vanish as Mum nodded and then said,

'Well, we'd best get going then as they're only open til four thirty today.' She reached into her vast handbag and produced a bit of paper with her neat handwriting on it, 'I expect that you forgot your list so I made my own. There's a H&M just down here.' True to her word, there was indeed a H&M and we trudged around picking out clothes for Beth before repeating the exercise in M&S and Debenhams. I always thought females loved shopping but, as we picked out dresses and jeans and jumpers, Beth was, at best, indifferent until, whilst wandering around Debenhams, she spotted a pink top sporting an image of Mickey Mouse and, for the first time, she became animated and I happily added the t.shirt to the not insubstantial haul that we already had. It was about two hours later when, all shopped out, Mum suggested that we adjourn to the nearby branch of TGI's for something to eat and I realised, with some surprise, that she was enjoying herself. Although I'm fairly sure that it was something she hoped for eventually, she was never one of those mothers who go on and on about waiting for Grand-kids and she'd certainly never shown more than a passing interest in Adele but I realised, as we were seated at a garishly coloured table in the restaurant and handed menus, that she was enjoying Beth's company and it seemed that the feeling was mutual. Although still not exactly chatty, Beth seemed to come out of her shell a little in Mum's presence and I welcomed the change as well as the relief of not having to go it alone with Beth, at least for a few hours.

'So, I said after we'd given our drinks order, 'I suppose Dad's got a fair bit to say about all this?' Like most blokes of my age, a lot of important conversations are filtered through to my Dad via my Mum - Dad and I will talk about general stuff every couple of months at the football but we hadn't had a home game for a little while and we hadn't even had a chance to speak since Beth had crawled out of a tunnel and into my life.

'Your Dad thinks that we tried to bring you up to do the right thing and that we've obviously succeeded. He's very proud of you.' Although I was undeniably touched by this declaration, the way that she averted her eyes at the last moment suggested that Dad had had a great deal more to say before getting to the 'proud of you' part but I had the good sense to let it go.

'So, what do you fancy, Beth?' I asked, glancing at the girl who was studying her menu with interest and Mum rolled her eyes,

'Will, although I'm sure that she's a very clever girl, I very much doubt that Beth can read yet!' She scanned her own menu, this time from the bottom where the children's options were listed before turning to Beth and asking,

'How about some spaghetti bolognese?' then, when she was met with no more than a steady gaze, 'a burger?' Nothing. 'What about a wrap?' I was beginning to despair that the kid who had eaten her breakfast happily enough, was going to turn out to be a picky eater but suddenly a smile broke her face as Mum suggested fish fingers and chips and this was followed by a shy nod. Result.

'You know, Will,' Mum said as we handed the menus back to the waiter, 'you're going to have to have a look at your shopping habits - from now on, you're going to have to be buying things like fish fingers and spaghetti hoops and frosties.' Taking off my jacket as the heat of the restaurant filtered through, I grinned at her,

'Mum, I'm a single bloke - what the hell do you think I eat anyway?' She smiled, acknowledging my joke and then turned serious,

'Shandy's a nice girl, Will, and I know that you had plans for the two of you,' But. 'But, I'm not sure she's right for you - can I take it that she's not been exactly supportive about Beth?'

'Yes,' I sighed, 'You can take that. I suppose I can't blame her really, it is all a bit strange.'

'So what?' She paused as our food was delivered to our table and I watched as Beth immediately tucked into her fish fingers, oblivious to the conversation we'd been having. 'Life is strange, Will. Man plans, God laughs, your other Nana used to say and she was right. If you're gonna be with somebody, it needs to be somebody who'll back you up, not get her back up every time you do something she sees as stepping out of line.' She stopped and then, 'You know, she reminds me a bit of your Grandma Shelly - Shandy I mean - when she was younger, she had that same mad curly hair, not when you knew her, of course.' I smiled, remembering that the Grandma Shelly I had met always had sensibly short curls that were set every week at the hairdressers - as a kid I'd been fascinated by it's immovable texture that I was convinced would withstand a tornado, let alone the wind and rain of England. 'All I'm saying is that I'd like to see you with somebody who values you, Will. Your Dad may have his faults,' she rolled her eyes, 'God, does he! But he's always on my side. Always.' With that, she turned to her plate, stabbing her fork into her chicken and it appeared that the conversation was over, although I had a feeling that it would be back. To my relief, we then moved onto the safer topics of what else Beth would need while she was staying with me and we put together a list of final items to buy before heading home. After coffees for me and Mum and a Babyccino for Beth, Mum asked for the bill, waving away my protests as she paid with her debit card, 'Keep your money, Will, you're going to need it - kids are great but they're bloody expensive, I can tell you that for nothing!'. As she took back her card and receipt, we rose to leave the table and Beth paused, puzzled,

'What about your book?' She asked Mum and we both glanced at each other before I asked,

'What book Beth?'

'You need your book,' she insisted and Mum laughed,

'Do you mean a cheque book Beth? Blimey, I haven't used one of those for about ten years - I don't know anybody who has!' As Mum hustled us out of the increasingly busy restaurant I saw that it had already started to get dark and I was about to suggest that we head for the tube station when I realised that we'd left the shopping bags inside the restaurant and so I jogged back inside to retrieve them, an exercise that involved apologising to the raucous party of twenty somethings who had already taken over our table and then fishing the bags out from underneath the bench, excusing myself so many times it almost became an incantation before I finally had the flimsy plastic bags and was able to extricate myself from the booth. Exiting the restaurant for the second time, I struggled at first to see Mum and Beth and then I spotted them standing by an ornamental fountain talking to a woman who looked to be in her late sixties and who was handing out flyers for something or other. Hurrying over to them, I held up my arm to indicate that I had the bags, expecting them to break away from the flyer lady but, when that didn't happen, I joined them, curious about what it was they were talking about.

'Clever little thing isn't she?' I heard the woman say as I moved into earshot and I glanced at Beth whose expression was subdued but with a hint of a puzzled smile.

'Got 'em,' I announced, stating the bleeding obvious once again and Mum gave me a distracted smile. The woman turned her attention to me, favouring me with a little wave before stooping to speak to Beth,

'Have you been learning about this in school love?' She looked up at Mum, 'I think it's great that kids are being taught about their own history still - too many schools these days are so scared of offending somebody that they forget how important that is.' I couldn't read Mum's expression as she nodded tightly and I took my cue to say,

'We'd best be off now Mum, it's nearly dark and I think Beth's tired.' As I reached for Beth's hand, I saw that she was clutching one of the flyers that the woman was giving out and I reached for it,

'What's that you've got there?' I asked,

'Bug hole,' Beth replied and I smiled, certain that I'd heard her wrong.

'That's what she said before,' Mum said, 'when she first saw the flyer - bug hole. What does that mean?' I glanced at the piece of paper which was advertising a special retro showing of Bambi at a local cinema.

'Would you like to see this film Beth?' I asked, assuming that she'd been attracted by the picture of the famous deer and she gave me a curious look,

'Saw it.' The frown remained for a moment and then she smiled, 'Saw it at the bug hole with Ellen, I liked the animals'.

'Who's Ellen, Beth?' I asked, my heart starting to race at the thought that we may be about to get a clue as to where this strange little girl came from but her attention had been stolen by a group of skateboarders being pursued by a harassed looking security guard.

'The bug hole,' the flyer lady said with a strange smile, 'Now that's not a name that I've heard for quite some years, brings back some memories that does but,' she shook her head, 'this little 'un was certainly never there.'

'Bambi at the bug hole,' Beth insisted and the woman smiled uneasily at me,

'Kids, they don't miss a thing do they? She must have heard that from her Gran or Granddad. Bit of a trip down memory.....'

'I saw Bambi at the bug hole with Ellen,' Beth reiterated, her voice getting louder and I gripped her hand tighter, anxious now to get us away from this before she went into full on meltdown mode. Throughout this whole, odd, conversation, Mum had been standing quietly, her attention fully focussed on Beth as a frown threatened to knit her eyebrows together.

'Where's Ellen now Beth?' She asked and the girl gave her a stern look,

'We don't talk about Ellen any more. Mustn't.'

'Oh, but you can tell us, can't you?' Mum tried, 'That can't do any harm can it?'

'Loose lips sink ships,' Beth stated and then grinned, seemingly delighted at the rhyme.

'Another blast from the past,' the elderly lady said but, this time, there was no trace of the kindly smile that had been evident throughout this whole exchange. 'Your daughter certainly is an unusual one,' she remarked faintly and I shrugged and said,

'She's not my daughter,' instantly regretting it as the woman's expression sharpened.

'It's a long story,' I hastily explained, 'but I'm her legal guardian for the time being.'

'For the time being,' the woman repeated, not bothering to hide the tone of disapproval in her voice, 'Well, I must be getting on, nice talking to you,' she nodded curtly at Mum and then was off but she might as well have not spoken as Mum was still gazing intently at Beth.

'Why are you not supposed to talk about Ellen, Beth?' She asked and the kid gave her a stern look,

'Because of the baby,' she said and then, almost in a whisper, 'the black baby.'

'You mean Ellen had a baby?' Mum asked and Beth's eyes darted from side to side as though any one of the strangers around us might overhear and uncover this deep, dark secret.

'Ellen had a black baby and now she's not allowed to live with us any more,' she said and Mum's face brightened as she asked,

'So, is Ellen your sister, Beth?' During all this, my mind was already whirring, wondering if there would be some way of tracing this Ellen through local maternity wards and reuniting her with our Beth Green but Beth simply repeated,

'Not no more. We don't talk about Ellen no more,' and then covered her ears as though to ward off further questions and I shook my head at Mum to tell her to lay off for now - the last thing I wanted was for Beth to have one of those awful kiddie tantrums in the middle of a busy shopping centre. I wasn't getting my hopes up that Beth's family would or could be traced that way and that was just as well as, later on, when Beth was asleep, a headache-inducing number of telephone calls would result in the information that, seemingly, not a single woman named Ellen had given birth to a baby of any colour or description in any of the four hospitals in the East End that offered such services. I had just concluded my telephone tour of the hospitals and popped open a can of Stella when Mum rang, her voice uncharacteristically subdued without her normal rush of questions and gossip and I frowned, hoping it wasn't bad news - Dad's ticker's always been a bit dodgy and there was always the low level dread of receiving *that* phone call.
'Everything all right Mum?' I asked and there was an uncharacteristic pause - and one that I didn't like much - before she replied,
'Me? Yes, I'm fine Will but there was something bugging me about earlier, at Westfield. Well, a couple of things really and so I did a bit of research - you know, on the internet?' I assured her that I was aware of the concept and she went on, 'So, I was looking for something that Beth said this afternoon, about going to a place called the Bug Hole and I found it. It turns out that the Bug Hole was what people used to call the Empire cinema on Roman Street in Bethnal Green.' I shook my head and then, realising that she couldn't see the gesture, I said,
'The Empire? There's no Empire cinema in Bethnal Green Mum.'
'I know,' Mum said impatiently, 'that's the thing. There was one once but, Will, the Empire closed for good in nineteen fifty nine.'

CHAPTER 14

First Andy and now Mum and I wondered who would be the next to suggest that there was something weird about Beth. Of course I had no choice but to agree that some of the things that Beth said were a bit odd but, did I really believe that she was anything other than a normal little girl who had found herself in a new and scary situation? Not then, I didn't but that would all change in a matter of days. For the next couple of days it was just me and Beth, spending quality time together as we navigated the terrain of this strange new relationship. For a little while, we had no real contact with anybody else apart from phone calls with Mum and a brief and uncomfortable visit from Andy who managed to very quickly annoy and frustrate me with his repeated questions about how long I was likely to be 'stuck with Beth.' I was surprised to discover that Shandy had decided to keep our curry-house double-date but decidedly unsurprised to learn that she had not spoken fondly of me during the evening and so I tempered my side of the conversation on the assumption that what I said would be reported back to her. So during those couple of days, Beth and I played games, cooked and generally got to know one another. Although she still refused to say any more about the mysterious Ellen and her black baby or any other family, I did discover that she loved being read to from Winnie The Pooh and had a violent and total dislike for chili con carne so my time wasn't entirely wasted. On the afternoon of the third day, a Wednesday, we were due a visit from our social worker or whatever the hell they call themselves these days and so I decided that we'd have a nice morning out and a spot of lunch beforehand. I was already nervous about that afternoon's meeting as I'd been warned that they would need to speak to Beth alone and, although we'd reached a stage where I was able to go take a shower or make a cup of tea, Beth was still uncomfortable if I left her for too long and I had no idea how long the social worker would want to talk to her without me. As I bundled Beth into her new pink parka and fastened her shoes, I realised that she was muttering to herself and I listened more closely before realising that she was repeating a bit from the Winnie The Pooh book we'd be reading the last couple of nights.

'Pooh's first idea was that they should dig a Very Deep Pit, and then the Heffalump would come along and fall into the Pit,' she muttered in a strangely flat voice and I smiled,

'But there wasn't any Heffalump was there? It was just silly old Pooh with his head stuck in a jar of honey.'

'Fall into the pit, dig a very deep pit, fall into the pit,' Beth murmured and I shook my head,

'Well, never mind. Let's go now, eh.' I turned off the TV and put out the lights, leading Beth through the hallway and out the front door. We walked down Columbia Road, past the imposing Shoredich Church which, famously, is featured in the well known rhyme 'Oranges and Lemons' - something that pops into my head every time I walk past it and thinking it would amuse Beth, I sang a little bit of it out loud as we crossed the street;

"When I am rich, says the bells of Shoreditch,"

'When will that be, say the bells of Stepney,' Beth immediately responded and I laughed out loud as we finished the rhyme together, raising our voices on the part where the chopper comes to chop off your head. It felt like the first proper interaction between us and my mood was instantly lifted as we passed the flower market and reached the gates of Hackney City Farm and went inside, Beth wrinkling her nose as the smell of the animals reached us and I smiled.

'You'll soon get used to it. What shall we see first, the rabbits?' She nodded enthusiastically and I happily led us through to the enclosure which housed four rabbits who came to greet us, little pink noses twitching in the hope that we'd brought something tasty with us.

'What's up Doc?' I quipped and Beth giggled, a sound that truly was music to my ears and I peered at the information board by the enclosure, reading aloud as I was informed that a group of rabbit burrows is called a warren and then, that a burrow is an underground rabbit hole and, at this last, Beth's face darkened,

'Why?' She asked and I frowned, puzzled,

'Why what hon?'

'Why would they want to live underground? Why is everything underground, all the time?'

'Well,' I explained, 'They live underground to protect them from other animals, because it's safe there.'

'NO!' She yelled suddenly, startling a Sloaney type woman who was standing nearby with her two kids and I gave her what I hoped was a reassuring smile before returning my attention to Beth,

'It's OK, they just.......'

'No,' she repeated, thankfully in a more normal tone of voice, 'It's not safe. Never safe.'

At a loss as to this sudden change in mood, I gently led her away from the rabbit enclosure and toward the donkeys, Larry and Clover who were, apparently, the farm's stars and who, thankfully, lived totally, one hundred percent above ground in the sun. Beth's previous sunny mood returned as she fed them bits of hay provided by a kind volunteer and I informed her (with the help of the info board) that a donkey can hear another donkey braying from up to thirty miles away. To my relief, the rest of our visit proceeded without incident and we ambled our way from the farm to the Counter Cafe by the canal in Hackney Wick and ate huge sandwiches in the weak November sunshine until it was time to head back to the flat and the visit from Child Services. Despite the brief bunny blip, Beth had seemed to enjoy our little trip and our mood was light as we made our way back to my flat although I still harboured a low level dread of the forthcoming meeting, certain that my child-care skills would be examined and found wanting. We'd only been back about half an hour when I heard the buzz of the doorbell and opened the front door to find a petite smiling woman of about thirty standing on the doorstep. Whereas the odious Judith had been exactly what I had expected from somebody in her profession, this woman was the exact opposite and I took to her immediately, as did Beth who happily chatted away with her as I put together a pot of tea and dug out the only packet of biscuits in the flat that didn't have happy faces or animals iced onto them. If I'd been worried about being judged then that worry was misplaced as JoJo, as she introduced herself, after a brief tour of Beth's new residence, complimented me on the flat and on my decision to snatch Beth away from the jaws of the foster system. Unsolicited, she told me that she was the latest generation of a family that had lived in Bethnal Green for more than a hundred and fifty years, adding that she was a distant ancestor of a well known bantamweight boxer from the area.

'His name was Richard Coleman, although he boxed professionally under Bobby Corbett,' she said, pride colouring her East End accent and I smiled even though I wasn't and never had been a fan of boxing as I never could see the point of two blokes hitting each other until one fell down then calling it sport.

'Bobby,' Beth suddenly cried, her little face lighting up, where's Bobby?' JoJo smiled sweetly, although her face was instantly alert as she asked,

'Do you know somebody named Bobby, Beth?' Obviously hoping, as we had with Ellen, that a name might lead to Beth's family being traced.

'Bobby,' Beth repeated as though JoJo were slightly dim, 'Bobby the boxer. He gave me sweets.'

'That's nice,' JoJo said, 'and do you know where I can find Bobby, Beth. Do you know where he works maybe?' Beth shook her head firmly,

'No work. He's just home on leave, just for a little while but he gave us sweets and he found threepence behind my ear and gave it to me.' She paused to take a monster bite of her biscuit before adding, 'Mum took it to the Turk cos he had a bit of tongue put away for us,' she suddenly stopped, looking startled as she implored JoJo, 'You won't tell anyone though will you?' JoJo attempted a smile, her tea all but forgotten as she leaned closer to Beth,

'No, of course not. Beth, do you think you might be able to help us find Bobby. You said he was on leave, do you mean from the army?'

'Bombing the jerries,' Beth yelled jubilantly, 'Bobby says that's where he's been.' JoJo's face had turned almost as white as the milk in Beth's glass but she gamely continued,

'You said that he gave *us* sweets, do you remember? Who else did you mean, did he give sweets to your friends?' Beth thought about this for a moment and then shook her head,

'No. Just me and Jenny.' JoJo leaned forward further until I began to fear that she would topple out of her chair and onto the floor as she continued to prod,

'Who's Jenny , Beth?'

'Jenny!' Beth stated and then, gathering that more was required, 'Jenny Rowe. Bobby the boxer is her daddy. I like seeing Bobby but I don't see Jenny no more.' I had been sitting inbetween the two, looking from one to the other as this peculiar conversation progressed and as I, again, registered the fact that JoJo was starting to look decidedly peaky, I decided to jump in,

'Why not Beth? If Jenny's your friend, how come you can't see her anymore?' I turned to JoJo, 'This isn't the first time she's mentioned a name - the other day she was talking about somebody called Ellen who, from the sounds of it, might be her sister. With that, and now Bobby and Jenny, surely it can't be that difficult to figure out who she belongs to.' A strange smile appeared on JoJo's face and I persisted, 'I mean, how hard can it be? We find out where Jenny and her Dad Bobby live and then they can tell us who Beth is.'

'That simple eh,' she replied in a voice that was suddenly hoarse, 'except that Bobby has been dead for more than seventy years and Jenny is now in her nineties and living in an assisted living centre in Tower Hamlets.'

CHAPTER 15

Although I'd been told to expect the visit to last for at least an hour, it was less than twenty five minutes in when JoJo grabbed her coat and announced that she needed to be on her way.

'They told me you'd be wanting to talk to Beth on her own for a bit,' I said, following her down the hallway to the front door and she gave me a tight smile,

'No need, I've got all I need already.' I shook my head, bewildered as she yanked open the front door and, before she could leg it to her car, I touched her arm briefly and said, 'Listen, I know that Beth sometimes says some strange things - she seems to have quite the imagination but, you know, you won't need to tell anybody about any of that stuff will you?'

'Course not,' she called, too brightly, as she hurried down the street, but she would - I knew she would and, as it happened, before the day was out. If Judith's problem was that her time in the business had made her jaded then it was the opposite for JoJo; she was too keen - too determined to save the world one waif or stray at a time and Beth had gotten to her just as surely as she'd gotten to me. I slowly closed the door and walked back into the living room where Beth was flicking through one of her picture books, oblivious to the turmoil that she had just created in the young woman's mind. As I went to sit down, I noticed something on the seat opposite and, reaching over, I realised that it was JoJo's file on Beth, left behind in her haste to flee this flat and the strange child that it contained. My first thought was to try to remember if JoJo had given me her number - she seemed like a nice woman and I didn't want her getting into trouble for leaving a confidential document behind at a client's home. My second thought was that, although I knew that I shouldn't, I also knew that there was no way that I was not going to open the file and take a sneak peek. I had a couple of hours before Mum was due to turn up to, firstly, find out how things had gone with the child services and, secondly, to watch Beth for a couple of hours while I popped out to meet Andy for a couple - a meeting that had been engineered by Andy although the venue choice of Number 90 Hackney Wick told me that not only was it the choice of his partner, Dawn, but that she was likely to be there too and it wasn't an evening that I was looking forward to. Checking that Beth was still absorbed in her picture book, I carefully opened the file, noting immediately that JoJo's business card was tucked into the bottom left hand side and I felt a brief stab of smug satisfaction at having had a legitimate reason to open the file. Turning to the first page, I saw that it was a very simple tick box form with questions about how the child was living and I was gratified to see that JoJo had answered all of these favourably but then, halfway down, I saw that the last four or five boxes had been left unchecked and, in the margin, she had written two things, "eloquent but confused" and then "Disturbed?" Plucking out the business card and then slapping the file shut, I picked up my mobile and dialled the mobile number on it and it only rang twice before JoJo picked up, sounding harassed.

'JoJo,' I said above the static that told me that she was currently driving, 'This is Will Thorn, Beth Green's guardian. You missing something?' There was a pause during which I could hear the sound of sirens and then,

'I'm on my way.'

While I waited, I put on another pot of tea and the kettle had just boiled when I heard the doorbell ring again and I answered it to find JoJo, once again, standing on the doorstep. As I stood in the doorway, she looked at my hands as though she expected me to be holding her folder and, without a word, I turned and beckoned her inside, closing the door behind us.

'I'm making more tea,' I said as we reached the living room and she nodded then I heard her asking Beth about her picture book as I returned to the kitchen to make the drinks. As I returned, I saw that she was perched on the edge of the chair that Beth was sitting in, seemingly to better see the book but, as I walked into the room, I heard her say,

'Beth, do you remember earlier, when we were talking about Bobby the boxer and about Jenny?'

'JoJo,' I began and she gave me a reassuring smile,

'It's OK, we're just talking, I'm not going to upset her.'

'Bobby and the sweets when he came home from the pub.' Beth confirmed and JoJo nodded,

'Do you know which pub he goes to?' She asked and Beth nodded, still looking only at her book,

'The Cabin. It's his favourite,' Beth replied and JoJo gave me a sly look,

'Do you know The Cabin, Will?' I shook my head,

'Not offhand, no, but there's a new pop up pub or restaurant turning up around here every other week these days, isn't there?' The look she gave me told me that I hadn't convinced her - which was fine as I hadn't even managed to convince myself and she went on,

'Beth, can you tell me what Jenny looks like?'

'I don't see Jenny no more,' Beth said, repeating what she had told JoJo earlier and JoJo quickly nodded,

'I know - and that's a shame, but can you tell me what she looked like when you used to play together?' Beth shrugged,

'Same as me, she's little.' I hid a smirk as JoJo continued,

'OK, is there anything else you can tell me about what she looks like?' For the first time, Beth looked up from her book as she seemed to consider the question and then, glancing to me as though for reassurance, she said,

'She's got brown hair and a blue dress with poppies on it.' JoJo sighed and picked up her tea as though she were disappointed in this lack of information from a traumatised child and, she'd just picked up her wayward folder and stuffed it into her bag when Beth suddenly smiled as a lightbulb moment struck her and she said triumphantly,

'I nearly forgot, there's another thing. She's got this mark on her face - Bobby says that it's a beauty mark but I think it's ugly; it looks like a pimple - right on her chin!' I had been barely listening as I ran through everything that needed to be done - I needed to leave the house in less than an hour and Mum would be here any minute and so Beth's words barely registered with me until I heard the clatter of tea cup on saucer and turned to see that JoJo had, again, gone deathly pale and was staring at Beth in wonder as she said,

'You know what this is, Will? It's a miracle!'

CHAPTER 16

I managed to settle the miracle down with a chicken sandwich and yet another episode of Peppa Pig and was out the door within minutes of Mum arriving to take over. Although the evening had been pitched to me as a couple of beers and a catch up, I had the feeling that it would be more of a kind of intervention, the intention of which was to make me see the error of my ways regarding my situation with Beth and I wasn't wrong. Stepping through the doors of the oh so trendy Number 90 Hackney Wick which is a pub - or 'Bar and kitchen' as they like to call themselves - perched on the edge of the canal and tends to be packed to the rafters most of the time with young men sporting beards and skinny jeans drinking things that have been 'infused'. As I walked inside, my mind was still very much on the troubling meeting with JoJo and it took me a minute to spot Andy and Dawn sitting at a table in the corner with untouched beers in front of them, telling me that they had either just arrived or that these beers weren't their first. I shook Andy's hand and did the double cheek kissing thing that Dawn was, for some reason, so fond of and then said that I would grab a beer and be back in a minute - giving myself a precious few moments to allow me to gather my thoughts before, over-priced beer in hand, I wove my way back to their table. As I sat down again, I noted with dread that Dawn was wearing what she, presumably, thought was a sympathetic expression and I took a long sip of my beer to delay the inevitable.

'So, how's everything going?' Andy asked and I laughed,

'I don't think that's really what you got me here to ask, is it?' I said and Dawn sighed,

'It's just that we don't really understand what you're doing, Will.' I shrugged,

'Me neither - I didn't choose for this to happen but it did.' I took another swig of my craft beer, 'With any luck, it won't be for long anyway and, in the meantime, I'm managing.'

'You're managing,' Dawn repeated flatly, 'Will, you do realise that this is not normal and,' she held up a hand as I started to interrupt, 'And that you're going to lose Shandy if you don't do something about all this.' I looked at my drink, noting with slight alarm that it was almost dry and then finished the job in one long gulp.

'Firstly, if by 'do something about all this,' you mean chucking Beth back into the care system then that's not going to happen so that's off the table. Secondly, right now, I honestly couldn't give a rat's arse about "losing" Shandy in fact, I don't even know what I was thinking when I wanted her to move in with me. She's selfish, manipulative and,' I paused, 'to be honest, just not really a very nice person so,' I pushed my chair back from the table with a screech, earning myself dirty looks from the hipsters whose game of chess I'd disturbed, 'So, if that's all……..'

'Don't be a dick, Will,' Andy said quietly and I sighed and sat back down as Dawn ran a hand through her over-done bob as she stared awkwardly at her drink.

'Look,' I said as Andy signalled to the barman for another round even though he and Dawn had barely touched their drinks, 'I know how weird all of this must seem - and, believe me, it's getting weirder by the minute but,' I paused, trying to find the right words, 'it just feels like the right thing to do. Beth needs me - or, at least, she needs someone - and I'm just doing what I need to do until the police pull their finger out and find out who she belongs to.' Dawn's more natural smile told me that I had, at least, gone some way toward explaining what was going on and, as Andy collected the new drinks and then delivered them to our table, he shrugged and said,

'Well, you're right about one thing anyway, Will. I've always thought that Shandy was a bit of a C….'

'Character,' Dawn finished with a wry smile and, with that, the atmosphere was lifted and we went on to talk about less touchy subjects such as Dawn's new job with Hackney Council and the dismal performance by West Ham that season. As I wove my way home along the canal, I reflected that, all in all, it hadn't been a bad evening - which was just as well as, the following morning, all hell broke loose.

CHAPTER 17

When I woke up, I thought that the most challenging part of my day would be looking into childcare options for Beth for when I went back to work - the night before, Mum had tentatively offered to step in, at least for a little while but, as much as Beth seemed to like her, I didn't think it would be fair and so had set myself the task of researching local childminders. Other than that, I'd planned a day of doing really very little and that plan started well enough until, just after I'd washed up our breakfast dishes, there was a knock on the front door. Quickly drying my hands, I hurried through the hallway and opened the front door to find a woman who looked to be in her thirties standing on the doorstep and, behind her, a bloke holding an expensive looking camera.

'Mr Thorn?' Lynn Reeves from the Hackney Herald, have you got a moment?' I stared from her to the camera bloke who was shifting from one foot to the other, eager to get on with whatever it was that they were here for.

'What?' I asked, bewildered, 'Why, what's this about?' As I've said before, I knew that my situation with Beth was 'irregular' but I couldn't, for the life of me, fathom why it would have any interest for the local press.

'I'd like to talk to you about Beth,' the reporter pressed on, 'the Miracle Child of Bethnal Green!' Confused, I shook my head,

'Sorry mate, I think you've got the wrong end of the stick from somewhere - Beth's just a little girl,' I frowned as another thought occurred to me and one that should have come to me sooner, 'Who told you about her anyway?' Ignoring my question, she moved toward me, causing me to involuntarily move backwards and to inadvertently give her a peek inside the house, which of course was the exact moment at which Beth came wandering down the corridor. Having been left alone longer than she was comfortable with, she'd given in to her natural curiosity and decided to come and see who I was talking to and the camera bloke snapped off a picture before I could tell her to go back inside.

'Look,' I said, starting to get annoyed, 'there's no story here and I'm really busy so I'd like you to go now.' I started to close the door and, raising her voice, Lynn Reeves called,

'Can you at least let me have a comment on the story from London 24 this morning?' Ushering Beth back into the living room, I fired up my laptop and waited impatiently for it to boot up before logging onto London 24. Typing "Bethnal Green" into the search box, the story was at the top of the list as the page loaded and I quickly clicked on the link, scanning through it in disbelief as I struggled to comprehend what I was seeing. I had barely finished reading the piece when the phone rang, and, noting that the caller display showed an unknown number, I let it run to the answering machine and, after a couple of moments, heard,

'Hi Will, I'm sure you must be very busy but I'd just like a few minutes of your time,' the voice was young, female and entirely unfamiliar and I listened with increased bemusement as she went on, 'this is Diane King from the Bethnal Green News Ezine - we're all very excited about Beth and would love to meet her. Give me a call on......' I silenced the machine with a vicious stab of my finger and then pressed 'delete', having no intention of calling Diane King back to talk about Beth or anything else. I glanced over at Beth who had taken only a slight, passing interest in the answerphone message and then returned my attention to the article on London 24. I didn't recognise the name of the writer but I did recognise the name of the source - Joanne Forbes of Bethnal Green; better known to me as JoJo and I read the story again from the beginning. In a nutshell, the story told of how Joanne Forbes had 'come across' a child who knew things that she couldn't possibly know - who had an ethereal air about her like she wasn't from this world and who spoke accurately and convincingly of things that happened over seventy years ago. My first instinct was to call the Child Services HQ and speak to JoJo's boss to see if he or she was aware of what I was sure was a gross breach of confidentiality at the very least but I resisted for the moment, choosing instead to read the article one more time.

"Beth Green may just be the answer, Joanne told us, her eyes shining, not just to what happened that fateful night but also to some of the bigger questions that we all ask ourselves every day."

'What a load of crap,' I said aloud, instantly covering my mouth but Beth was oblivious as she poked at a game that we'd bought at the shopping centre; something that involved a ladybird whose wings opened to provide spaces for coloured bits of plastic. 'Just nonsense,' I added, aware even as I said it that my words didn't have the intended conviction. There were questions, I knew - ones that seemed to have no simple explanation but, I thought, simple or not there must be one - there had to be something that made more sense than what Joanne 'JoJo' Forbes was suggesting in this ill-written missive on an obscure website.

'Beth,' I began and she looked up from her game with a slight frown at being interrupted, 'Do you remember yesterday when the nice lady was here, JoJo?' Beth nodded and then went back to her game, clearly uninterested and I took a moment, unsure of how to continue then, 'Do you remember talking to her about Bobby and about Jenny ?'

'Bobby the Boxer,' Beth replied promptly, 'everyone likes Bobby.' I nodded,

'I'm sure they do. Beth, can you remember when you last saw Bobby?' A small frown again crossed her face but was then replaced with a sly smile as she shook her head,

'Nope. He said he'd give us ten bob if we didn't tell. No harm in it, he said, just a bit of fun but she would be cross.'

'Who would be cross, Beth?' I asked, 'What was it that Bobby wasn't meant to be doing?' My questions were met with silence and I forced a smile, 'It's alright, you can tell me - I won't tell Bobby, it'll just be our secret.' She considered this for a moment and then, lowering her voice even though only the two of us were in the room, she said in a semi-whisper,

'Going to the bookies. She's always cross when he goes but there's no harm in it, that's what Bobby says.' I thought for a moment then,

'Beth, this bookies that Bobby goes to, is it in Bethnal Green?' Immediately she shook her head,

'No silly,' she giggled, 'it's up West!' She paused then, in a strange, deep voice, added, 'You don't shit where you sleep!' Shocked, I stared at her and she shrugged, 'I know that's a bad word but that's what Bobby says.' She turned back to her game and I tried to keep her attention,

'Beth, you said that Bobby was on leave from the army, remember? Jenny must have been sad when he had to go back to war.' Although she continued stubbornly messing with bits of plastic from the game, it was as though a cloud passed over her features and her previously relaxed posture tensed.

'Did something happen to Bobby?' I asked quietly and, this time, she flung the pieces of her toy onto the carpet and stood up,

'I don't want to talk about Bobby anymore.' She headed for the bathroom, pausing as she got to the door, 'If he hadn't have been going where he shouldn't then he wouldn't have been where he shouldn't have been - that's what Jenny's Mum says - and he wouldn't have left his wife and kids to struggle along on their own.' She looked directly at me then, her stare trying to direct a message beyond her words as she added, 'He tried to help - Right until the end, Bobby tried to help.' She left the room and about a million questions and I turned back to my laptop, snapping it shut in disgust as I reached for the phone to give JoJo several pieces of my mind that, quite frankly, at that moment, I could ill afford. Just as my hand closed over the receiver, it rang and I pulled my hand away as though the phone were a living thing that might pounce and bite at any moment. Leaving it again to run to answerphone, I waited and listened as another unfamiliar voice - male this time - tried to solicit just a moment of my time and I had a brief urge to just unplug the damn thing, only resisting due to the fact that shutting out the unwanted calls would also mean missing out on the ones that I needed to take. When Beth returned from the toilet it was as though the previous conversation had never taken place and she picked up her game, stacking the pieces neatly on the coffee table before turning to me with a smile and asking,

'What shall we do today then?' Which, of course, was a very good question. An hour before, I had been contemplating a few possibilities including a walk around Bethnal Green Gardens and the surrounding area to see if anything jogged Beth's memory but now I was loath to even make the trip out to the front door for fear that more uninvited guests would be waiting for us. And they were. Using the reasoning that JoJo's misguided (and hopefully career destroying) move couldn't yet have spread that far - and that we would have to leave the house at some point anyway - I ventured down the hallway about ten minutes later only to spot the outline of a couple of people through the glass of the front door and I retreated quickly, ignoring the doorbell when it rang, despite Beth's questioning looks. I had absolutely no experience of the press other than what I'd seen in films where they're always portrayed as tenacious self-serving vultures who will do anything to get a story but, I reasoned as I resolutely tried to blank out the doorbell, that sort of thing only applies to celebrities and corrupt politicians, not ordinary people. I was also fairly sure that there were rules about children for the press, concerning what they could and couldn't do but then, as soon as that thought appeared, I remembered the furore in the media over the fact that some of those tenacious self-serving vultures once hacked into a murdered child's mobile phone in order to try and get to a story. It had only been about ten minutes since the first ring on the doorbell but, already my nerves were wound tighter than violin strings and I was starting to get a headache.

'Why aren't you answering the door?' Beth whispered and then urgently added 'Is it the rent man?' making me laugh out loud and blessedly relieving some of the tension that had gotten a grip on me,

'No hon, not the rent man. Just some silly people who want to talk to us about something they've got the wrong idea about.' She mulled this over for a second then,

'So, why don't you just tell them that then?' I forced a smile as I tried to figure out how to word it in a way that she would understand.

'Well,' I began, 'because they're not very nice people and, if I don't tell them what they want to hear, they'll just make up some lies so that they have something interesting to put in their newspaper.' She glanced at my copy of the Evening Standard from the day before which had a perfectly innocuous picture of some actress getting an award on the front and then asked,

'Like with Joan Barry when they wrote all those horrid things about her having Charlie Chaplin's baby?' I took a moment to process this, the name being only vaguely familiar to me and then I nodded,

'Yeah, a bit like that. But, Beth, how do you know about that?' She rolled her eyes, giving me a glimpse of the teenager-in-waiting before replying,

'Who doesn't know about it, EVERYBODY has been talking about it although,' she frowned, 'I don't see what all the fuss is about,' she paused, 'Like with Ellen and the black baby - babies are nice aren't they!' That again.

'Beth,' I began hesitantly, 'wouldn't you like to be able to see Ellen and her baby? They're your family aren't they?'

'I can see Ellen,' she replied promptly, 'but not the black baby. Not yet.'

'Did the baby go away?' I asked, thinking once again of the charms of Child Services but Beth shook her head,

'No, Ellen went away but not the baby. Not yet.' Trying - and failing - to make sense of that, I decided to change tack,

'What about your Mum and Dad, Beth, can you tell me where they are?' This time, she stopped to look at me as she replied,
'Of course, silly, they're right here!'

CHAPTER 18

"They're right here." Unable to stop myself, I glanced uneasily around the room which, apart from Beth and myself, was empty and yet I felt the hairs on my arms stand up as Beth smiled at something - or someone - that only she could see. Of course I knew that kids have imaginary friends - I had one myself when I was little; a little boy called Tom who liked adventures and who, I realised later in life, was loosely based on a kid in The Never Ending Story but that was the thing - Imaginary friends tend to be fantasy figures; the version of yourself that you'd like to be, not parents who were supposed to be safe, dull and, most importantly, there with you. Before I could ask Beth what she meant by that, the phone rang and, glancing at the caller display, I noted with relief that this time it was Mum and I grabbed it on the second ring, eager to hear a familiar voice although, coming from her, her first words were so alien that it took me a moment to assemble them into anything that made sense,
'Will, have you been on the Facebook this morning?' I blinked at the phone, apparently pausing so long that she felt that she had to repeat herself and I stopped her,
'No, I haven't, what….?' Although I have a Facebook account, I tend to visit the site only sporadically, spend five minutes sending birthday wishes to people I haven't seen since school and then, having no desire to see hundreds of pictures of people's babies, holidays or dinner, log off and, to be perfectly honest, I had no idea that Mum was even on there.
'Why?' I asked, finishing, 'what's on there?' Although, by that point I had a pretty good idea what the answer to that question would be .
'People are saying things,' Mum said in an uncharacteristically quiet voice, 'about Beth. Some woman called Joanne is saying that Beth is some kind of miracle.' For a split second, I had the urge to laugh it off - to tell Mum that it was all just silliness and that she should take no notice of anything that she sees on Facebook but then, glancing at Beth, I sighed.
'Mum, I think I need your help.'
As I was still unwilling, for the time being, to brave the outdoors, I asked if Mum could come round and she agreed readily enough although her tone was still troubled; we're not a family who attracts attention or drama and I could tell that she was already wondering what people would think about all this - had probably been wondering that since the moment that Beth came into my life but now we had the kind of attention that had breached the walls of our close circle. By the time she arrived, the doorbell had

rung another three times and the telephone five and it was on the fourth ring of the doorbell that I recognised, with relief, Mum's outline through the glass of the door and hurried to let her in.

'Will,' she said as she hurried inside, 'there are some people outside, they asked who I was but I didn't say anything, who are they?'

'I don't know, Mum,' I sighed, 'there've been a few journalist coming round trying to talk to me - no doubt having seen what JoJo's put on the internet, they've been phoning too.' Whilst waiting for Mum to arrive, I had logged onto Facebook, instantly wishing that I hadn't as I quickly saw what Mum was talking about - a post that JoJo had put on about two hours before had started to trend and had been shared by at least three people on my friends list that I could see during a quick scan of my news feed. In the post, she mentioned that she "probably shouldn't be talking about something work related" (this was the bit that I sincerely hoped would come back to bite her in the worst way possible) but that she'd come across a miracle and one that the world needed to know about. Thankfully, despite JoJo's best efforts, I very much doubted that "the world" did know, or indeed care, but I had enough experience of Facebook to know that if a story is sordid enough or gory enough, it doesn't take very long for it to reach a mind numbing number of people. I also noted, incredulously, that JoJo had "friend requested" me and I stabbed viciously at the button that would decline her request. Several people had, of course, gleefully pressed JoJo for more details which she had been only too willing to provide, along with a link to the article on London 24 and so by the time that I logged on, the story was gaining traction and, unless it was nipped in the bud, would no doubt be "viral" before the day was out. I've never quite understood why a word that describes something that spreads quickly, destroying everything in it's wake is now a term describing something that most people consider to be good - of course I understand the basic reasoning but it depresses me that the human race, with all the tools at its disposal, can sometimes be so unimaginative. Part of me wanted to respond to JoJo's post with a view to shutting it down for good but I was smart enough to realise that this would quite possibly have the opposite effect. By participating in the conversation, I would, effectively, be putting myself into the game and I didn't want to do anything that would give the story legs and, in turn, give JoJo further attention which was obviously what she was craving. Still, it was tempting to come up with some withering comment in order to mock her professionally and personally, although I knew that probably the only purpose that this would serve would be to put me in the position of troll - an internet term that I, incidentally, find wholeheartedly fitting. In order to resist the temptation, I closed the laptop and turned to Beth who was messing about with the charger for my phone, staring at it with a fascination that seemed to be all-consuming and so I went into the kitchen to put the kettle on in preparation for Mum's arrival. As I busied myself with the kettle and cups, I was making enough noise that, at first, I didn't register the sound of voices and so it took me an ill-afforded minute or so before I realised that what I was hearing wasn't the television but real live voices - and ones that were inside the flat. Hurrying from the kitchen, through the living room, I arrived in the hallway to find Beth with two men, one of whom had a camera which I made a grab for as he clicked off a couple of shots of Beth and then of me.

'What the fuck? Get out! Who let you in?'

'She did,' the non-camera-bearing bloke shrugged, but he was already retreating toward the open front door and I followed quickly, making sure that they completed the journey through the door and back out onto the path.

'Beth,' I said too loudly as I closed the door, 'don't ever EVER open the door unless I'm with you!' I took a breath and lowered my voice, 'Look, there are some not very nice people who might want to talk to you, remember the ones we were talking about before?' She nodded and I mirrored the gesture, 'OK. I know that you didn't know that you weren't supposed to but, from now, just don't open that door, alright?' Another nod then,

'Why did that man have an earring in his lip?' That was a question that I really, honestly, did not know the answer to but I tried to explain the nuances of fashion as I understood them as I finished putting together the tea tray. By the end of the explanation, Beth didn't look convinced and I knew just exactly how she felt. Now that Mum was here, we needed to come up with some sort of a plan. Until all of this, I hadn't been overly daunted by the task of looking after Beth, figuring that the job just involved feeding, clothing and sheltering her and, generally, just keeping her alive until a more permanent solution was arrived at but it seemed that now, the responsibility also required me to shield her from the attention of the press and, on that day, I felt woefully ill-equipped for the job.

'Well, if you're not going to report this JoJo, then I will!' Mum said as though we'd been discussing the subject at great length although, in reality, this was the first time that the topic had reared it's ugly head.

'I still might,' I shrugged, 'I haven't decided yet although I'm not sure I really see the point - Getting JoJo fired isn't going to undo any of this mess, is it?'

'Probably not,' she sniffed, 'but it might at least discredit the things she's saying - if she's exposed as someone unprofessional enough to put a child in harm's way then people might decide that she's not worth listening to.' That had, of course, crossed my mind, as had the slightly less noble thought of the satisfaction that would be had from seeing her crash and burn but I still wasn't sure that either of those things were worth the hassle.

'I thought she was nice,' Beth interrupted me, pointedly reminding me of my responsibility in all of this. And, so had I, which was maybe part of the problem - I'd thought she was nice too and that we'd got on, making what she'd done seem like even more of a betrayal. Or maybe I'm just not a very good judge of character. By the time the doorbell rang again, we were no nearer to a solution and we were all quiet for a moment until we heard the distant sound of footsteps retreating and then the squeak of the gate.

'Another lot buggered off,' I said with satisfaction and Mum nodded,

'Well yes, for now,' she paused, picking bits of lint from her skirt, 'but Will, maybe getting rid of them isn't the answer.' I looked at her, puzzled,

'What? I don't see what else I can do at the moment.'

'Well, I do,' she replied, giving me a pointed look, 'getting rid of them only convinces them that there's something here for them, something we're trying to hide so, what we can do is go to them instead. I gaped at her,

'Go to them, you mean……..

'Yes, Will,' she said firmly, 'I'm saying we call one of them and tell them they can come here and speak to us and to Beth. We grant them an interview and then they go away,

CHAPTER 19

The idea was so simple that, at first I couldn't believe that I hadn't thought of it myself - Let them come round with their cameras and their questions and it would soon become apparent to them that Beth was just a little girl, a bit strange perhaps, but certainly nothing to write home about. I imagined that, after getting their fill of whatever Beth decided to talk to them about, the interview would be quietly shelved and become nothing more than an embarrassing reminder of how their eagerness for a story had caused them a wasted trip. I'd even thought about briefing Beth on what she should talk to the reporters about but the idea of putting words in her mouth didn't sit well with me and I decided against it in the end. Of course things might have been different if I had but then again, maybe not - if you stitch a hundred what-ifs together, you still won't have enough cloth for a pair of pants as my Nana used to say. Flicking through the list of media people who had left messages, I came across one from Looking At London, a small television network that broadcasts largely factual programs of interest to the people of the capital and, although I had my misgivings at the idea of putting Beth on television, I also realised that it would be the quickest and most effective way of shutting this thing down. And so it was that, the following morning, Mum, Beth and I found ourselves trawling the tiny maze of streets in Soho, looking for the studios of Looking At London.

'From the directions she gave me, it must be just down here,' I said after our third wrong turn, 'she said it's toward the end of the street, just past a sushi place.'

'What's sushi?' Beth asked as the three of us jumped back in tandem when a black cab sped around a corner towards us.

'It's fish,' I explained, 'but served raw with rice and vegetables,' and Beth gave me a look that told me that she might just be a kid who still believes in fairies and magic but she wasn't about to believe that people would willingly eat raw fish. Five minutes later we were outside the unassuming building and, after announcing ourselves into the tiny little intercom, were buzzed inside and into a large bright reception area where a young woman with pink hair sat behind a reception desk with a huge mirrored wall behind her. I noticed that I still needed a haircut.

'Mr Thorn, yeah?' she asked and then, without waiting for a reply, stabbed a button on the console in front of her and informed somebody of our arrival before offering us a dizzying array of drinks including a selection of teas, coffees and mango or pomegranate juice. As we were led through to a kind of ante-room in which we would be kept before going on air, I had expected the presenter to be some perma-tanned and hairsprayed fifty-something so I was slightly taken aback when the door opened and a woman in her twenties, red haired and freckled, introduced herself as Lydia and told us that, although she was there to brief us on the whole procedure, she preferred not to get 'on topic' before going on air as repeating things was likely to make Beth sound stilted. I had to admit that this made sense and so, after being told to 'just act natural', Beth and I were whisked into another room where a young woman indifferently slapped a bit of make-up onto us both before ushering us back through the ante-room and into the studio. Although my nerves had been twanging away from the moment I woke up that morning, Beth looked calm and composed but so so tiny as she took her seat on the television set and the crew fussed about lighting and angles, whatever the hell they were. If she was nervous at all, she hadn't shown it once - when we got up, I'd gone through the whole thing with her again just to make sure that she understood what was going to happen and her only response had been a firm nod and then to tell me precisely which of her new dresses she intended to wear for the occasion. Now, as we sat under the hot bright lights, I wondered again for perhaps the hundredth time if this was a good idea - I'd seen enough shows like Jeremy Kyle and Jerry Springer to know that, a lot of the time, the set up was to make the normal folks look at worst, deviant and at best foolish and I could only pray that this wasn't going to be the case here. Sweating and itching under the lights and make-up, it was a relief when we were told that we were about to start and I smiled reassuringly at Beth as we sat through the theme music to the show and then Lydia's impossibly up-beat introduction. I had been expecting a Jeremy Kyle style studio audience full of whooping and gasping people with nothing better to do but the studio we found ourselves in was, in reality, tiny and completely empty apart from Lydia, Beth, myself and four or five members of the crew operating the lights and cameras. The whole thing was set up to seem intimate and private and I cautioned myself against trusting that impression, ever mindful that this would be a cosy chat between Lydia, Beth, myself and a few thousand strangers.

'To begin with,' Lydia began with a smile, 'Will and Beth, I'd like to thank you both for taking the time to come and talk to us this morning, I'm sure that you've had a very busy few days.' I smiled and nodded, unsure how to respond and Lydia ploughed on,

'Now, for those who haven't seen this story in the press, Will works for London Underground and, a few days ago, found Beth here alone in one of the tunnels in Bethnal Green station, is that right, Will?' I confirmed that it was and she gave me a smile before going on, 'And, unfortunately, as yet, the authorities haven't been able to trace Beth's parents and so, Will, you made the decision to take Beth in and give her a home, at least temporarily,' she paused with a look that I suspect was aiming for surprise but managed only to look slightly owlish. 'May I say, Will, that was an incredibly generous gesture on your behalf!' I shrugged, already uncomfortable with the "hero" angle and the fact that that we were talking about Beth as though she weren't sitting right between us.

'Not really,' I said in what I hoped was a matter-of-fact tone, 'Everyone is very confident that we'll find Beth's family sooner rather than later and this seemed like a better solution than having her plugged into the foster system.' There was a pause and then Lydia leaned forward slightly, subtly alerting her viewers to the fact that things were about to start heating up.

'That's really good to hear but, Will, Beth's not just an ordinary little girl is she? She....'

'Not at all,' I interrupted having been anticipating this direction change, 'She's funny and extremely clever, as are many many of the little girls out there that you refer to as "ordinary". In the few days that I've known her, I've discovered that Beth has many special qualities, including a resilience during what must be a very upsetting time for her.' Lydia paused a beat or two too long as she re-programmed her mental satnav to deal with this then,

'I'm sure that's true and, of course every little girl - and boy for that matter - is special but I am, of course, referring to the recent reports about Beth. People are saying that she has spoken about things that she can't possibly know about - things that happened decades before she was born,' she paused for effect as one of the camera-men zoomed in on her, 'Spoken about these things as though she had actually been there.' I sighed,

'Yes, I have, of course, seen the stories. Firstly, by "people", we're actually only talking about one person - an employee of Child Services who, I have to say, has behaved incredibly unprofessionally. Secondly, although I will admit that Beth does have something of a vivid imagination, the stories published by this Child Services *professional* are, of course, nonsense and we are currently working to have them removed from the internet.' Lydia nodded, her expression turning serious in order to take into account my comment about JoJo's behaviour but I caught a sly smile as she turned to Beth, the cameras following her so that only the two of them were now in the frame. 'Hello Beth, thank you for coming to see us today, I know that all of this must be a little bit scary.' The camera zoomed in on Beth whose expression was placid but watchful as Lydia continued, 'Now, I know that Beth isn't your real name but is it OK if I call you Beth for now?' Beth nodded, her hands folded primly in her lap, exuding a self-possessed confidence that made me release the breath that I was holding. 'OK, that's lovely,' Lydia carried on, 'Now, Beth, do you remember talking to a lady called JoJo when she came to see you at Will's flat the other day?'

'Yes, she was nice,' Beth replied and Lydia smiled, pleased,

'Was she? Well, I'm very happy to hear that and, Beth, do you remember what you talked about with JoJo?' There was a pause as Beth gazed directly into the camera that was trained on her, blue eyes huge in her pale face and freshly washed hair shining, before she turned back to Lydia,

'Bobby. We talked about Bobby and Jenny .' Every fibre of my being itched to intervene but I held my tongue, confident that Beth didn't need my help, at least not yet. 'You talked about Bobby,' Lydia smiled, 'that must have been nice. Beth, can you tell me who Bobby is?'

'Bobby the boxer,' Beth replied promptly and then, looking around at the cameras, 'Bobby was on television too. He was bleeding but it wasn't scary cos you couldn't see that it was red.'

'Why was Bobby bleeding?' Lydia asked and Beth rolled her eyes,

'Because he was boxing and the other man hit him.' Lydia nodded,

'How come you couldn't see that the blood was red Beth?'

'Because there was no colour of course, just dark bits and light bits.' She paused and then, 'We saw the King on television too - at Christmas at Bobby's house.'

'The King?' Lydia asked eagerly, 'Which King did you see Beth?' Beth did the eye roll thing again, suddenly seeming much older than she was,

'King George of course, Bertie. He said that we have to make a world where we can all live together in justice and peace but Bobby said that's bollocks.' I let out a snort of startled laughter, earning myself a dirty look from JoJo and I guiltily turned it into a cough as Beth's eyes widened as she realised that she'd said a bad word.

'King George, of course,' Lydia continued undeterred, 'Beth, do you know who the Prime Minister is?' Beth nodded and answered too loudly as though it was an answer in a test,

'Winston Churchill. I haven't seen him on television but I've seen him in the newspaper.'

'So,' Lydia clarified, 'George is the King and Winston Churchill is the Prime Minister, is that right?' Beth fixed her with a level gaze but said nothing and I decided that the time had come for me to jump in,

'She's probably been learning about all this at school,' I butted in, 'I would imagine the schools have been teaching a lot about our monarchy what with the Queen's ninetieth birthday coming up.'

'Beth,' Lydia carried on, ignoring me, 'Who's your favourite actress?'

'I like Rita Hayworth,' Beth again replied promptly, 'but we don't go to the pictures much cos it's too dear - everyone says we have to make sac......sacrifices cos there's a war on.'

'I think this has gone on long enough,' I interrupted again and began to pluck at the microphone attached to my shirt and Lydia put up a hand to stop me,

'I'm sorry, I didn't mean to bombard Beth with questions, Will. I couldn't help but get a bit carried away as Beth is so very interesting to talk to and, I think we'll all agree, a very unusual little girl.'

'As I said before,' I replied, 'Beth has a very vivid imagination but I assure you that she's not unusual in the way that you're implying - as I said, kids learn things in school and they see things in films and on television and that's all that this is.'

'Well,' Lydia said, the sly smile back on her face, 'If you'll give me just a few more minutes of your time, we have a short video of somebody who seems to very much disagree with that statement and I'd like to play it for you now.'

CHAPTER 20

This was a mistake. That wasn't the only thought in my head but it was certainly the predominant one as a screen on the wall behind us burst into life and the picture sprang into focus to show a seated woman who looked familiar although I couldn't place her at first. The idea behind bringing Beth here and putting her through this had been to mock and discredit the things that had been said on the internet but, as the woman on the screen began to speak and I finally recognised her, I realised that I'd probably only made things much much worse.

'Well, I only met Beth the once,' the woman on the screen who had been introduced as Margaret said, 'but I could tell that she was different straight away - you could just tell that there was something special about her.' I closed my eyes as if, in doing so, I could block out the woman from the shopping centre, the one who had been handing out leaflets, but she continued regardless,

'I knew it was her, right away,' she said glancing around as though she were unsure of where she should be looking, 'you know, when I saw the story on the internet - I said to Terry, that's my husband, that's her, the one I was telling you about.' A disembodied voice on the recording said something that I couldn't make out and the woman, Margaret, nodded in response.

'Well, I met her when I was giving out leaflets at the shopping centre in Stratford - she was with Will who, I believe, is looking after her at the moment and, as soon as I saw her, I knew that there was something other-worldly about her.' I let out a snort of derision but still didn't seem able to make good on my earlier plan to unplug myself and Beth and leave the studio as Margaret carried on,

'I was helping to promote the showing of Bambi at the local cinema you see and the little girl, Beth, said that she'd already seen it,' she paused, her expression intense as she looked directly into the camera and said, 'She said she'd seen it at the Bug Hole in Bethnal Green which simply isn't possible. I'm seventy six years old and I'd completely forgotten about the Bug Hole until that day. You see, the Bug Hole was a cinema that I used to go to as a child but Beth couldn't have ever been there - I don't even know how she knew about it - the Bug Hole closed decades before my children were born and they're in their thirties now!' The screen froze and, as the lights in the studio brightened, Lydia turned to me with a smug smile as she said,

'Will, I realise that your main goal here is to protect Beth and I have to say that you're doing an admirable job but, you have to accept that there are a lot of people with questions that, as yet, simply do not have a logical answer!' I sighed and, this time, did extricate myself from the equipment attached to my clothes as I said,

'What I will accept, Lydia, is that people need something with which to fill up their sad little lives and, this time, they've decided to target a frightened and confused little girl for their own entertainment and,' I dumped the microphone onto the chair that I had just vacated, 'I think that enough of mine and Beth's time has been wasted on this ridiculous story.' As I stood, I realised that I'd been so intent on my little speech that I hadn't noticed that Beth had also stood and had wandered over to one of the cameras, her fists clenched so tightly that the knuckles stood out white against the dark of the camera pit.

'Beth, come away from there hon,' I said but she ignored me as, gazing into the huge lens of the camera she began muttering something to herself.

'Can we turn those cameras off now please?' I snapped but was again ignored by Lydia and the camera crew who were all staring at Beth, eagerly waiting to see what she would do next. With an irritated sigh, I crossed the studio in a few large strides and went to take Beth's hand. I'll admit that, at this point I was angry - at the studio for exploiting an innocent little kid for ratings, at the old busybody trying to get her fifteen minutes of fame but, mostly at myself for putting Beth in this position in the first place so I was probably rougher than I meant to be as I grabbed her hand and attempted to pull her away from the intrusive gaze of the camera.

'What's she saying?' Lydia called from where she was still seated on the studio set, apparently still eager to get as much out of Beth as possible before we finally took our leave and the cameraman shrugged,

'Dunno, I haven't been able to make any of it out, but we'll probably be able to amplify and clean it up on the playback,'

'Don't bother,' I snapped, pulling Beth away, 'I'll be doing everything in my power to make sure that you don't broadcast any of this anyway.'

'Good luck with that,' Lydia said dismissively as she stood and began to walk off the set, 'you signed a contract agreeing to today's recording and giving us the right to broadcast however much of it that we see fit.' Unable to believe what I was hearing, I lost concentration for just a moment but it was long enough for Beth to pull her hand out of mine and shove the camera dolly in front of her - although she can't have used much force, the cameraman wasn't expecting it and he staggered backwards as the dolly caught him in the chest and, rather than rushing to help their fallen colleague, the other two camera blokes zoomed in on Beth again as, still muttering at first but then getting louder, she yelled something that I only understood when she repeated it in a shout,

'They can't hear us! Why can't they hear us?'

'It's OK, Beth,' this was Mum who had pushed her way past the two cameramen at the side and was reaching for Beth as she repeated, 'Everything's OK, we're going to go home now.'

'Why can't they hear us?' Beth repeated, this time in no more than a whisper and, grasping her hand, Mum asked, puzzled,

'Who Beth? Who can't hear us?'

'The ones down there,' Beth moaned, her face a picture of misery as she added,

'The ones down in the tunnel. Why can't they hear us here on the steps?'

CHAPTER 21

'Did you get that?' These were the first words spoken after Beth's outburst and they were spoken, of course, by Lydia. Knowing already that the camera-man had, in fact, got that (part of me had noted that flashing green light on the camera throughout the whole thing), I didn't wait for his response as I grabbed Beth and strode through the studio, Mum right behind us almost tripping over one of the thick camera cables in her new high heels bought especially for the occasion, and we didn't stop until we were outside and blinking in the sunlight.

'I didn't like that lady,' Beth said matter-of-factly, no sign of the recent storm and I smiled grimly,

'Neither did I, hon, I'm sorry I made you do that.' She smiled widely, sunshine after the rain, and shrugged,

'S'alright, I liked the funny tea though.' I couldn't help but chuckle, thinking that I supposed at least one good thing had come out of the whole debacle and I was so busy concentrating on getting across the busy Soho street and heading for home that I didn't notice the young bloke with the camera until he was right in front of us. Thinking that he was just another rude and harried office worker, I swerved to move around him and it was only when he shifted again to block our path that I recognised him for what he was. 'Do you wanna get out of our way, mate,' I asked in a reasonably calm tone, 'I can assure you that we're all really not in the mood at the moment.' Ignoring me, the journalist who can't have been more than twenty four, twenty five, ignored me and gave Beth what he probably thought was a winning smile although it won nothing from Beth but a fierce glance and then dismissal as she followed my lead to try to get around the human obstacle.

'Just a couple of minutes of your time, Mr Thorn,' he persisted and I frowned, amazed at how, all of a sudden, everybody wanted "just a couple of minutes" of my time, as though that would be all that was required to get the whole complex and weird story.

'As I said,' I reiterated, giving him a light but firm shove, 'we're really not in the mood at the moment so I really do suggest that you get out of our way. Now.' Reluctantly, he stepped aside but, apparently, couldn't resist clicking off a couple of pictures and I really didn't have the energy to take issue with him about it - the street was lunchtime busy and we were being buffeted from all sides by hard-faced media types hurrying to the nearest Pret or EAT with the urgency of paramedics hustling to the scene of an accident and all I wanted was to get Beth, and myself and Mum, away from there as quickly as possible. It was times like that that I regretted never having gotten around to owning a car but then, I reasoned, it wouldn't have helped much in our current situation as I would have had the choice of either parking about ten miles away or taking out a mortgage to pay for parking in one of the NCP spots. Although already depressed at the thought of the expense, I flagged down a passing cab and the three of us climbed inside and, as we sped away from the scene of the prime media location, I was just grateful that it was mid morning meaning that, at least, the meter wouldn't be ticking away while we sat snared up in traffic. Although Beth seemed unperturbed, I was shaken by the experience and just wanted to get us home as quickly as possible but I got the driver to drop us at the Tesco Metro just down the road from my flat, figuring that I would do well to get in some provisions in the event that we needed to hole ourselves up for the next few days. Mum hadn't said much during the drive from Soho to the East End and I raised an eyebrow as, during our amble around the shop, she picked up a large bottle of red and deposited it in my trolley - it appeared that she did have some things to say - about a litre's worth!

'You asked me once what your Dad thinks about you and Beth,' she said and I nodded, 'I did. And you said he was proud of me.' We were back at the flat and, after settling Beth down for a nap, Mum had opened the wine and the floodgates.

'I know - and he is, you know, very proud of you for taking on the responsibility simply because it was the right thing to do but, the thing is,' she took a large gulp of wine, 'This.

This new situation with Beth....' She sighed and then, 'You know that your Dad's health's not great these days don't you Will?' I nodded and jumped in to save her from saying it,

'I know and, believe me, that has already crossed my mind but, I promise you, I'm going to do everything I possibly can to make all this stop,' I took an equally large slug of wine, 'I was thinking you and Dad could go and see the Hiddlestones in Spain.' I had been expecting her to veto the idea immediately but, instead, she nodded thoughtfully. The Hiddlestones were long term friends of Mum and Dad's and they'd moved to Loret De Mar a few years back when they retired - Mum had often talked about going out there to visit and I figured that this would be the perfect time. I still imagined that this whole thing would be forgotten within a couple of days but, in the meantime, I thought it was unlikely that the press would follow my parents to Spain. Just one more thing for me to be wrong about.

'That's not a bad idea,' Mum said, brightening a little, 'It'd get your Dad away from all this and,' she smiled, 'it would be nice to have a proper chat with Penny, not just on the phone.' I nodded, relieved,

'You deserve a holiday anyway and,' I topped up our glasses, 'maybe Beth and I will come out there to join you for a few days.'

'That would be lovely,' she said and then frowned, 'but what about work, won't you have to go back soon? You don't want to lose your job.' I shrugged, that was a very good question - I had told them a couple of weeks but, after the last few days, it all seemed a bit pointless to be honest but Mum was right, I needed the job and Jim was a nice bloke but he wouldn't wait forever.

'We'll see,' I said vaguely, 'I'll speak to Jim tomorrow, let him know what's going on.' As it turned out, I didn't need to as Jim saw for himself what was going on when the Looking At London programme about Beth aired that evening.

CHAPTER 22

It was past midnight and I was stood in the hallway trying, with limited success, to unscrew the doorbell. I knew that this wouldn't stop them from hammering on the door but anything was better than the harsh buzzing sound of the doorbell waking Beth every fifteen minutes and winding my nerves ever tighter with each buzz. Although she'd offered, more than once, to stay, I'd reluctantly sent Mum off in a taxi about nine o'clock - there was no point in her being trapped in the flat too and, as she'd said herself, arrangements would need to be made if she and Dad were to fly off to Spain. I gave the plastic casing of the doorbell a last tug and it finally came apart allowing me to quickly disable it with a sigh of relief. It wasn't great but it was better - even then I don't think I had any idea how mental this whole thing was going to get; I was still convincing myself that it would all blow over within a day or so and the press would move onto bigger and better stories and so I went back to the living room confident that, if nothing else, Beth would now be able to get some much needed sleep. Alright for some! Without a shred of experience to prepare me, I had absolutely no idea how to deal with something like this, who would? I'd already called my local police station to tell them that I had half of London's press turning up on my doorstep and ringing the bell and was sympathetically but firmly told that, unless they were trespassing on my own personal property, there was nothing that could be done. I'd turned the phone's ringer to silent, choosing not to disable it completely in case Mum called to let me know her travel plans meaning that my evening was punctuated with message after message coming in from various media outlets, all of whom simply wanted a few minutes of my time. And so it was that, at about eleven o'clock I caught a message from a Spencer Hall telling me that he was calling from a PR company called, amusingly, Hall and Oakes and that he was able to help me with the peculiar situation that I now found myself in. After only a few moments hesitation I picked up the phone and dialled the number that Hall had provided in his message, eager to connect with somebody who could maybe help make all of this go away. The phone only rang once before it was picked up and a man with a plummy Oxbridge accent introduced himself as Spencer Hall. In a conversation that only lasted about three minutes, Spencer assured me that he knew exactly how to handle my situation and asked if I could come into his office. When I explained that this wasn't practical (I can't go for that, no can do) he sighed and agreed to come to the flat instead and, after I gave him directions, he hung up after promising to be on my doorstep promptly at nine o'clock the following morning. The way things were going, I was tempted to mark a corner of the doorstep with a "reserved" sign for him. In the meantime, I settled myself in for what promised to be a very long night, figuring that sleep would be impossible and so it was with some surprise that I awoke on the sofa to see the first thin tendrils of daylight through the living room window. Looking at the clock, I saw that it was just a little before seven o'clock and so, after checking on Beth, I decided to hit the shower and get a head start on the day. A quick peek down the hallway confirmed that I still had company, some of whom had no doubt been there all night and I closed the door, cheerfully hoping that they were as cold and bored as I imagined them to be. True to his word, Spencer Hall arrived at nine o'clock on the dot, calling as he made his way up the drive to alert me of his presence and I gratefully let him in and ushered him into the living room where Beth was engrossed in yet another episode of Peppa Pig. After fixing some coffee, I settled down on the sofa opposite the man who was dressed uber-sharply in a navy pin-striped suit, making my jeans and ancient Oasis t.shirt seem even scruffier than they actually were.

'Firstly,' he said without any preamble, for which I was grateful, 'have you spoken to anybody about this since the Looking At London programme aired last night?' I shook my head and he nodded, 'Good. Let's keep it that way until we have a game plan.' He took out a complicated looking electronic organiser and, after stabbing at the screen a few times, stared at it for a moment before continuing.

'From now on, the media gets only what we drip-feed them - To begin with, I'm working on getting an exclusive with one of the glossies as they tend to be the highest payers…..'

'Hang on,' I interrupted, alarmed, 'I'm not interested in making money out of Beth!' He gave me a pitying look,

'Understood. But, Mr Thorn, it is, unfortunately, what makes the world go round and, I don't imagine that you'll be going back to your job at London Underground….' he held up a hand to silence my unvoiced protest, brown eyes stern behind his sensible rimless glasses, 'and, even if that were your intention, they are not going to want you back, not with the kind of attention that you're currently attracting. No,' he straightened an imaginary crease from his impeccable trousers, 'I'm afraid that will simply not be possible and so the money part is just common sense.'

'But,' I replied miserably, 'It just seems totally wrong,' and he gave me a sympathetic smile,

'Mr Thorn',

'Will,'

'Will, these people are going to be watching you and Beth and writing about you anyway so, you might as well at least have something to show for it.' I had to reluctantly admit that that made sense and I freshened our coffee as Spencer gave Beth a speculative look that I didn't much care for, guessing (accurately) that he was mentally sizing her up for magazine photographs and God knew what else.

'Now,' he continued glancing again at Beth but, this time, to ascertain how much of our conversation she was listening to - although she seemed entirely absorbed by her TV show, I had a feeling that she was still tuned into the two of us and I smiled uneasily as he pressed on with, 'What I'm going to need to know about is anybody with any kind of grudge against you, anyone who might,' he paused, shifting awkwardly in the narrow armchair, 'dish the dirt as it were.' I thought for a moment before answering,

'Not that I can think of,' and then I remembered Shandy, 'I mean, I just broke up with somebody - over this…..situation….but I can't see her talking to the press about it.'

'Name,' Spencer barked and I replied,

'Shandy. Shandia Washington.'

'Shandy,' he repeated as though it amused him and I felt a brief stab of dislike toward this man who, it appeared, made a considerable amount of money from people like me, ordinary people who, through no fault of their own, find themselves in extraordinary situations.

'I apologise if I come across as a little harsh,' he said as though reading my mind, 'but these people are vultures and they will not hesitate to jump on any and every piece of salacious gossip that's presented to them. Our job here is to make sure that anything presented to the media shows you - and Beth - in a positive light and so, if you were unfaithful to this Shandy, or mistreated her in any way, it's best that I know about it before the press do.' I shook my head, defeated,

'No, nothing like that. As I say, we broke up a few days ago because she didn't like - didn't understand - why I felt that I had to take Beth in but, other than that, everything was fine between us.'

'Good,' Spencer repeated and I ploughed on, suddenly unable to stop talking despite mentally advising myself of caution,

'She's got a little girl,' I said, 'Shandy - she's got a daughter called Adele. Not mine. The father doesn't have anything to do with them. Married.'

'That's helpful,' Spencer responded and I squinted at him,

'Is it?'

'Yes,' he gave me a frank look, 'If, for whatever reason, she does decide to speak to the press unfavourably about you, we have some ammunition to fire back with.' He smiled, 'Oh, don't look so appalled Mr Thorn, Will. I know that you think that Shandy isn't the type of person to go to the press but I've been doing this a long time and you would be surprised at how the idea of their fifteen minutes of fame makes some people do funny things.' Actually, I wouldn't - I'd seen enough copies of The Sun to know what people are capable of, I'd just never imagined that one day it would be me. As though to punctuate the subject of our conversation, there was a loud banging at the front door and, without hesitation, Spencer rose and strode down the hallway and through the open living room door, I heard him bark, 'My client has nothing to say to you right now. Leave your cards with me and I will contact you if and when Mr Thorn decides to speak to you.' To my amazement, the clamouring outside died down immediately and, when Spencer returned to the living room, it was with a fistful of business cards which he tucked indifferently into his briefcase as I mused on the fact that the guy was worth keeping around even if just for the particular magic trick that he had just performed.

'Now,' he said decisively as he snapped the locks on his case shut, 'I will be in touch later today but I will repeat what I said earlier - you do not speak to anybody - Anybody! - other than your very close friends and family without consulting me first, are we clear?' I nodded dumbly and he slid a sheet of paper over to me, 'This is our contract which states that I now speak on your behalf as far as the media are concerned. I realise that you may want your solicitor to look it over but I will need this back pronto if you want me working on your behalf.'

'That's allowed, is it?' I asked and he gave me a questioning look, 'I'm allowed to talk to my solicitor as well as my close family and friends?' For a brief moment, Spencer Hall looked annoyed but then he chuckled,

'Absolutely - but not his receptionist, secretary or any other such minion.' He stood to leave and repeated, 'I will need that back signed and sealed as quickly as you can, Will. Get it checked if you must but it's just a standard partnership agreement.' Standard. As though I actually had a solicitor and as though I were constantly deluged with legal documents that required such a person to check them through. In reality, the only contracts I'd ever signed were for my mobile phone, the lease agreement on my flat and the hefty document from TFL detailing what I can do and when, not only during my working hours but including the several hours leading up to the start of a shift. This was entirely new territory for me but, then, so had the entire past few days and, after a cursory glance which told me that Spencer Hall would be running interference for me and Beth in return for which, he would receive a weighty but fair commission from any monies earned, I signed and handed it back to him, solicitor be damned !

'Very good,' he said mildly, posting the document through a slot at the top of his suitcase, 'as I mentioned, I'll be in touch later, in the meantime........'

'Don't talk to anyone, I know, I know.' He smiled,

'What I was going to say was, try to get some sleep - you look dreadful Will.' Good advice, I thought as I walked him down the hallway and closed the door behind him, but there was more chance of me running for Prime Minister than there was getting any more sleep and so I stuck the kettle back on as I tried to figure out how I would keep a small child occupied in a small flat for a couple of days. I was just pouring the (extra strong) coffee when I heard Beth say something and I called through to the living room, 'Hang on Beth, I'll be back in there in just a second.' There was a moment of silence and then I heard her repeat it, although I still couldn't make out what it was that she was saying and, thinking that it would no doubt be another of the random but mainly inconsequential things kids talk about, but urgent to them at the time, I called again for her to hang on for just a minute. Again, there was a moment of silence before she repeated it, loud enough for me to hear this time and, as I hurried through to the living room, still holding my scalding cup, she began repeating it over and over like a chant, her voice increasing in pitch and volume until, by the time that I reached the living room, her voice seemed to be bouncing off - and coming out of - every wall as she repeated, 'Am I dying? AM I DYING?' and a chill swept through me as I realised that, although I could hear her voice loud and clear, there was absolutely no sign of Beth.

CHAPTER 23

I'm standing on the beach watching some kids playing hide and seek and the "seeker" is cheating. He's supposed to count to a hundred but I watch as he reaches seventy five and then races through the rest in a single breath before setting off on his quest. That's OK, I used to cheat too. I remember playing the game when I was about his age; finding some obscure place to hide and then waiting, trying not to giggle but also in the grip of an illogical but very real terror of the moment that the tablecloth or curtain would be pulled back to reveal my presence. Of course, being the seeker was even more terrifying as a part of me was always convinced that, in childish conspiracy, my friends, instead of hiding and waiting to be found, would have taken off to the Rec or to McDonalds and would be sitting there laughing at the image of me trying, fruitlessly, to find them. It did happen once or twice. During her time with me, Beth never expressed a desire to have other kids to play with, partly I think because she was aware of the pressure we were under with the press and all that but, also, I think she was just content to play by herself. She certainly never showed any interest in playing hiding games in fact, just the opposite, usually she seemed to have a need to keep me in sight at all times or, at least, as much as was possible. My therapist - I have one of those now, a woman in her sixties called Tracey, with a kind face and bright red hair - has told me that, of course, Beth didn't really vanish; that she was there the whole time and that my over-tired mind just kind of edited her out of the scene for a bit. She doesn't really help, this therapist, but it's soothing to sit in her quiet, cosily lit office for an hour every week and so I keep going - the good old NHS are paying for it, so why not? There is a shriek as the seeker finds one of the hiders behind the closed ice-cream hut, a little girl with dark hair in uneven pigtails who, in her pique at being the first to be found, blurts out the location of one of the other hiders and the game is declared void, all of the others reluctantly emerging from their hiding places and glaring at the pigtailed traitor. I move away from the little gang, aware more than anyone these days of the dangers of being a lone male in the presence of children but, as I walk back toward my hut, I can still hear the kids arguing the finer points of Hide And Seek law, one particularly squeaky voiced girl insisting that it's wrong to dob somebody else in just because you've been caught out. She's wrong though - not the little girl, the therapist. Although my mind was, almost certainly, tired, I know what I saw, or rather didn't see, Of course, I didn't tell her that - arguing with her highly trained and, no doubt expensive, explanations is, apparently, not in the spirit of wanting to get better and so I just nodded and mumbled, 'S'pose you're right.' She wasn't though, she wasn't right and she wasn't there.

CHAPTER 24

For a moment I couldn't move - couldn't breathe - the sound of Beth's voice was deafening, chasing every thought out of my head, and yet the room was empty.

'Beth?' I finally managed, 'Where are you hon?' As I spoke, the sound of her voice faded and then grew silent as though somebody were using a remote control to turn down the volume on a TV set and, for a second, the only sound was that of my heart which was beating way too fast.

'Beth, stop this now, where are you? I'm worried.' I took a step toward the bedroom, even though logic told me that her voice had been way too loud for her to have been in another room and it was then that I heard her voice again, at a normal volume and, this time, from right behind me and I swung around to find her standing in the doorway between the kitchen and the living room, a small smile playing on her lips as she announced,

'I'm here.'

'What......? Where were you?' I asked and she simply shrugged and repeated, 'I'm here,' as though that were all that I needed to know and, for the time being, I suppose it was.

'You shouldn't just go off like that,' I scolded, 'I was worried about you!' She nodded as though this was just exactly what she had expected as she said,

'OK,' and then, 'Who's that?'

'Who's what?' I asked and, a split second later, there was a loud knocking at the front door.

'How did you.......? I started and then stopped - all I seemed to be doing was asking Beth questions to which I never got an answer. I hoped that sometime soon that would change but, for the time being there were more pressing matters and I frowned as I looked toward the front door; Spencer Hall had made himself very clear when he told me not to speak to anybody but close family and friends but I thought I would go mad if I was forced to just wait it out every time one of the press boys or girls decided to do a bit of a Phil Collins on the front door. After a few seconds of indecision, I grabbed one of the business cards that Spencer had left behind and, strode down the hallway toward the door where a quick glance through the glass was enough to confirm that this latest visitor was another crusader for the truth or, at least, a juicy story. Prying the letterbox open (not easy from the inside), I poked the business card through and yelled to the reporter that any and all queries should be directed to Spencer Hall then I returned to the living room, relieved that at least one task had been taken out of my hands. On my return, I was half expecting Beth to have vanished again but she was still sat in the armchair playing with another of the expensive bits of tat that we had bought at the shopping centre and I took a moment to just appreciate the quiet and calm. Having a quick tidy up, I came across one of the school prospectus leaflets that I'd picked up and laughed softly to myself - at least for the time being, it was unlikely that Beth would be leaving the house at all, let alone five days a week in order to attend a school. I supposed that I should be thinking about starting on some kind of home learning routine but, for the moment, it was a concept that I had neither the time or the inclination to give much serious thought to. As I mentioned, Jim had, of course, seen the programme when it aired and it was about lunchtime when he called, sounding uncharacteristically nervous to tell me that it might be best if we extended my leave by at least a month or so as, apparently, Head Office were concerned that all the attention would prevent me from doing my job to the best of my ability. The good news was that, at least for now, I would still be paid, something that came as a relief as my meagre funds were dwindling rapidly.

'You know, I've got kids, Will,' Jim said apropos of nothing and I smiled,

'I know that, Jim, I've met them, remember? Several times.' And I had, at least once a year at the work barbecue, Siobhan who was fourteen and Owen who was eleven or twelve - nice kids as far as I could tell although I didn't really see what they had to do with my current situation.

'Yeah, course,' Jim replied and then noisily cleared his throat, 'I just wanted to say that what you're….you know, what you're doing is really admirable Will. I love Siobhan and Owen to bits but the idea of having to look after them by myself, let alone with all this fuss going on, well………' He let the rest of the sentence hang and I decided to put him out of his misery;

'Thanks Jim but I'm not completely on my own - Mum's been great and, as for the press and that, the extended leave is a good thing as we're thinking of getting away for a bit, all of us.'

'Good, good,' Jim said suddenly sounding distracted as I had visions of a customer arguing that he did buy the right ticket but the machine got it wrong or, somebody insisting that TFL are responsible for the laptop that they carelessly left on the platform and I wrapped up our conversation with a good old British 'Well, I'll let you get on then.' And that was that. All of a sudden, I was disconnected from the thing that had been the one constant in my life for my entire adult existence and I felt a momentary sense of panic at the strange, ungrounded feeling that overcame me. Then Beth told me that she needed a wee - how's that for grounded? As hard as it was, I made a vow to get through the rest of the day and night without even glancing at the television or the internet and so, with this mission in mind, I devised a game for myself and Beth whereby each room in the flat was a different country. As lame as it may sound, the game involved the two of us standing in each room in turn and talking about what that place might be like and we enjoyed ourselves, particularly in France (aka the bathroom) where Beth seemed delighted by my dodgy French accent and silly talk of snails and frogs legs. Finally, exhausted, I made us the Will Thorn version of a croque Monsieur and found The Jungle Book on Netflix for us to watch. When I put Beth to bed, it was only nine o'clock and I itched to log onto the internet - just to have some form of contact with the outside world but I resisted, instead picking up a James Pattterson paperback that I'd started months before and then abandoned. Although the antics of The Women's Murder Club did distract me for a while, I still felt restless and discomfited by the idea of being trapped in my own home and the walls seemed to close in a little more every time the phone rang or there was a knock at the door. It's times like that that social media is most tempting - the urge to connect with other people if only in the most tenuous way and I glanced several times toward the laptop, itching to log on but I knew that doing so would rob me of the little sleep that I was likely to get that night and so I did the next worst thing - I called the one person that I hadn't yet spoken to since this whole circus began.

CHAPTER 25

Although the phone only rang two or three times before it was picked up, it was long enough for me to almost hang up at least twice. I told myself that I was just calling to say hello, how are you, been a long time etc as I could still hear Spencer Hall urging me to speak to nobody, but I knew better. I wanted to talk. I wanted to talk and talk and talk, and not about the weather or work or any of the other inconsequential things that people engage themselves with to avoid the bigger issues. There was a click as the phone was picked up and then a pause that I remembered so well, even though it had been over five years since we'd last spoken and I took a breath as I prepared to announce myself, unsure as to how she would react to this blast from the past at eleven o'clock on a Thursday night.

'Will,' she said before I had the chance, 'I'm not sure this is a very good idea.' As understatements go, that was a pretty good one but it was too late for that now - it had been too late for that from the moment that I dialled her number, despite the couple of almost hang ups.

'I know,' I said quietly, 'and I'm sorry, but I really need to talk to you.' I was treated to another of those pauses and I heard the tell-tale click of her lighter as I pictured her shifting to a more comfortable position, preparing herself physically and mentally for the conversation ahead.

'How are you?' She asked after almost a minute and I resisted the urge to make a flip comment, aware that she was probably the only person that I knew who, when asking that question, was genuinely interested in the answer.

'Not good,' I replied honestly, 'Out of sorts and out of my depth.' I sighed, 'This is such a weird situation for me - for anyone - and I'm scared. Scared that I'm ruining my life and,' I ran a hand through my hair, 'scared that I'm ruining Beth's. I mean, she seems OK but she's only a kid'

'She's not though, is she Will. Only a kid.'

'No,' I admitted, 'no, she's not.' I hesitated, unsure of how much to tell her, 'It's real Shelly. Everything they're saying is real and there's so much more that they don't even know about.'

'Are you scared of her Will?' I froze, floored by the unexpected question that had, honestly, never crossed my mind before then but then answered immediately and honestly,

'No. Not even a little bit, but I'm scared for her. Of not knowing how to help her. She's not a ghost, Shelly and she's not an illusion. I don't know what she is but I do believe - know - that she was there; somehow she was there that day at Bethnal Green.' This time, the pause was so long that I worried that she had hung up and then,

'We can't see each other you know Will. I mean, I want to help, I really do but…….'

'I know,' I replied quickly, 'and I'm not asking for that. I just needed to talk so you have helped anyway, really.' It was the truth, she had helped - just talking to her was a balm on my frazzled nerves and I felt stronger, more able to cope.

'I'm glad,' she said warmly, 'As soon as I saw all the stuff on the internet and in The Sun, I wanted to reach out but I wasn't sure that I should - wasn't sure if you would want that after everything that happened,' a pause during which I heard her lighter being brought into service again, 'After what I did.'

'Shelly look……'

'I tried to call your Mum but she wouldn't take my call. Not that I blame her of course but I just wanted to know how you were. How's she taking all this?' I smiled into the phone,

'Brilliantly - you know how she is - but I'm trying to get her and Dad to get off to Spain to visit some friends til all this dies down. They shouldn't have to be mixed up in all this, not with Dad's dodgy ticker and all that.'

'That's a good idea, you're a good boy Will and you'll figure out what to do about all this, I know you will. You can call me again but now I'm tired and I need to……'

'Who are you talking to?' Startled, I swivelled round in my seat to find Beth standing in the doorway between the bathroom and the living room although I hadn't heard her get out of bed or move from the bedroom to the bathroom and I smiled,

'Nobody hon. Sorry, did I wake you up or did you have a bad dream?' She shook her head,

'No dreams. Not any more.'

'Listen Shelly,' I said into the phone and there was a low chuckle,

'Nobody. That's who I am, isn't it Will?'

'No, I didn't mean….' I flustered, trying to find the right words which is why I didn't hear Beth cross the room, didn't realise that she was beside me until she took the phone from my hand, holding it awkwardly in both hands, seemingly unused to the sleek

design. She studied it closely for a moment before holding it to her ear, the handset casting a dark shadow across her face as she gently said,
'It wasn't your fault.'

CHAPTER 26

Grandma Shelly. Dad's Mum and the reason, I suspected, that I had been chosen. I don't, of course mean 'chosen' in any kind of Messiah kind of way, I'm not delusional, but chosen by Beth as the one to help her. To help her do what was, back then, a question that I still didn't have any idea of the answer to. Throughout my childhood, Grandma Shelly had only really been a name, someone that, by the age of fourteen, I'd met only once or twice. Usually at funerals which were the only occasions that she deemed important enough to break her self-imposed exile from the world. Had she been born in a different time, Grandma Shelly would no doubt have been sent to various mental health professionals who would have coaxed, counselled and coddled her before casting her, all fixed, back into the world but back in her day there was none of that and so she simply walked away from her life, a weight of guilt and grief driving her to leave her husband and remaining child and begin a life of seclusion and loneliness. You see, my Grandma Shelly was *that* woman. Until that fateful day, she had been a perfectly ordinary woman, girl really, of twenty four, raising two children in war time Bethnal Green and working in a shop to supplement her husband's meagre army salary. She'd just finished work that day and had hurried to pick up the baby from the child-minder - Dad was five by then and in school and so she wouldn't have to worry about picking him up until a couple of hours later. She was heading for home and was just turning into Bethnal Green Road when the siren went off and so she changed course and hurried into the entrance to the station and down the steps. It had been raining that day, the grey day only adding to the oppressive atmosphere of the East End at that time but, afterwards, nobody could say if it was because the steps were wet from the rain or she simply lost her footing in her rush to get the baby down into the relative safety of the make-shift shelter down below but, to be honest, the reason doesn't really matter. What matters is that Grandma Shelly tripped only a few steps down from the entrance and, a couple of horrified onlookers coming down the steps behind her saw her twist her body sharply round in an attempt to shield her baby from the fall. Unfortunately, apart from a few, nobody noticed that she had fallen in their panic to get down to safety and so it was that, having just gotten back on her feet, she was knocked back down by the steamroller like mass of people following her down the steps. As she was kicked and trampled on, a hand appeared and pulled her roughly to her feet and dragged her to the side of the steps that her rescuer considered to be safer but the kind stranger either couldn't hear or was too panicked to register her screams for her baby -

my Auntie - as she struggled in vain to escape his clutches in order to wade back into the fray. When the whole thing was over - a matter of minutes, although it seemed like a lifetime to Grandma Shelly as she could do nothing but watch in helpless horror as more and more people fell and disappeared into the teeming mass of flailing bodies. Outside the station, a distance of only a few feet and the whole world, Thomas Penn, an off-duty policeman, arrived and, seeing the commotion, tried to get past the dead and dying to try to assess the situation but the only light was a dim 25-watt bulb partially painted black. Twice, Officer Penn fainted as he tried desperately to help those that were trapped. On the heels of PC Penn, fifteen year old James Hunt reached the ARP (Air Raid Precaution) depot where he was due to report, and was told to head to the tube station to give assistance. "I was small for my age, see, so I could only manage the little ones," James said afterwards, the shock clear on his white face where patches of soot and blood stood out in sharp relief. Most of the babies and children James pulled out had turned blue. One of the blue babies that James pulled from the crush of people was Grandma Shelly's daughter, Nancy. Although Shelly escaped the carnage with only minor cuts and bruises, the psychological wounds would prove almost fatal and, after a failed suicide attempt a week after the tragedy, she walked out of her neat little house in Bethnal Green and out of the life that had made her so happy only a short while ago. She told me about what happened that day only once, many years ago now, and, afterwards, made it clear that, despite my unlimited questions, the subject was now off limits forever. Although I saw her only rarely as a kid, we had a connection and so I saw her secretly and kept her secret - a fact that my parents were blissfully unaware of as she was persona non gratis as far as the rest of the family were concerned. The real tragedy was that, despite her continued sense of guilt, nobody would or could ever blame her for the baby's death but Dad did, and still does, blame her for walking out on the child that was still living. There were many times when I wished that things were different but none more so than during that phone call when I wished wholeheartedly that she could come round and tell me what to do or, at least just listen - really listen - like she always does when we talk on the phone. Who knows, I remember thinking at the time, when all of this was over there would be many changes to be made and, maybe, the situation with Grandma Shelly would be one of them.

'She's there!' Shelly whispered and I nodded pointlessly,

'Just now,' I said, 'She was in bed until about a minute ago.' Although she had just confessed to feeling tired, Grandma Shelly now sounded wide awake,

'What does she want, Will?' I glanced at Beth who was hovering behind me, her eyes fixed on the phone.

'I don't know. What is it Beth? Do you want a drink of water?' There was a sigh from the other end of the phone, from a ninety four year old lady somewhere in Surrey.

'No, Will, I mean what does she *want*? Why is she here?' There was a pause and then, 'Why has she come back?' Until that moment, I hadn't realised how important it was to me that Grandma Shelly was in my life and I let out a breath that it seemed I had been holding for about a week as I said,

'So, you believe,' I said, 'but, Shelly, how can it be? How is this possible?'

'Will,' she replied immediately, 'I don't believe - I know! I remember her. She was there.'

CHAPTER 27

It was two days later that they shot Beth. Once again, we found ourselves in a studio, sitting under hot bright lights, but this time it was an upmarket and tastefully decorated studio in Bloomsbury; a large loft type space with walls decorated with discreet pictures from some of the celebrity photo shoots that had taken place there. The last couple of days had been relentless as the press endeavoured to find new and innovative ways of getting to Beth after I stopped answering the phone and door - the afternoon after my conversation with Shelly, I opened the blinds in the kitchen to find a journalist perched on the ledge of the garage of the house next door, camera trained on my kitchen window just in case the blinds were opened, giving him a fifty centimetre glimpse of my kitchen. It was shortly after that that Spencer Hall came round again (once again doing his neat parting of the red sea thing as he made his way through the reporters lurking outside) to inform me that he had agreed - for a staggering amount of money - to a feature and photoshoot with Beth and myself for 'Taste' Magazine. I have to admit that, until that point, I'd never even picked up a copy of the magazine, let alone bought it. From what I understood, it was the domain of people who bought multi-million pound homes in Holland Park and the content was largely celebrities and minor royals showing off their homes, yachts and private jets. As somebody who rented a one-bed in Hackney with the nearest I came to a yacht being a rowing boat on the Serpentine, I don't mind admitting that I was feeling more than a bit like a fish out of designer water. I needn't have worried though; when we arrived, we were treated impeccably - in fact, with a reverence that embarrassed me although, as usual, Beth took the whole thing in her stride. Before the talking part, they wanted to get some photographs of Beth and, to my relief, the set had been decorated tastefully to resemble a Victorian park (my over-tired mind half-expected them to have recreated the scene at Bethnal Green station) and, in a new dress, green with white piping, Beth sat on a swing in the pretend park as the photographer gently directed her. While all this was going on, Spencer stood at the side of the studio - although he was talking almost constantly on his mobile, I could tell that he wasn't missing a thing as his eyes remained trained on Beth and anybody who approached her and I got the feeling that I wouldn't want to be in the shoes of anybody who might dare to displease him. Spencer had explained to me that, once the magazine was on the shelves in a few days time, we would slowly begin drip feeding the press, starting with just the major tabloids to begin with. Although this prospect made me nervous to say the least, I trusted his judgement - I had to; my only alternative was to go it alone and barricade myself and Beth in the flat whilst the press bayed at the door. When we arrived, the Producer's Assistant had given Beth a doll, a no-doubt expensive thing which, quite frankly, gave me the creeps with it's blue staring eyes and pursed lips but Beth had been delighted, not cynical enough to realise that, rather than just a nice present, the doll would add the extra 'Aaah' factor to the photographs. While the photo shoot was in progress, I was fed endless cups of designer coffee and, inevitably, about forty five minutes in, I needed the loo. Weaving my way back through the labyrinth of corridors, I finally found the 'facilities' as an Assistant referred to them when I asked for directions and I was about to go inside when I heard people talking and I retraced my steps to peek around a corner where two seemingly junior members of staff were deep in conversation.

'Do you think it'd be tacky if I asked to have a picture with her?' This was from the one closest to me, a tall lanky girl with hair cropped short on one side, long on the other and what I think they call "half sleeve" tattoos on each arm. A picture - a selfie - as though Beth were Britney Spears or someone.

'God, Bella,' the other one (surprisingly prim with long blonde hair in a ponytail and a dark coloured all in one shorts suit) replied immediately, 'I wouldn't. She's a miracle - it might be, like blasphemous or something!' Jesus, rather than Britney Spears, Beth was now God. I pushed open the door to the "facilities" and went inside, taking a moment to identify the urinals as they were discreetly molded into the tile wall and, instead of white, were made of some dark grey faux marble type material. As I conducted my business, I brooded on the conversation that I had just overheard. I was already very much aware that there would be people who would want to get their hands on Beth to prod, poke and interrogate her and, even people who may mean her harm and I was overwhelmed again for a moment by the weight of the responsibility that I had taken on. I'd been more than happy to let Spencer Hall take over when it came to the media but, as I made my way back to the studio, I reminded myself that, press aside, Beth's well-being was my department and I thought again about maybe taking her off to Spain to join Mum, Dad and the Hiddlestones - the only thing stopping me being the thought that I might, inadvertently, take the press with me, an outcome that I wasn't willing to risk for the time being. As I arrived back at the studio, the atmosphere was relaxed and light and I felt some of the tension leave my body as I heard Beth laugh at something that the photographer had said to her. It may sound like I was, for the most part, taking all of this in my stride but that most definitely wasn't the case. Looking back, I think I was probably in a kind of shock for the most part, just reacting to every new incident and then managing it the best that I could. As I watched the last few minutes of the photoshoot, my phone beeped and I smiled as I read Mum's text,

"Wish you were here." I fired back a reply that I felt likewise and updated her on that day's proceedings and she fired right back telling me that the weather was lovely, that Tom Hiddlestone had just had some gallstones removed and that Dad was existing on omelettes as he didn't trust any of "that foreign food." I had just slipped the phone back into my pocket (I'd long since disabled the internet function in a bid to avoid the temptation to check what rubbish was being said on the World Snide Web), when Spencer strolled across the studio to join me.

'How are you doing Will? More coffee?'

'God no!' I laughed, 'I've had so much I probably won't sleep for a week!' I neglected to mention that sleep hadn't exactly been my thing for the last week or so anyway as I added,

'But I'm fine, thanks. Are we nearly finished here?' Spencer nodded, managing somehow to give the impression that I had his full attention even though I could see that he still had at least one eye on what was happening on the photo set.

'Absolutely, just a few more shots then we should have what we need.' He pressed a tiny button on the wire protruding from his ear and then frowned, 'I need better, Anthea - go back and tell them if they won't go to a hundred thou then Hello will. Will, what we need now,' he said, still looking at the set and it took me a moment to realise that he was back talking to me again, 'Is for Beth to have a little chat with Ros, the interviewer so, once Travis is happy with the snaps, we'll whisk her away to get that muck off her face - there's something obscene about the sight of a little girl with make up on, don't you think?' I privately argued that Beth would disagree with that one - she'd seemed utterly delighted as she stared into the mirror after the make up girl had done her thing and I thought we might have a bit of a fight on our hands when it came to getting it removed. See, that's the thing; the thing that made it all so weird and the thing that probably explains why, in some ways, I seemed so unaffected by the whole thing. We knew that Beth was different; we knew that by some force that we might never understand, she'd been brought to me from a time decades before I was born but, then there were times like with the make-up when she was just a little girl. A regular little girl who liked Peppa pig, biscuits with chocolate in (but not raisins) and dressing up and putting make-up on. Travis, the photographer, signalled to Spencer who excused himself and then trotted over to the set and the two of them stood huddled over the camera for a moment, presumably reviewing Travis' work before Spencer nodded briskly and patted Travis' shoulder and, the next thing I knew, the hot bright lights on the set were being switched off and the production assistant strode onto the set, handing Beth a juice carton before leading her by the hand to where I was standing. As she skipped, beaming, to me I noticed that she'd spilled juice down the front of her new dress and I remember thinking that it was a good thing it hadn't happened before the shoot even though, as instructed, I'd brought another one along with us in case the one she was wearing clashed with the set or something.

'Listen Beth,' I said, 'there's a lady called Ros who wants to talk to us for a bit but first I think we should sponge the juice off your dress and take off the make-up, OK?' To my surprise, she just nodded happily,

'OK,' and then, in a conspiratorial tone, 'It itches!' I nodded sympathetically, remembering not too long ago when I'd had to wear the muck myself for the disastrous TV programme (Spencer had not minced his words in telling me how foolish an endeavour that was, without representation) and I hurried Beth through to the wardrobe room where Sally was ready with her sponges and wipes. Although he wasn't in the room with us, I could almost feel Spencer's presence somewhere nearby and, to my surprise, this was a comfort; he could be abrupt, ruthless and, at times, unbearably pompous but for all that, I sensed that he was very very good at what he did and there was something very reassuring about having him on our side I was jolted from these warm and fuzzy thoughts when the make up girl, Sally, suddenly screamed and scrambled back from the chair. Although I didn't scream, as I swung round to face Beth, I felt myself take an involuntary step back from her, almost colliding with Sally in the process. The right side of Beth's face which Sally had not yet started on looked just as it had when Beth was on set, pale with an unnaturally bright blush on her cheeks and lips, the make up not quite able to disguise the glow of little girl skin underneath. The left side, where the make-up had been removed, was a mass of cuts and ugly bruising, the eye swollen almost completely shut and a weird flatness to her face. A flatness that I would later realise came from the cheekbone having been shattered by a careless or panicked shoe. Even though, really, I knew what I was seeing, I still couldn't help blurting out,

'What have you done?' to Sally who just stared at me in horror and I immediately felt ashamed as I saw she was close to tears. 'I'm sorry,' I said as I moved toward the make-up chair and then, 'Stop this now Beth.' For a moment, she just looked at me, her expression placid despite the horror of her face and then she smiled. For all the affection that I had for the girl, it was a smile that made me take a step back as Sally fled the room and I repeated quietly, 'Stop it now.' Looking back, I've no idea what made me so sure that Beth had the power to do as I asked but, as I watched, her face blurred for a moment and then she was back and, once again, her face was one half little girl skin and one half thick stage make-up but the smile remained.

'What's going on in here Will?' Without taking my eyes from Beth, afraid of what might happen if I did, I replied,

'Everything's fine, Spencer.'

'Not what I heard,' he said calmly and I risked a glance at him before turning back to Beth.

'Sally's gone home. Apparently, something in here gave her quite the fright.' I shrugged and grabbed the pack of wipes that Sally had discarded,

'Sorry to hear that but we can finish up in here ourselves.' I plucked one of the wipes from the packet and began inexpertly wiping the make-up from Beth's face as I had seen Sally do.

'Well,' Hall muttered, sounding unsure for the first time since I'd known him, 'whatever it was that happened, I hope we can make sure that it doesn't happen again during the interview.' I hoped that too and wished that I could reassure him but the strange smile that was still on Beth's face made me feel as unsure as the man sounded. As I finished wiping the last of the make-up from her face, Beth reached out a hand to gently grab the back of his jacket and he swung round, surprised as it was the first time that she had made direct contact with him since he had entered our lives a couple of days before.

'It'll be alright, Mr Hall,' she said and then smiled - this time her normal, sunny smile - as she amended, 'I'll be alright.' After gazing at her for a moment, he nodded briskly and smiled back,

'That's wonderful, Beth, I'm very happy to hear that.' With another brief smile, he glanced at me and said, 'Well, I'll be waiting for you in the interview room. Whenever you're ready - take your time.' He turned and strode from the room, seemingly confident that he had 'handled' this latest crisis with his usual efficiency and I watched him go, blissfully unaware, as he was, of the sticky, bloody handprint that had been left on the back of his jacket.

CHAPTER 28

As it turned out, the interview was fine. Surreal but fine. Ros, the interviewer and mother of two girls of her own was gentle and patient with Beth and expert enough in her job to know when to gently press a point and when to move on and Beth responded by being chatty and charming as she answered Ros's questions clearly and, at times, elaborately. I, on the other hand, came across as a sweatily nervous idiot but then, it wasn't about me, was it? The whole thing only took about an hour and, once finished, we were herded once again through the ante-room to be 'de-briefed' by Spencer before being released, Beth chatting excitedly the whole time about seeing herself in a periodical.

'Now, you need to realise,' said Spencer who, I noticed, had taken off his jacket which was now nowhere to be seen, 'that once the magazine hits the shelves, the level of attention from the media and the public will increase quite considerably and we need to manage that.'

'But,' I protested, 'I thought the whole point of all of this *was* to manage the attention - I mean, to, well, make it go away.' For a moment, Spencer looked at me as though I were a particularly dense child or possibly, chimpanzee and then,

'Yes, Will. That is, of course, the point but first we need to give them a little bit of what they want. As I've said before, the idea is to drip-feed them only the information that we want them to have and this interview is going to be giving them rather a lot of new information - by the way,' he gave Beth an awkward smile, 'you did splendidly young lady, splendidly indeed!' I thought again of the bloody hand-print and then pushed it out of my mind as I tried to figure out what it was that Spencer was trying to tell me.

'What I'm saying,' he continued, 'is that, for the time being, it might be best if the two of you stayed away from the flat.' He said "flat" in a tone that some might use to say "ghetto" or "hovel" but I chose not to take offence as I tried to grapple with what it was that he was trying to get at.'

'I've booked the two of you into a suite at The Dorchester - they're used to handling the press there and, if you give me your keys, I'll have somebody fetch whatever you need from the flat.' So that was it. Having really only just settled into my place, Beth was now going to be shunted on to somewhere new.

'I've never been to a hotel before!' Beth piped up from behind me and I thought briefly of the City View in Bethnal Green and the unfortunate child that had gone missing from there and wondered briefly what had become of him - had he been found and returned to that fleapit and his mother or was he still out there somewhere, just another kid joining the ranks of those living under bridges and public toilets? Despite the inconvenience, I felt a stab of gratitude that Beth's fate was my flat and The Dorchester, of all places, rather than the unknown fate of the equally unknown boy.

'Not just a hotel,' I told Beth, 'but a super posh one!' I picked up a cup from the table and held it delicately with my pinkie finger sticking out, 'we're going to have to drink our tea like this and talk like this,' I said putting on a plummy accent and she giggled, imitating my gesture with the cup but not the accent.

'Right, that's settled then,' Spencer smiled as he signalled to the Production Assistant who gave him a thumbs up and then jerked the same thumb toward reception, 'there's a car waiting - once we get through the front door, I'll go first, then Beth, then you, Will, and then Winston behind you.' Winston? I thought but didn't get to ask the question as we were already on the move and, as we reached the front door and fell into formation, a black guy who was built like a WWF wrestler but dressed in a smart black suit fell into step behind me. That would be Winston then. Spencer was just about to open the door when there was a shout from behind us and the PA hustled through the reception area carrying the doll from the photoshoot which she handed to Beth who clutched at it like a long lost friend, then we were off. Once outside, I immediately understood the need for Spencer's choreography as the entire pavement outside was crammed with people;

some just onlookers who had come to see what all the fuss was about but, mainly it was reporters from TV and radio as well as the newspapers and, with them, their camera-men, all jostling and shouting as we emerged from the building. 'Keep your head down Beth,' Spencer called over his shoulder, 'try not to let them see your face!' But it was like she hadn't heard him as she followed Spencer to the car, head held high as she smiled sweetly at the frenzy of media people surrounding us. On reaching the car, Spencer turned and picked Beth up, lifting her into the car and out of sight before ushering me inside and climbing in after me and then we were away, watching through the tinted windows of the car as the press tried to get a last couple of desperate photographs before we were out of sight. Throughout it all, Beth sat with her nose pressed against the window and I resisted the urge to tell her to come away, knowing logically that nobody could see inside but not really being convinced, believing, as most of us do, only in what I could see which was a mass of people whose attention was all fixed on the window that Beth was peering out of. As we joined the snarl of traffic in the West End and the press were left behind, I began to relax a little. Unlike Beth I had, of course, stayed in a hotel before but never The Dorchester and, as we drew close I began to even tentatively look forward to the experience, figuring that a little bit of pampering would be quite welcome after the last week or so and so I was puzzled when the car didn't slow as we approached the hotel but then I understood as I spotted the crowd of people huddled at the end of the driveway. Oh goody, more press.
'We're going in the back way,' Spencer explained, 'there'll be somebody there to meet us.'

And there was. As we swung away from Hyde Park and the busy bus-clogged Park Lane, the driver took us to a vast back entrance where the car was ushered through a set of industrial looking gates leaving the press firmly behind - it seemed that we wouldn't be getting a celebrity red carpet entrance after all and that suited me just fine. We got out of the car and were ushered through a kitchen which was bigger than my entire flat, filled with white uniformed staff who projected a professional aloofness and then we were whisked all the way up to the Oliver Messel suite on the eighth floor; a sprawling opulent suite with a terrace boasting views of Hyde Park although, frustratingly, we were warned not to go onto the terrace under any circumstances in case the press had their zoom lenses primed and ready. I would later learn that the suite would generally cost almost five thousand pounds a night and I wondered who would be picking up that particular tab. After what seemed like only minutes, a tall, immaculately dressed woman arrived with a couple of bags containing the items that I'd asked for from the flat and I started setting our our clothes and other bits and pieces, partly to establish some kind of familiarity but mainly just for something to do as Beth was engrossed in exploring the suite. By this time, it was about five o'clock and, having seen that we were settled - or as settled as we were going to get - Spencer announced that he would be off and he swept out of the room after admonishing us once again not to venture out onto the terrace, or to open the door even for hotel staff until the code word had been provided. It seemed that, once again, we were prisoners of a kind but this time with room service and a turn-down service, whatever that might be. Once I had us squared away in terms of our meagre belongings, I consulted the room service menu and picked up the phone to order club sandwiches for us both (at twenty four quid a pop), some orange pop for Beth and a much needed beer for myself followed by a piece of chocolate tart for Beth (a snip at just thirteen pounds!) Once I had finished reciting our order, the man at the other end of the phone asked if I would like a newspaper for the morning and, if so, which one and I cringed, not looking forward to the pictures of today's press bun-fight as we left the studio. I needn't have worried though; on perusing the internet the following morning I found the world discussing the phenomenon that, although there must have been hundreds of photographs taken of Beth the day before, not a single one of them was useable. In every single picture taken, Beth's face was nothing but a blurred halo of light.

CHAPTER 29

I don't keep photographs out on display on anymore. In my old flat - my old life - I had a couple; one of Mum and Dad taken a few years back in Brighton and one of Nana when she was about twenty and wearing her Wren's uniform (I did briefly have another one taken a couple of Christmas's ago but she made me put it away, insisting that if she wanted to look at that old woman, she could just look in a mirror). These days I only have a room rather than a flat and there's hardly anything in it; minimalist I think they call it these days but I just call it necessary. The less things that I have, the less likely I am to be reminded of everything - you'd be amazed by how many memories can be conjured up by something as insignificant as a chair or a cup, memories that can send a good day crashing into nostalgia and depression. And, anyway, I find that life is just simpler without a lot of things to look after - I have what I need; a couple of plates, cups and glasses, a bed and an old chair that I got from the local charity shop when I first moved up here. My room is small with a little kitchenette unit and just one tiny window that looks out onto a sliver of beach and I share a bathroom with a Scottish bloke called Mark who works in IT and mostly keeps himself to himself other than occasionally lending me books that he orders from Amazon. If he knows who I am, he doesn't let on and, in turn, I respect his privacy by not asking questions or mentioning the fact that he never sleeps, prowling endlessly instead around his room and the bathroom in the early hours. Of course my landlord knows who I am, I knew that from the start as, during my interview, he made a nervous reference to my 'past situation' and then followed up by saying that none of that was any of his business and that he only cared about whether he gets his rent every month or not. I always make sure that he does. Although I no longer have the picture of Mum and Dad displayed in a frame, I talk to them every couple of weeks on the phone during which Dad confidently predicts that I'll soon be over all this and be on my way back to London and Mum worrying that it might never happen. It won't, or at least I don't think so and, what would I do if it did; go back to my old job on the tubes? Resume drinking with Andy in The Salmon And Ball? Maybe patch things up with Shandy? The idea of any of that happening is so ludicrous that it would make more sense for me to think about moving to the moon than it would my old life and everybody in it. I can't go back to my old life, I patiently explained to Mum during one of these conversations, because it's not there anymore. She's not there anymore. Beth.

CHAPTER 30

'Please, you don't understand……..just let me touch her, just for a second!' I'd opened the door to the suite for the delivery of our breakfast, after, as instructed, requesting the code word ("Tea-Set" if you must know) and the minute the young woman was inside, she'd dumped her trolley just inside the door and made a lunge for Beth who was sitting on one of the huge armchairs in the suite. Despite the early hour, my reflexes were already awake and I managed to grab her before she got anywhere near Beth but I struggled to keep hold of her as she strained toward the bed.
'Beth, push the red button,' I yelled as the woman caught my cheek with her fingernail as she flailed, trying desperately to escape my grip. On Spencer's insistence, the hotel Manager had had a couple of discreet panic buttons installed in the room and I had showed them to Beth, carefully explaining that although everything was, of course, going to be fine, the buttons were there in case any reporters tried to get onto the balcony or into the room. It was a carefully thought out security plan, along with the code word and the private phone line, all of which of course meant nothing in the event that, as now, the intruder was on the hotel staff and therefore privy to all of the protocols set in place.
'Please. I have cancer - breast cancer - I just need to touch her. I need the miracle!' I stared at the woman who went limp on seeing Beth push the red button, at first baffled before I slowly began to understand that she thought that Beth could somehow cure her, like the people who think that they can be cured by touching a statue at Lourdes.
'I'm sorry,' I said and I meant it, 'but she can't help you, she's not a………healer, she's…..' I stopped, unable to finish the sentence, she was what? A miracle? A ghost? An angel? I was saved from trying to answer that question as the manager and a security guard burst into the room.

'It's alright,' I said quickly, 'just a misunderstanding, everything's fine.' Although I tried, I knew that the girl would be gone within the hour - she had breached the rules and I could save her from being sacked no more than Beth could erase her cancer with just a mere touch. I still felt bad though and I poured myself a strong cup of coffee from the tray, ignoring the bacon and eggs that had started to congeal as Beth nibbled on one of the sweet pastries that had been artfully arranged on a plate with some strawberries.

Spencer had said that he would be in touch today to brief me on what would happen next but until then I wondered, as I gazed around the room, just what the hell we were supposed to do to occupy ourselves in the meantime. I didn't want to switch the TV on for obvious reasons and we weren't supposed to leave the room which left a seemingly endless number of hours ahead of us to fill. As though summoned by the thought of him, the telephone rang and I picked it up to find Spencer on the other end of the line.

'I just heard what happened,' he said and I didn't even bother to ask how - I already knew by then that he had his ways and that I would do well to remember that there was very little point trying to keep anything from him.

'Everything's fine,' I said, 'it was just a girl from the hotel. She thought Beth could help her with something but she's gone now.'

'She most certainly is,' he replied grimly, 'and with an extremely generous severance on the understanding that she says not one word about anything she heard or saw over there.' I didn't bother explaining that, in my opinion, talking to the press was the last thing on the mind of the young woman who was living with a ticking time bomb inside of her - in Spencer's world it seemed that all there was was the media and the people trying to make a quick fortune from it. 'I called to see that you're both alright,' he continued, 'and also to let you know that the photographs are fine.' For a moment, I stared blankly at the phone without a clue as to what he was on about now and then he expanded with, 'From the shoot yesterday, the pictures are fine. After today's, ah, revelations, I was concerned that the same thing might have happened as with the media's pictures but.......' he let the sentence trail off, seemingly confused as to why I wasn't as delighted about this as he was and there was a pause and then he cleared his throat and when he spoke again his tone was businesslike and I found myself matching it as we discussed "the next trench of the campaign" and "managing the media's expectations." I thought we were almost done when he cleared his throat again and said, 'There is one more thing.' I waited, fairly sure that for the foreseeable future, there would generally always be "just one more thing" and he went on, 'I don't know how much of the news you've seen this morning but there was a piece in The Sun. It seems that your friend, erm, Shandy, has been speaking to them and.......' I zoned out on the rest of his sentence as I fired up my laptop and accessed The Sun's online edition. Sure enough, there it was on page two, an awkward looking photograph of Shandy and Adele accompanied by an article that, at first skim, appeared to be an account of 'My life with Will and The Miracle Of Bethnal Green' by Shandia Washington. Apparently, the fact that Shandy only met Beth that one brief time in the station was no reason to ruin a perfectly good story. Having said a hasty goodbye to Spencer with a promise to check in later in the day, I pulled the laptop onto the desk in the suite and read the article again properly. Interestingly, not only had Shandy neglected to mention to the reporter that we had broken up but had also promoted herself from girlfriend to fiance and, as I read about how she could tell that Beth was special from the start, I was tempted to risk the wrath of Spencer Hall by placing a comment pointing out just how full of rubbish she really was. I looked again at the photograph - sitting with Adele in her lap, Shandy was wearing a red halter type top which she no doubt thought looked glamorous but was, in reality, ill-fitting and accentuated all the wrong bits. Her wild curls were scraped back from her forehead in a tight ponytail and, simpering for the camera, she looked hard-faced and cheap and I wondered, not for the first time since all this began, what the hell I had been thinking. I was so intent on thinking unkind thoughts that I didn't notice that Beth, having finished her breakfast, had climbed off the bed and was now standing by my shoulder as she said,

'Why is that bad lady on the telly?' I had tried, a couple of times, to explain to her the difference between the TV and the computer but she seemed stubbornly determined that if it's square and has pictures on it it's a TV and now wasn't the time to go through it all again.

'She's not really a bad lady,' I said faintly whilst wondering if that were actually true, 'but she's not somebody we're going to have to worry about any more.' That last part I certainly hoped was true and Beth smiled vaguely, having already lost interest in the subject,

'OK,' she thought for a moment and then, 'Can we go to the park again?' I sighed and then reminded her that we weren't supposed to leave the suite and, for a moment, a cloud passed over her face.

'I know,' I sympathised, 'I don't like it either but it's just for a couple of days. Why don't we play a game?' For a moment, the frown remained in place and then she smiled,

'Can I pick?' Maybe I should have seen that smile as a warning but, as I replied,

'Course,' I was only relieved that her attention was diverted from Shandy and her unexpected re-appearance into our lives. I finished the last dregs of my coffee and moved the cup further onto the table before moving the breakfast trolley safely out of the way to minimise the risk of breakages should Beth decide on a game that was a little more boisterous than the old travel favourite, I Spy. Although it seemed unlikely that the ornamental touches in the suite were real antiques or masterpieces, I thought it prudent to move or secure anything that could be damaged as I wouldn't welcome either the replacement bills or the disapproving looks from the hotel management.

'So, what's it to be?' I asked once I had Beth-proofed the room as much as I was able to, 'Freeze? Treasure Hunt?' Ignoring me, she wandered away from me, trailing a hand along the desk as she went before, very deliberately, announcing,

'I want to play "show and tell".' And what I really wanted was to curl up and go back to sleep and not wake up again until all of this was over but I nodded and smiled,

'OK, how do we play that?' I only had the vaguest notion of the game; something that they like to do in schools where the kids bring in something from home and then tell everybody about it and I found myself glancing at the scant few things of Beth's that had been brought over from the flat, wondering which of them she planned to tell me about, bearing in mind that we'd bought each item together.

'You know!' She said playfully and, before I could respond, the room suddenly went dark and the huge flat-screen TV burst into life revealing first a clean blue screen before blinking white and then the resolution cleared to show a picture forming. As I watched the screen change from a still image to a form of video action, I was dimly aware of a commotion outside of the room and I would later discover that these were shouts from the press huddled outside as, although nothing was caught on camera, they would all later swear, to a man, that the building wavered and shimmered as though in the grip of an earthquake. For the moment though, I was aware of none of that as I watched the action on the screen. At first I could only make out vague shapes, the blurred outlines that slowly began to clarify and brighten until I could see that they were people - at least a hundred of them, mostly women and children with just a handful of men, all sitting on the floor of what looked like some kind of hall, a random selection of belongings in neat piles amongst them. As the picture cleared further still, I saw that it wasn't a hall but a kind of tunnel and, after a moment or so, I was finally able to see that it was the platform of a tube station, the track just visible past the people, some of whom were sleeping and others who talked and laughed amongst themselves. The image opened out until I could see almost the full length of what I now recognised as a temporary air raid shelter inside a London tube station and goose-bumps sprang up along my arms as I realised that I was about to witness something that maybe nobody else currently alive knew about. If I'd known then just how right I was about that, I would have looked away, left the room or gouged my own eyes out - anything to avoid seeing the scene that was about to unfold in front of me. From the eery yellowish lighting on the platform, there was no way of telling what time of day or night it was but, the fact that most of the children and some of the adults were sleeping gave me the impression that it was night-time, an idea that was reinforced as I watched several women yawn one after another as though it were a highly contagious disease. As those already in the tunnel prepared to bed down for the night - or, at least, for as long as the current danger dictated, still more people were arriving from the stairs and I watched, transfixed, as two people, one a familiar face, emerged from the darkness of the staircase into the jaundiced light of the tunnel. The woman and little girl made their way slowly along the platform, stepping over coats and bags, some of which had people sleeping underneath them, until they reached a point just past the halfway mark when the woman gestured to the girl to sit down before handing her what looked like an apple from her large old-fashioned handbag. I expected the woman to sit down beside what was surely her daughter but, instead, she remained standing, gazing first one way and then the other as though looking for something or someone. Due to the panoramic view that I was now seeing, I was able to watch as the woman's gaze lit on something in the middle distance and I saw a roughly dressed man who looked to be in his forties catch her gaze and tip her a little wave before gesturing in the direction of the mouth of the train tunnel. Belated realisation dawning, I watched, appalled, as the woman followed the man not into the train tunnel but through a door which I could only assume led to some kind of store cupboard or staff room and then they were gone and I didn't have to use too much imagination to figure out what it was they would be doing in there. Having lost sight of the woman and her temporary customer, my attention was drawn back to the little girl who was still sitting where her mother had left her but, a moment or two later, her eyes grew wide and she began to frantically look around herself, first on the dirty floor and then patting the pockets of her pink dress - a perky pink thing with a dropped waist. After a second search of herself and the immediate area, she cast a fearful glance toward the steps from where she had just come and then, after a quick check in the direction her mother had disappeared, a resolute look came over her face and she stood up, dusting the platform dirt from her dress before marching, head held high, back toward the steps. Having already seen spoilers as it were for this particular drama, I wanted to shout to her to stop, to go back and sit down again in the relative safety of the underground cavern but I was powerless to make a sound as she marched resolutely along the platform and then disappeared into the mouth of the staircase. Thankfully I was spared from watching the next - and last - few minutes of Beth's life but not the angry shouts and then the panicked screams of her mother as she returned from her business transaction to find that her daughter was nowhere to be found. Neither was I spared the look of despair on her face as she ran to the stone mouth of the staircase only to find her way blocked by an impenetrable mass of bodies or the knowing, judging looks of the women who came to her aid, urging her back onto the platform before she too could be swallowed by the crush.

'So,' I said, unable to stop my voice shaking as I dragged my eyes away from the screen, knowing that it would make no difference as what I had just seen would stay with me for a long time to come, 'You've shown me, now....' Beth simply stared back at me, a small smile playing at her lips as she whispered,

'Never tell!'

CHAPTER 31

My first thought was that there was a kind of symmetry to it - the little boy belonging to a lady of the night going missing from the City View on the same day that I found Beth, whose mother shared the same profession. My second thought was that I now knew Beth's real name. Although Beth's impromptu home video had included no sound, my limited lip-reading skills were enough that, as her mother raced up and down the platform, increasingly panicked as she called her daughter's name, I was able to tell, with a reasonable amount of surety, that she was calling the name Annie and I repeated that name aloud in the sudden quiet of a suite in the Dorchester hotel. If I was expecting a reaction from Beth / Annie, I was disappointed as she simply gazed at me and gave a small nod as though it were entirely unimportant that I could now, at least, call her by her correct name. It did occur to me that, now that I had a first name as well as an approximate age, it probably wouldn't be all that difficult to fill in the blanks - her full name would be available from a number of sources - including the Stairway To Heaven memorial which features the name and age of each and every victim of the tragedy but, even though my laptop was within easy reach, I hesitated, a vague sense that it would be obscene to look into her life and death while she was sitting right in front of me, stopping me for the moment. I also wondered how and when, if at all, to share this information with Spencer and, therefore, the rest of the country. A furtive peek through the closed curtains told me that the press were not even nearly bored of this story yet, primed and ready as they were for even the merest glimpse of Beth and, when the magazine hit the shelves in a couple of days time, I knew that the frenzy for more would reach fever pitch. My main job, dictated by morals was to protect the kid but, I had also signed a contract which now sat somewhere in Spencer's Hall's office, stating that I would co-operate with a PR campaign which would, essentially, remove any right of privacy for myself and Beth. It wasn't quite selling our souls to the Devil but, at that moment, I felt it was within the same postcode. I glanced at Beth - Annie - I never would get used to calling her that and she never seemed to mind - although surely impossible, she seemed entirely un-moved by what had just happened and was fiddling with the remote control for a double set of lamps over the desk, deliberately turning them on and then off again in a way that was likely to become quite annoying quite soon. Aiming to distract her from this latest game, just before my nerves snapped entirely, I put aside my better judgement and flicked on the television, flicking through channels at such speed that the constant onslaught of photographs of Beth moved past like one of those flip books where you draw a picture at the corner of each page and then flick through really fast to create a moving image. Finally, I came to a channel that was showing an ancient episode of The Monkees and Beth seemed happy enough to sit and stare at Davy Jones and his pals as they mugged and sang through their latest adventure. For the first real time since Beth had entered my life, I found myself craving time alone - not long, just half an hour or so to think about what I'd just seen but I knew that was impossible. The closest thing I was going to get to 'alone time' for the time being was a visit to the bathroom attached to our suite and, even then, haste was the keyword as I worried that, in my absence, Beth would try to get the door to the suite open or, worse, venture out onto the balcony and into the line of fire of a million shots from the waiting cameras. I knew that the antics of The Monkees wouldn't keep Beth occupied for long, even though they apparently don't have time to get restless as there's always something new, and it was still a few hours from lunchtime which would, at least give us something to do for a short time. For the first time in my life I was having to divide the day into little blocks of time that needed to be filled or, at least to be managed, and I thought wistfully of a time of fast days on a tube platform and, even faster nights spent in the pub with Andy or watching the footie at home. It was right about then that my mobile phone chirped and I picked it up to see that it was a new message from Mum and I swiped the screen with my thumb to open it, not understanding at first what it was that I was seeing until I moved the phone away from my face (I'd been avoiding a visit to the opticians for months and I had a feeling it wasn't going to be on this month's list of priorities either) and I saw that what I was looking at was a ragtag group of reporters standing around and sweating in the fierce sunshine outside the Hiddlestones Spanish villa. After swearing quietly under my breath, I fired off a text in reply telling her that I was going to speak to Spencer to see if there was anything that he could do and hit send. As it turned out, there wasn't but he did, after a little bit of research, point me in the direction of a group of ex-pats near the Hiddlestones who had set up a kind of task force or support group and I fired off an email to somebody called Greg who promised that he and 'a few of the boys' would go and see what they could do, but not before asking a bunch of questions about Beth which I reluctantly answered in the interests of getting him on board. And it passed a bit of time. The Monkees had given way to an old episode of Taxi and I paused for a minute, smiling as Andy Kaufman did his ludicrous unidentified accent as Latka Gravas. Kaufman is believed by many to be alive despite documentation of his death from cancer in 1984 and was being watched and, presumably, enjoyed by Beth who, despite being crushed to death in 1943 was drinking juice and watching TV in an over-priced hotel suite in 2016. It was enough to give you a headache if you thought about it for too long. Thankfully, I was saved from just that by the sound of my phone and I picked it up expecting either Mum or the mysterious Greg but, this time, it was Spencer, exuberantly informing me that This Morning were desperate to have Beth on the show and that he was confident of a substantial payout seeing as it would no doubt net them a bigger viewer turnout than all of the Euro 2016 matches put together. Personally, I couldn't give a stuff about either the money or This Morning's ratings and the idea of sitting on a sofa while Holly Willoughby and Phillip Schofield simpered at us made that morning's coffee burn in my oesophagus but I told him that was great and to let me know when he had a hard tick on that (see how I was already picking up the lingo?) As it was, due to the murky waters that are This Morning's rules on child exploitation, this would all be over by the time that hard tick arrived. I spent the rest of the morning working out what additional items from the flat we would need if we were to be here another couple of days whilst an increasingly restless Beth, now bored with TV programmes that were made decades before or after she was born depending on which way you look at it, played aggressively with her ultra-annoying bashing frogs game which had arrived mysteriously with our other stuff despite my not having asked for it. I still harboured a desire to grab Beth and escape to Spain to see Mum and Dad but, when I mentioned that to Spencer on the phone, he dispassionately asked if I really thought it was a good idea to make Beth run the gauntlet of the press through Heathrow airport, not to mention the trauma of the aeroplane itself, the only experience of which Beth had were the ones that used to fly over London dropping bombs. I had to reluctantly agree that he was right, although a traitorous part of me couldn't help but note the fact that it was very much to Spencer's benefit that Beth remain in England. With this thought in mind, I took a little bit of vicious pleasure in noting again the eye-watering prices on the menu as I ordered lunch for us both, the choosing, ordering and eating of which at least passed another hour or so and then it was back to being busy doing nothing. Which is my roundabout way of explaining why it was that, around two o'clock, I finally gave in to the urge to log onto the internet. My first glance at Facebook was almost reassuring as, with it being the tail end of the nation's lunch hour, I found myself scrolling through four or five posts featuring photographs of people's food, drinks and, in a couple of cases, the exotic locations in which they were dining but then it kicked in and I shook my head as I saw page after page set up solely to document Beth's story, each one more ridiculous than the next. One page claimed that Beth was an alien sent to Earth on a kind of fact-finding mission and, another was written by a woman who claimed that she was Beth's mother and that she, too, had been brought back to life because of unfinished business in Bethnal Green - the fact that she had apparently been born and raised in Glasgow was something that she had, I saw, dedicated an entire section to explaining; an explanation that I declined to read at that time. Although ludicrous, these pages were essentially harmless and I found myself relaxing a little but then I saw it. At first I almost snapped the laptop shut in shock but I managed to hold myself back, vaguely aware that it would draw the attention of Beth who, at that time, was doodling on a drawing pad and showing absolutely no interest in what I was doing. I shifted in my seat and moved the laptop on the desk so that it was at an angle where Beth wouldn't be able to see the screen and then sat back to read it properly. As much as I'll never understand why people enjoy trolling celebrities, I do of course understand why certain kinds of people want to be a part of something, even if it takes lies and deceit to do so. Still, I found myself becoming angry as I read an account by some woman called Diana who claimed to be some kind of clairvoyant and, who also claimed that Beth had contacted her before transporting to "this realm" and had told her that, contrary to being a miracle, she was here to avenge the deaths of everybody who died on the steps that day. I was so incensed by this idiotic nonsense that I almost missed the other thing and I was just about to flick over to the BBC news site when I spotted it and, this time, I did close the laptop but it was too late - even with my eyes closed, I could still see the picture that had been at the top of a cluster of photographs. It was a picture that I knew well, one that I'd been fascinated by as a kid. A photograph of Grandma Shelley in her Wren's uniform.

CHAPTER 32

'And so you didn't think to tell me about this? Or, are you going to tell me that "it just never came up?" Rather than sounding angry, Spencer sounded one part exasperated and two parts jubilant - as well he might as, as far as he was concerned, this story had just grown legs and was set to run and run once the press got hold of the fact that Beth's rescuer was related to the woman whose misfortune had triggered the entire disaster.

'Both of the above,' I said simply, refusing to rise to the sarcasm in his tone, 'it's private. A private family matter.' I didn't add that once this private family matter went viral it would probably send my Mum ballistic as, that too was private. Unfortunately, that didn't appear to be a word that Spencer was familiar with, something that was evident in the way that he swept my explanation aside with an impatient,

'Well, no matter, we can simply incorporate this from now on. Do you have photographs of the lady? I can send somebody back to your flat and then.......'

'Spencer,' I interrupted sharply, 'I mean it. This is personal and not something to dangle in front of the newspaper people.' I sighed, 'I signed your contract on the understanding that it was about Beth and, maybe, about me a little bit but I didn't sign up for this.' I paused, feeling the need to offer something to balance out the harshness of what I was saying, 'Look - I may have something for you. A breakthrough of sorts. If you can get over here at some point, I'll tell you all about it.' I heard the faint beeping of an electronic device and got a mental image of him tapping away at his PDA and then,

'I'll be there around four but, Will, you need to understand something. The press find out things and they print those things in their newspapers. Regarding your

Grandmother, it is your decision as to whether they print whatever they like or, we give them a story and thereby control what they put out. Think about that for a while and I'll see you in a couple of hours.' And I did think about it but it didn't really help much. I thought about Shelly sitting alone in some flat that I'd never seen - and about having to tell her that the one thing that she had been running from all these years had found her again and that it was my fault. Spencer had talked about controlling what was printed in the papers but he'd said nothing about protecting a very old lady from unwanted questions and prying eyes. I picked up my phone to call her then put it down again; what exactly was I going to tell her? That somebody on the internet had done their research and found her picture? That somebody out there had found a little piece of the truth but that, at the moment, it was all but buried as it wasn't nearly as interesting as the alien and revenge theories? By the time that Spencer arrived, I had picked up the phone and put it back down again at least a handful more times and was still no nearer to an answer, deciding eventually to wait until Hall got there and see what he thought although, at the same time, I cautioned myself against relying on the man for too much - and crediting him with too much integrity.

'She already knows,' was his surprising response and I stared at him, confused,

'But how could she.....' I had assumed that she would still be blissfully unaware of a lot of what had gone on so far, an assumption that had been largely correct until about four hours ago.

'She knows because, when I saw the story, I knew that it was only a matter of time before the press found her and landed on her doorstep so I got my people there first and had her moved.' Had her moved, as though she were an old sofa or out of date wardrobe.

'Had her.....to where?' I spluttered, trying to picture Grandma Shelly being forced into interaction with strangers and being removed from her home.

'Not far,' he smirked, 'In fact, she's just downstairs on the next floor. Not as grand as this of course but still not too shabby. Will, are you alright.........' For a moment, I was unable to answer as the full picture of what he was trying to do fell into place and then I stood and strode toward the bathroom, beckoning for him to follow and, once we were out of Beth's range, I hissed,

'You will not bring her here, do you understand?' If Spencer was uncomfortable with my tone - or with being in a bathroom with another bloke - he didn't show it as he shrugged, 'As you wish. I brought her here for her safety Will, first and foremost, but it did occur to me that you may like to see her. If that's not the case then......' I rolled my eyes but forced myself to de-clench as I said,

'Good. As long as I've made myself clear - I do not particularly like the idea of Shelly and Beth being under the same roof but as long as it's understood that they will not, under any circumstances, ever be in the same room, I can live with it for the moment.'

He nodded, eyes downcast, letting me think that I was in charge and I relaxed a little further although the idea that Shelly was so close by, separated from me by just a few feet of concrete was like an itch that you can't quite reach and I tried to focus on something else - anything else - to distract myself. Thankfully, this wasn't difficult as, when we returned to the living area of the suite, we discovered that Beth had figured out how to use the remote control for the television and was sat on the edge of the bed watching, fascinated, the footage of the reporters outside, a superimposed photograph of herself in the corner of the screen as the newsreader updated the viewing public on the non-story of a bunch of blokes with cameras standing out in the cold. Gently taking the remote from her, I clicked the TV off and dropped it onto the desk and there was blessed quiet for a moment until, a couple of seconds later, the screen burst back into life.

'Must have dropped it on the button,' I said, convincing nobody, particularly myself and I clicked it off again before looking pointedly at Beth who smiled sweetly, seemingly now fascinated by the bow on her dress.

'You had something you wanted to tell me,' Spencer said, lowering himself into a chair that looked antique, rigid and uncomfortable and I felt pretty much the same as I poured glasses of water from one of the bottles supplied in the little fridge, stalling for time. It wasn't that I had decided for definite to never tell him about Beth's true identity, just that I was annoyed at the way that he had tried to manufacture further drama by throwing Beth and Shelly together and so, for the moment, took a childish pleasure in not only denying him this extra scoop but also keeping something for myself if only for a little while. I handed him a glass of water as I pretended to weigh my words - eager not to seem too eager - and then,

'That thing that just happened with the TV? It's happened before. Something like it happened in the dressing room at the photo shoot and that's what made whatshername freak out. I think sometimes Beth can control things that way but,' I added hastily as I watched a frown appear on his face, 'not all the time, in fact, not often at all.' The frown remained for a moment and then cleared as he nodded,

'Right. Well, that's certainly something to keep an eye on when she's in the public eye - the people want a miracle not cheap magic tricks.' He cleared his throat as he replayed what he had just said and then, 'not that that's what this is, obviously but...' he let the rest of the sentence trail off and I decided to take pity on him and change the subject to one of his favourites.

'So,' I said, 'You told me about the thing with This Morning, is there anything else that I need to prepare Beth for?' He smiled, suddenly looking more comfortable as he replied, 'There will be - I'm currently talking to the tabloids to see what kind of offers come in for the next exclusive,' he looked up at me, 'Tasteful, of course, no splashy shocker stuff and,' he took out his electric organiser and frowned at it and then put it away again,

'Needless to say, we're starting to hear a little noise from various book and film people. Will, by the end of all this, you're going to be a very rich man - you and Beth, of course.' By that point, I'd given up on trying to explain that profiting from Beth was the last thing on my mind and so I just nodded, my mind, despite Spencer's words, picturing the circus of headlines, books and merchandise ahead of us. Although I had signed the contract willingly enough, I couldn't help feeling that I was on a kind of rollercoaster whose brakes had just failed and that I was dragging Beth with me toward whatever disaster waited at the end of the line. Shelly had asked me why Beth was here and it was a question that I had no idea how to answer. Because I hadn't asked. I didn't know whether it was fear or something else that had held me back from asking Beth that question and now I was starting to feel that it was too late and I suddenly felt indescribably weary with the weight of the whole thing.

'Are you still with me, Will?' I jolted myself back to reality and cleared my throat,

'Yes, tasteful. That would be good.' I eased myself down onto the bed beside Beth,

'So, how much longer do you think we'll have to stay cooped up in here?' I realised that this probably sounded ungrateful as most people wouldn't consider a stay at The Dorchester to be exactly a hardship but I refused to allow myself to apologise for the ingratitude, ignoring thirty eight years of upbringing that urged me to do just that. The fact was that, however opulent our surroundings, we both felt like we were being held captive and longed to join the outside world if only just for a little while.

'Let me see what I can do about getting the two of you out for a while,' Spencer nodded, 'I imagine you could both do with a bit of a break from all this.' I nodded, suddenly ridiculously grateful for this small concession to what was, basically, our basic right in the first place,

'Thank you. That would be great.'

'Can we see the donkeys again?' Beth asked and I smiled,

'That might not be possible,' I began hesitantly, not wanting to get her hopes up but, at the same time, not wanting to say no outright to what was, after all, a pretty reasonable request but, before I could continue, Spencer jumped in, his tone jovial as he announced,

'Oh, I think we can do a bit better than donkeys!' He stood and held out a hand to me, 'Let me make a few calls and see what I can do.' His entire demeanor in the short time that I'd known him suggested that what he could do was probably rule the world but, still, I didn't want to get my own or Beth's hopes up too much so I just shook his hand and said,

'We appreciate it Spencer, I know you must have a lot on at the moment.' Once he'd gone, seemingly buoyed by the idea of something that was better than donkeys, Beth set about laying out her tea-set for pretend tea for herself, me and her doll and I busied myself with catching up with the world's news that didn't involve Beth, something that it turned out there was quite a lot of as the country had begun to reach fever pitch in the run up to the EU Referendum and the sporting world mourned the loss of boxer Muhammed Ali. A little while later we added to the already substantial room service bill by ordering dinner and then it was time for Beth to go to bed and, once again, I found myself with several empty hours to fill. Keeping the volume low, I flicked through the movie channels, dismissing one after another as my mind kept returning to the surreal fact that Shelly was somewhere below us, maybe even flicking through the same boring channels and no doubt sneaking cigarettes on the balcony if she had one. Not able to concentrate on anything on the TV and too fidgety to read a book, I eventually dozed off in an armchair about eleven o'clock, not waking until just gone four when I was disturbed by the sound of talking. For a moment I sat perfectly still, not sure if I was actually awake or dreaming then, heaving myself out of the armchair, I walked into the bedroom which which was illuminated by a soft glow although none of the lamps were currently turned on. I stood for a second or two in the doorway, taking in the scene in front of me; Beth was kneeling on the bed, eyes shining in the soft light as she appeared to hold a conversation with the wall. Moving closer, I tried to make out what she was saying but could only make out the occasional word, "soon" and "dark". As I approached the bed, she finally seemed to notice my presence and turned to me with a smile, briefly pausing in her one-sided conversation before resuming and, this time, I heard her clearly as she said, "She's beautiful now. So beautiful.'

'Beth,' I said softly, the dim thought that she might be sleep-talking making me reluctant to startle her, 'It's late. What are you doing?'

'Talking,' she replied immediately in a tone that suggested that it was, in fact, perfectly obvious and I nodded.

'I know, I can hear. Who are you talking to?' This time, she looked at me properly for the first time since I'd entered the room and she smiled as she said,

'I'm talking to the lady. The lady from the steps.'

CHAPTER 33

The following morning, Spencer made good on his promise and so, after breakfast, Beth and I found ourselves once more being sneaked through the cavernous kitchen of the hotel. After being fooled once on our original arrival at the hotel, the press were unwilling to make the same mistake again and so many of them were tag-teaming with one at the front and one stationed outside the back entrance meaning that getting away undetected was not going to be easy. After some deliberation, it was decided that, dressed in the blue and white uniform of the junior kitchen staff, I was to load a laundry trolley onto a hotel van - a laundry trolley containing Beth who, delighted at the idea of this game, had been instructed not to giggle. Accompanied by an actual member of staff, we then drove out of the back gates unmolested and then through the park to the Lancaster Gate exit where Spencer was waiting for us in an entirely inconspicuous looking dark blue Nissan. As we got out of the van, Richard, the hotel guy gave us a smile and a little salute and then was gone, driving back the way we had come and Beth and I climbed into the Nissan where I resisted the urge to attempt to high-five Spencer in congratulation for such a well planned escape. Once we were buckled in, I lost the kitchen garb only to be handed a bag containing another disguise; this time a baseball cap and nondescript coloured hoodie. Although she scowled when she saw her own disguise, the purpose of which was to essentially turn her into a little boy, Beth soon cheered up as we were driven through the West End, down past Brent Cross and then onto the motorway, the snarl of traffic suddenly giving way to clear road ahead. Although I had tried, Beth had refused to be drawn out on her conversation with 'the lady from the steps' and, in the end, I hadn't pressed her on the subject, figuring that she would, as always, talk when she was ready. As field after field sped past us, I was amazed at how good it felt to be out of the hotel - even speeding along the drab M40 and, after an hour or so, I realised that we were headed toward Chester. Although I hadn't been there since I was a kid, the one thing I knew about Chester was that it had a zoo - a big one - and I smiled to myself as I anticipated Beth's reaction when she found out where we were going. We stopped around ten o'clock for a toilet and coffee break and then were on our way again and so it was about half past twelve when our driver eased us into the carpark of Chester Zoo and Beth's face lit up as she spotted the huge model giraffe and hippo outside the entrance. Once inside, I found myself on edge, steeling myself for the shout of recognition every time somebody glanced at us but after an hour or so I started to relax. True to his word, Spencer did quite a bit better than donkeys and we saw monkeys, lions and tigers before decamping to one of the on-site cafes for plasticky sandwiches and disastrous coffee. While Beth chatted excitedly about what we would see next, I just luxuriated in being outside in the cold but bright sunshine and I felt more cheerful than I had in days as we placed our rubbish in the bins provided and made tracks for the penguin enclosure. As we arrived, I saw from the notice board that we were just in time for feeding hour and Beth clapped as I hoisted her onto my shoulders so that she could see over the crowds of people already waiting impatiently - the school Christmas holidays were still a couple of weeks away so the zoo didn't have the frantic feel that it would when full of jostling, shrieking children, it was still busy. As we watched the Australian zoo-keeper start to feed the penguins - teasing the odd little trick out of them as she went, Spencer stayed a couple of steps away from us as one call after another came through to his earpiece and, for a while I was so buoyed with gratitude for our little field trip that I felt bad that he was missing out on some of the fun. I snapped off a picture of the penguins on my phone and sent it to Mum and asked for an update on the press situation. I was hoping that the mysterious Greg and his mates had been able to do something to despatch that particular problem but was keen for confirmation. It was getting toward the end of feeding time and the Aussie woman gathered up the strays that were waddling around at the end of the pool then, as a final flourish, gave some kind of signal and, to a man (or, to a penguin), they all jumped into the pool, causing an almighty splash as a finale and Beth shrieked with delight, clapping so hard as she sat on my shoulders that her baseball cap, which was at least one size too big for her, tumbled off her head and her long blonde hair that I had tied up loosely and inexpertly inside the hat, fell free onto her shoulders. At first I didn't notice, caught up in the penguins performance myself, then a twenty something woman standing next to us who happened to be glancing in our direction, did an honest-to-God double take, her mouth falling open in surprise before she quickly and inevitably, whipped out her phone in order to snap off a shot of the miracle child. I waited for the woman to pounce, to maybe want to touch Beth like the poor woman at the hotel but she seemed, at least for the moment, to be rooted to the spot as she groped behind her, trying desperately to attract the attention of her companion without taking her eyes off Beth. I noticed with relief that Spencer too had spotted this unwelcome attention and we took advantage of the woman's temporary inertia and, without a word, began to push our way through the crowd toward the car, Beth still on my shoulders as she protested being dragged away from her beloved penguins. Finally breaking through the crowd and out toward the entrance we began to jog and, as we went, I wondered miserably if this was how things were going to be from now on, only getting a few minutes of normality before, once again having to run from the press or people who would always want something from Beth. As we raced across the car park, our driver already had the engine running and, no sooner were we inside then we were off, our unsatisfactorily brief foray into the world already at an end as the driver accelerated out of the carpark and back onto the motorway.

'I'm sorry about that Beth,' Spencer said and she just shrugged, seemingly doing much better than I was at accepting the new world order and I made a mental note to find something penguin related to buy for her on our way home if, that was, we would be able to make another stop. I had little doubt that the woman with the camera phone had already posted onto Facebook or Whatsapp and I had a feeling that it would only be a matter of (not very much) time before the press were alerted to our impromptu outing and would be on our tail. To my surprise, most of the three plus hour journey back to London was uneventful as Beth fell asleep and the rest of us fell into an amiable silence, punctuated now and again by Spencer conducting conversations on his mobile phone. It was as we pulled off the M1 onto the Prince Of Wales Drive that I saw a car and a couple of motorbikes fall into place behind us and, with a sinking feeling, realised that we were likely to be stuck with this intrusive escort all the way back to the hotel. To give our driver credit, he did do his best to lose them and, for a short time, the car did fall behind although the bikes kept up easily enough. Besides, I realised, it didn't really matter anyway as they knew where we were headed and were tenacious enough to keep us in sight at all times. Thankfully, the driver had had the presence of mind to fill up with petrol when we stopped on the way to Chester so, although we couldn't stop to find Beth a penguin toy, it also meant that we weren't trapped in some petrol station forecourt surrounded by cameras for which I was grateful. By this time, it was almost five o'clock and traffic was sluggish as rush hour geared up and we crawled through Baker Street before finally reaching Park Lane and pulling round again to the back of the hotel. As we were once more ushered through the gates, it began to snow - only lightly at first but I still felt a clench at the thought that Beth was once more about to be confined to her five star prison whilst the snow piled up outside, just waiting to be played with. As before, we were taken through the kitchens and then spirited up to the suite in the lift, Beth looking around owlishly having only just woken up as we pulled into the hotel. Once we were ensconced back in the suite, Spencer checked his watch and then said,

'Will, I'll be in touch in the morning but I must be off now as my wife and I have theatre tickets.' I looked up, surprised, having not considered the idea that the man had a private life at all, let alone a wife and possibly children, somehow these things just didn't seem to fit into the picture of him that I'd been building up over the last few days.

'Of course,' I said quickly then, 'Spencer, thank you for today, despite, well, you know.' He gave me a wry smile,

'I do, indeed, know and, you're very welcome.' He smiled briefly at Beth and then, after reiterating the fact that he'd be in touch in the morning, strode out of the room and I felt a very brief stab of envy at the fact that he was on his way to a night out; just going out for the evening without having to worry about being followed or photographed but then I firmly pushed the thought aside, genuinely grateful for even the short respite that we'd been gifted that day. Suppressing a slight groan, I reached out and plucked the room service menu from it's ornate faux-wood holder already, believe it or not, slightly bored with the choices that it offered. I picked up the phone and was about to order a duck salad that I didn't really fancy when I had an idea and I hesitantly communicated this idea to the young dude at the end of the phone. About twenty minutes later there was a knock at the door, followed by the code word which had been changed that morning to "Penguin" and I opened the door to the room service guy bearing a trolley containing the haul that I'd persuaded them to get for us from the Marble Arch McDonalds. Despite the abrupt end to our zoo visit, we were both in good spirits and I munched happily on my Big Mac whilst Beth ate her happy meal as we both sat in front of an episode of the Beverly Hillbillies that was showing on the tireless repeats channel. Stretching out on the bed, I made the most of the relaxed feeling - the issue of Taste Magazine would be on the shelves the following morning at which point, I knew, the number of people congregating outside would probably treble and Beth would be required, as the hateful contract that I'd signed for Spencer, to be exposed further in order to feed the steadily growing media beast. The Hillbillies gave way to "I Love Lucy" and, losing interest, Beth wandered over to the drawer in which we were temporarily keeping the modest stash of toys that had been brought over to the hotel. I was told by Spencer that the public had been sending toys too - gifts for Beth that arrived in their hundreds but none of these had made it to the hotel yet as they were all being checked by the security company that Spencer had hired for that sole purpose. The idea of all those strangers going out and spending their money on presents for Beth freaked me out but not as much as the idea that there might be somebody who had done so with the express purpose of causing her harm and I knew that, even after being checked by the security guys, I would be reluctant to have any of the toys in the flat - which was fine as it wasn't like Beth was exactly deprived as it was. I had a vague idea that, if the security guys were sure about the safety of the toys then we'd probably end up donating them to a kids hospital or something - an idea that seemed to please Spencer a great deal; no doubt he was already thinking about the good publicity that could be had from such a move. I knew that none of this was Spencer's fault and that he was just doing what he does but it was good to occasionally have someone to direct my frustration at, even if it was only in my head. Spencer had said that he would arrange for a copy of the magazine to be delivered to the hotel that evening - although I had "as a courtesy" been emailed a rough draft of the interview, I knew that the magazine reserved the right to make changes after that and so I could only hope that they had been fair. When the call came to say that somebody was on their way up with the hot-off-the-press copy I was only mildly interested - I had no particular desire to see the pictures of Beth plastered in make-up sitting in a pretend park and, as I said, I had a fair idea of the content of the interview so, when the porter arrived with the magazine, I put it aside for the moment in order to take advantage of the fact that Beth was sleeping and have a shower and a shave. As I performed my "toilette" it occurred to me that other people, after a day like today, would be ending the day with photographs of their children grinning beside enclosures of penguins and chimps but I was ending mine with glossy professional ones in a fake setting. Once ready, I cracked open a beer as quietly as I could (not as easy as you may think) and then settled down in what I'd already come to think of as "my armchair" and picked up the magazine, flicking impatiently through features about some minor royal's new Buckinghamshire mansion and an ex pop star's new baby before finally getting to the article about Beth. The first couple of pages of the article held no surprises - there were a couple of large photographs of Beth that had been airbrushed to the point that she looked more like a doll than a child and an introductory paragraph or two and I skimmed through these before turning the page, my breath catching in my throat as I did. There were photographs on these pages too but much smaller ones;

two more of Beth in her "virtual park" and an even smaller one of me sitting in the interview room at the studio. These pictures were dotted around the edges of the article which was largely a true transcription of the interview with Beth and myself but, in the middle of the page was another photograph, black and white this time, showing a view of the platform of Bethnal Green Station, every inch of space taken up by people - mainly women and children - and their belongings. It was exactly as I'd seen it in the "vision" that Beth had shown me and there, in the middle, as I looked closely, was Beth's mother.

CHAPTER 34

My first instinct was to throw the magazine away, to simply pretend that it had never arrived - had never, in fact, even existed but I knew that it wouldn't work. From the moment that we arrived at the studio, Beth had been madly excited about seeing herself in what she called "a fancy magazine" and I knew that, although I may be able to stall her for a while, sooner or later she would insist on seeing the magazine and so any avoidance tactics would simply be delaying the inevitable. I had no way of knowing whether seeing the picture would distress her or if she would react to it in the same, placid way that she reacted to the images that she had shown me but I was less than enthusiastic about finding out. As I opened another beer and brooded on this latest quandry, I suddenly realised with a jolt that, although I now knew who and what Beth's mother was, I still had no idea at all about her Father and I wondered if she even knew herself, her Mum's occupation suggesting that Beth may not have exactly been born of true love. I thought back to the day in my flat when I'd asked Beth about her parents and she'd said, "They're right here, silly!". Had that just been a kid's wishful projection or had her Dad still, somehow, been part of her life? Either way, these weren't questions that were going to be answered that night so I flicked back the pages of the magazine and read the whole article from the top. Immediately, I realised I had been right to trust Ros, the interviewer, who had written eloquently and faithfully without succumbing to the urge to embellish or to pepper the piece with her own thoughts on what was, after all, probably the most extraordinary story to be broken within our lifetime. If it weren't for the fact that I had been put in the position of having to show Beth the photograph of her mother I would have, dare I say it, actually said that I was pleased with the article. Glancing at the clock on the wall, I saw that it was approaching midnight and so I used the bathroom again and then climbed, gratefully into bed after what had been a pretty long day in comparison to the couple before it. I knew that the following morning would bring with it a fresh wave of interest from the media and the people clamouring to get their hands on this latest edition of Taste Magazine and I would need the rest in order to deal with all of that. Still, as exhausted as I was, I tossed and turned as one train of thought after another kept me awake. First it was the previous, nagging question of Beth's Dad and then the thought of the added pressure that would come from the magazine going out and then, around four o'clock in the morning, the sudden realisation that Christmas was just around the corner and that I hadn't even given this the first thought as yet. For me, Christmas had, apart from the obligatory lunch with Mum and Dad, only ever meant the annual scrum to try to get as many shifts off as possible in order to consume more "Christmas spirit". I'd never had to think about Christmas in terms of kids and, in the pitch black of the early hours of the morning, a brief panic crept in as I thought about all the planning for presents and activities that I hadn't even made a start on. Finally, about five, bored of the ghost of Christmas coming fast, I got up and quietly ordered some coffee before once more picking up the magazine, this time taking the time to read about the lifestyles of the rich and famous as the world outside the curtains slowly lightened. It was still way too early to wake Beth and order breakfast so I turned on the TV with the volume low, steeling myself for the onslaught following the magazine going on sale and I was so prepared to be besieged by colour and images of people voicing their opinions (in this age of social media, it seems everybody has one on every subject and must, always be heard) that at first I could only stare dumbly as the screen remained mostly blank, just a dot of light at the centre which grew slowly to fill the screen before finally resolving into an image. As my eyes adjusted, I realised that my turning down the volume was unnecessary as there wasn't any sound included in this current programming, nor was there any colour. What I was seeing was a selection of major newspaper front covers but not the ones that I recognised with their glaring red banners and crude headlines. These were stark black and white, the text tightly spaced to fill up as much space as possible and photographs were used sparingly, the whole effect meaning that, on first glance, your eye wasn't immediately drawn to any one story but would bounce from one headline to another, none of the pictures vivid or shocking enough to immediately grab your attention. As I watched, three of the four pages vanished and the remaining one grew until it filled the screen and I now saw that this was the front page of The Daily Express, although by today's standards it looked as though it had been produced by a child's toy printing press rather than that of a major nationwide newspaper. A quick glance into the next room told me that Beth was still sleeping and I returned to the main room of the suite and to the TV which was still showing the same page as before. I now saw that there did, in fact, seem to be a main story and I frowned as I read and then re-read the headline Rzhev-Orel, a word or phrase that meant absolutely nothing to me. I would later discover that this refers to an operation led by the Red Army during World War II, the details of which I have since read about and then tried very hard to forget but, on that day, in a suite at the Dorchester Hotel, the very alien-ness of the word caused me to move closer to the television and my eye was finally drawn to the top of the page where the newspaper's price of one penny was displayed along with the moon's rising and vanishing times and the date of the issue which I saw, with a peculiar lack of surprise, was the fourth of March, 1943. At this point, there was no real shock at what I was seeing - although I was fairly sure that this was Beth's doing - one of her "cheap magic tricks" as Spencer had called them - it wasn't too impressive; you could, I knew, order copies of old newspapers online for less than a tenner although I'd never done so myself having never had the need. The shock would come only a few moments later as I looked more closely at the front page of the newspaper - a newspaper that landed on the streets of England the morning after what would turn out to be the worst civilian wartime disaster of all time.

Outside the hotel, I could hear the sounds of the city waking up; cars tooting their horns along Park Lane, the sound of whistling as a member of staff finished a night shift and the sound of barking as the early morning dog-walkers took to Hyde Park only a few hundred yards away from where I sat. Although I was, on some level, aware of all of these things, they only entered the very periphery of my consciousness as I stared at the page of the newspaper, struggling to understand what I was seeing. Although the day before had seen a human disaster of such proportions that the day had ended with one hundred and seventy three people losing their lives, there was not one single mention of the tragedy anywhere on the front page of one of the UK's most widely distributed newspaper.

CHAPTER 35

Although I had heard all the stories, I still couldn't believe what I was seeing and I scanned the page again. As you would expect, almost the entire, crammed page, was devoted to stories of war - one headline trumpeted that 'Berlin still burns, London gets brief reprisal,' going on to explain that the German capital was currently without light, gas or water. Another proclaimed 'Air Raid On One Stone Hut - We Hit Hitler's Molybdenum' and, further down, the impossibly jovial 'He Got Four In 20 Minutes!', a story about a Spitfire pilot, Paddy Chambers who had been awarded the DFC for shooting down four Italian bombers in twenty minutes. Right at the bottom, beneath all the blaring headlines declaring battles won and battles lost, was an advertisement, the only one on the page and it jarred badly with the theme of the day as it promoted "Style Shoes By Lotus", accompanied by a picture of an elegant piece of footwear that, these days, I believe would be referred to as a shoe-boot. There were nineteen or twenty stories altogether, all jostling for space on the all-important front page but nowhere in all that shouty text was a mention of the one hundred and seventy three people who had perished the night before in a tube station in East London. As it was, and as hard as it is to believe, it would be years before the English public would learn of the full horror of that night. Concerned that the incident would further damage morale in a war that had dragged on and, fearing that the tragedy may discourage people from seeking the relative safety of tube stations during air raids, the Government had demanded it be kept quiet, and so the people of the East End had mourned their fallen without so much as a footnote in the National press. In fact, afterward, the Government allowed the people to believe that the fatalities that night were caused by a direct hit on the station, despite the fact that not one single enemy bomb was dropped on London that night. As I rubbed my eyes which were blurry from staring at the small text on the screen for so long, I thought again of Shelly's question about why Beth was here. Although I can understand the horror and disbelief of the victim's families at the cover up, I didn't believe that Beth had come back for that reason - after all, the account of what happened that night was now public knowledge and was available to anybody who cared to look for it, plus, the recent publicity surrounding the unveiling of the memorial ensured that the tragedy would never again be Churchill's dirty little secret. Neither did I believe that Beth was here for revenge for the simple reason that there was no revenge to be had for what was an accident - a terrifying, horrifying one sure, but an accident nonetheless. No, whatever it was that Beth wanted, I was sure that it wasn't revenge - and particularly not revenge against a very old woman whose only crime was her haste to get her child into the safety of the temporary air raid shelter in Bethnal Green Station. In fact, as I heard a rustling and stirring from the other room, I was reasonably sure that the only thing that I knew for sure that Beth wanted was breakfast. For the first couple of mornings of our stay, I had taken a gleeful pleasure in ordering the Dorchester's version of a full English but, being unused to such a large meal so early in the morning, it had left me feeling heavy and dozy and so, this morning, much to the surprise of the guy on the phone, I ordered just pastries, fruit and juice and, of course, more coffee. After breakfast and showers for us both it was back to the waiting game. Although I knew it was simply delaying the inevitable, I didn't show the magazine to Beth and neither did I turn on the television - it was now well into the breakfast TV zone and I had no doubt that presenters on every channel with their fake smiles and even more fake relationships with their co-presenters (Gosh, we're just such good pals!) would be discussing and analysing every inch of the magazine article and I had an idea that watching them do it would give me indigestion even on a breakfast of pastry and fruit. As it was, we didn't have to wait too long. It was about half past nine when the phone rang and a triumphant sounding Spencer informed me that every single copy of Taste Magazine had sold out within twelve minutes of the stores opening and that "we were a hit". We may have been a hit but the idea of parading Beth in front of the public like some kind of circus freak did not put me in my happy place and so, initially, I was resistant to Spencer's next suggestion even though, deep down, there was a part of me that knew that, as always, he would bring me round in the end. It wasn't so much that the man's charisma was so magnetic that I agreed to everything he asked but more that I had to have confidence - hope - in the fact that he knew what he was doing and he did, I think. Looking back, the problem wasn't in Spencer's ability to do his job but just the simple fact that Beth was new territory not just for him and his company but for the world. Spencer was used to dealing with musicians and film stars, helping them navigate the stormy waters of the media as he convinced the world that whatshername's affair was due to an abusive marriage and whatshisname's creative accounting was down to a naive trust in his accountant. I suppose what I'm trying to say is that, if I was overly critical of Spencer's handling of the situation afterwards then I'm sorry - I don't blame him and, these days, I've even stopped blaming myself. My therapist told me that this is excellent progress. Spencer's idea was neat in its simplicity - we would give the world a few hours to digest the latest delivery from the Beth Green publicity machine and then, while they were still buzzing with this fresh information, we would hit them again, this time with an appearance by Beth herself The idea was that Spencer's people would collect a few questions from the journos crowded outside the hotel and then, by way of a PA system, Beth would make a brief appearance on the balcony of the hotel to answer a couple of these questions. When Spencer first pitched the idea, I was unconvinced - to me, the idea of a balcony appearance had shades of the Royal family or Eva Perone or someone and I worried that others would make the same association and react unfavourably to the comparison but, as always, Spencer's powers of persuasion won out in the end and, before I had completely accepted the plan, preparations were being made. Needless to say, the press, some of whom had been standing outside in the cold for over twenty four hours, were delighted by this new turn of events and Spencer's Assistant, Alec, returned to the suite clutching double handfuls of question slips, all of which had been filled in by the eager germs and rabies of the press and we set about sifting through them, discarding any that were overly personal or invasive. You see, for them, Beth wasn't a child at all, just a vessel, a seemingly endless gravy train of tidbits to print in their papers or to fill up dead space on their news programmes and, despite the last few days, I was shocked at some of the questions that these idiots felt were suitable for a little kid. I was still jealously guarding the secret of Beth's mother, although at that time I was telling myself that I was going to tell Spencer about it soon, that I was just saving it for when the time was right, as though there would ever be a right time for him to tell an eagerly waiting world that Beth died while her Mum was doing business on her back in a tube station store cupboard. The 'appearance' had been scheduled for three o'clock that day, a time chosen because there would still be just enough light for Beth to be seen clearly - and, of course, just enough time for the story to sneak into the evening editions. Due to the rapidly approaching appearance, I decided, out of necessity, to read the article to Beth and, if the words or the accompanying photographs, unsettled her she wasn't letting on as she gazed at the photos of herself with a faint smile playing on her lips. As the appointed time approached, I dressed Beth in the dress that she had chosen, a simple green shift with lace around the collar, and, although I was fraught with nerves as I listened to Spencer make his introduction on the balcony, she remained cool, almost detached as she waited for her cue and then stepped out onto the balcony with me directly behind her. As she stepped out into sight a hush fell over the crowd which, once just press and TV and radio reporters, was now easily over a thousand people, filling the pavement both on this side of the road and on the park side and, in fact, the road itself as traffic had been diverted to allow the people to congregate in order to hear a five year old girl speak. It had been decided that I would be the one to read out the questions that had been chosen then Beth would answer them and, as I thanked Spencer for his introduction, I made it clear to the waiting hordes that, once a question had been answered, there would be no further discussion on that particular point A good plan I thought and, standing next to Beth who gazed calmly out at her waiting audience, I picked up the first card and read out,

'Beth, where were you going that day, when the air raid siren went off?' Beth glanced at me briefly then returned her gaze to her people as my mind kept insisting on calling them.

'We were going to Nanny's,' she answered simply, 'Nanny Edna in Vallance Road. We were going for tea cos Nanny Edna had some ham even though Mum said even the Dorchester Hotel doesn't have that!' A polite titter went through the crowd and I could almost hear the buzz of electricity as hundreds of cameras and TV cameras recorded Beth's every word and gesture. Putting down the card that I was still holding and plucking another from the pile, I read out,

'Beth, in the magazine article, you said that you knew Bobby Rowe, the boxer. What was he like?' Beth smiled at me in response to Bobby's name and thought for a moment before answering,

'Bobby's nice. He plays with us and gives us sweets. Mum says he's loaded but a fool and his money are soon parted.' Again there was a good natured murmur from the crowd and I had just enough time to think that maybe Spencer was right, that this really was a good idea after all and then the first shot rang out.

CHAPTER 36

'Blasphemy!' Despite the thousand or more people gathered in front of the hotel, I heard the word clearly, the shrieky and hysterical tone cutting through the hubub of the crowd like a warm knife through butter. Then, the crack of the first gunshot followed by panicked screams from the crowd who were packed so tightly together that running for cover was close to impossible. It seemed like time stood still and I could only watch helplessly from above as the people congregated below us fought and struggled to break away from the confines of the crowd and then I finally came to my senses. I felt that hours must have passed as I stood inert after the first gunshot but, in reality, it was only a few seconds and then someone was grabbing my arm and dragging me back inside the hotel suite, having already pulled Beth to safety. I turned to reach for Beth and saw that she was already surrounded by paramedics who had appeared from nowhere and, as I watched, one of them jogged over to where I was standing.

'I'm fine,' I said faintly as he dumped his bag down by his feet.

'You're in shock,' he replied confidently and proceeded to lift my jacket aside, presumably looking for wounds that I may have overlooked. After a few minutes of prodding and asking questions which I assume were designed to give him some measure of my mental state, the guy, Ryan his name was, picked up his bag and sauntered back over to where his colleagues were examining Beth. As I stood, quiet and useless for a moment, I could barely think over the clamour of the crowd outside, Spencer barking instructions into his mobile phone and the white noise inside my own head. While I stood, frozen to the spot, men with complicated looking ear-pieces swarmed into the room, some barking instructions to unseen colleagues and others prowling the suite looking for God knows what as the Manager of the hotel hovered nervously just inside the doorway.

'Suspect has been disarmed and captured,' one of the ear-pieces said but I couldn't tell whether he was talking to somebody unseen or to the room in general. I knew that I should feel relieved but something was nagging at me - Just below the noise and thoughts crowding my brain, something was lurking just beyond my reach and I sat down heavily in the nearest chair, reaching automatically for Beth who was slowly wandering back toward the balcony.

'Stay away from there Beth,' I said and she shrugged and backed away to perch on the end of the bed, still eerily calm despite what had just happened. Taking a few deep breaths, I tried to compose myself, reminding myself that taking care of Beth was my main job and that I didn't have the luxury of falling apart. It had all been going so well; that's what I kept thinking - it was all just going so well, until it wasn't. From somewhere in the room I heard the sound of my mobile phone and I zoned the sound out - unlike a lot of people I'm perfectly capable of ignoring my phone when it rings, figuring that whoever it is will call back or leave a message if it's important enough and I refuse to be a slave to a small lump of plastic and metal. I thought about what the ear-piece had said; that the suspect had been captured; I hadn't gotten a good look at her but I did hear what she had yelled, loud and clear. Blasphemy, that's what she said, as in "against God". Was that what she thought Beth was? I glanced over at the little girl - one of the security guys had given her his ear-piece and she was giggling at something that someone at the other end of it was saying to her. What had the woman meant? Did she believe that Beth was, somehow, evil and, if so, had she really been trying to harm her? I closed my eyes trying to shut out all the questions that would once again remain unanswered and, when I opened them again, the security guys had silently left the room and the two medics were packing up their gear.

'Are you alright, Will?' Spencer asked and I smiled weakly and nodded as I glanced again at Beth,

'Yeah, I think so.' Having packed up their stuff the two medical guys headed for the door and, as they went, I heard one of them say some codey sounding stuff into his walkie talkie and then, less ambiguously,

'All clear up here, no injuries. The shooter was obviously a nut-job but thankfully she was also a lousy shot,' this was his parting shot as the door closed behind him. He was wrong though. Not about the woman's state of mind which was obvious, but about her being a lousy shot. Having had a chance to rest my brain for a few minutes, the stray thought that had been lurking just below the surface had finally broken through the shock and disbelief and, as I replayed those last few moments on the balcony, I saw clearly the moment when, just after the shot rang out, Beth turned to me and I saw the large ragged hole that had appeared in her dress just above her ribcage.

CHAPTER 37

I'm standing on the platform, if you can call it that, of a tiny train station on the beach. I know that sounds odd but it really is on the beach - when you're actually on the train heading North, you can sit by the window and see nothing but water for several miles of the journey, broken up by the odd cluster of salt marshes and small towns. There are no massive Virgin trains hurtling through this station, just the much smaller and slower Transpennine Express ones and there's no cavernous station building filled with Costas and mini Tescos, just a little cafe and a stall selling crisps, chocolate and soft drinks. From where I'm standing, I can look beyond the station to a little pier and people strolling along the promenade and, just behind me, a hill sloping up to picturesque gardens with a grand hotel perched at the top like the cherry on top of a cake. It's not quite the Dorchester, this hotel but it is pretty to look at and, although I've never been inside, I'm told that it's very grand and is, apparently, very popular for weddings. It's nearly May now but there's a nip in the air and I pull my jacket on and fasten it as I stare at the track to the left of me, in the direction from which the next train will arrive, its imminent arrival heralded by a trickle of people strolling onto the platform with backpacks and cans of lager. Hiking is a big deal around these parts and, every day, tourists turn up with their sturdy boots and fancy water bottles and equipment, expressions of steely determination on their faces as they board the train that will take them further North to the Lake District. Every now and then you'll hear about one of them going missing and the excellent local rescue crews will be deployed to bring them back safely - which they do, almost every single time. Hiking doesn't interest me though, nor does the majesty of the Lake District or the austere beauty of the fells and pikes that bring people here in their thousands every year. In the months since I've been here, I've been content just to be here by the sea, I find that it soothes me and so, apart from a couple of trips into Lancaster on the train for a few essentials, I've been happy with simply going nowhere but here where I can walk on the beach every day and not think. And there's a lot to not think about. I spend a lot of time not thinking about how it must have felt for the families to have woken up that day to the devastating loss of husbands, wives, mothers, fathers and children and for the government to have buried the tragedy so completely that their loved ones were not honoured by even the smallest mention in the press. I also spend time not thinking about the world that we now live in - a world where information is available at the touch of a screen and where anybody can publish an opinion or theory which quickly becomes fact as a post goes viral, reaching an enormous number of people within an impossibly short time. And, of course, I spend a lot of time - most of my time - not thinking about Beth and what happened on that balcony and then what happened afterwards. A small noise slowly invades my non-thoughts; a kind of whistling hum and I realise that it's the sound of subtle vibrations on the track indicating that the next train is on its way. For a moment, I have an urge to run - to just leave the platform and the station and to just keep moving, the desire to avoid anyone who represents a link to my old life being, for a second, so strong that fleeing seems to be the only option available, but I don't. Instead, I stare out to the water which is only just in sight at this time of day and, this small moment of focus calms me and I stay where I am. Standing well back on the platform, I watch as the little train - just three carriages - trundles down the track toward me, slowing and then finally coming to a stop and the nerves that I woke up with that morning return as the train doors open with a whine and a creak and the passengers start to spill out onto the platform. I watch as a couple of young women in uniform - clearly employees at the hotel - alight, followed by a couple of the hikers that I was talking about; their sensible shoes and rain macs giving them away just as surely as if they were wearing signs and then, here they are. I watch as, emerging from the last carriage, Dad steps down onto the platform and then reaches up to help Mum down before hopping back up to grab their cases; something that I suddenly realise I should have been doing and I finally walk forward, moving against the tide of people still disembarking until I'm in front of them. Awkwardly, I move in for a group hug, registering as I do the small gasp of distress as Mum gets her first look at me followed by a big smile designed to disguise her initial reaction as she returns my hug, all of us ignoring the curious glances from other passengers and platform staff. It's been nearly five months since I've seen them and those five months have changed us all, not just me and, as I finally break free and begin to lead them out of the station and up the hill to that cake cherry hotel, Mum is unable to stop herself from glancing at me constantly as we go. I don't mind that though, I'm just happy that, changed or not, we all survived.

CHAPTER 38

Directly after the incident on the balcony, Spencer demanded that security be stepped up both outside our room and outside the hotel and then promptly organised a brief press conference (which, thankfully, Beth and myself did not have to attend) where he thanked the public for their concern and assured them that Beth had been un-hit and un-harmed by the incident and, although I knew that at least half of that wasn't true, I kept quiet. Although I knew that my contract stated that I would furnish Spencer with any and all information I had regarding Beth, I couldn't shake the feeling that I had put her in harm's way just by contacting the man and I had no intention of making things worse if, in fact, that was actually possible. During the conference, Spencer urged the press and public to remain calm and promised that a further 'audience with Beth' would be organised in the very near future. While our PR man was doing his job, Beth and I were once again confined our luxurious prison - but this time with four bodyguards outside the room instead of two. I'm not generally one for video games myself but I'd had a couple sent up out of desperation and it turned out that Beth was surprisingly adept at both Paper Toss and Pixel Twist and she happily spent an hour or so beeping and blooping her way through the games like a girl who hadn't just been shot at whilst addressing the nation. I knew that I should probably be speaking to Beth about what happened but I also knew that I had no idea how to even begin and, as I put off the difficult conversation time after time, the weaker part of me argued that just letting her recover and move on was maybe not such a bad idea. Having eventually tired of her games, Beth took a nap and I took the opportunity to check out the usual news channels and websites, all of whom were playing the footage of the shooting over and over and I noticed that I looked pale and ill, particularly standing next to Beth and I realised as I watched myself on screen, just how tired I really was. It turned out that the shooter, one Georgina Hamilton, was a religious fanatic and had been arrested a number of times for taking part in violent protests against everything from abortion to gay marriage and it seemed that, if there was one good thing to come out of all of this it was that this particular individual would now be off the streets for quite some time. It still bothered me though; the idea that this woman, mad as she was, thought Beth was some kind of demon to be eliminated like a character in a computer game and I felt a wave of weariness wash over me as I contemplated the fact that I had been barely managing to protect Beth from the media so, what chance did I have of protecting her from gun-wielding zealots as well? I heard my mobile ringing and I picked it up guessing, correctly as it turned out, that it would be Mum again. Offering to come home again which was the last thing that I wanted just then. If there was one thing that I had managed reasonably successfully in this whole mess, it was getting Mum and Dad out of the line of fire (to an extent) of media scrutiny and I wasn't going to let them come back now. I didn't think that Mum really wanted that either and I worried that maybe the Hiddlestones, in the face of press outside their door, had been subtly hinting that Mum and Dad had outstayed their welcome. Thankfully, all of these fears were quickly nipped in the bud as I took Mum's call to be told that Craig Whatshisname had kept his word and that he and his pals had despatched the reporters who had gone away and, for the time being, had stayed away.

'I still wish you would come out here, Will,' Mum said for maybe the fiftieth time, although this was a slight variation - in previous conversations, it had been "I wish you and Beth would come out here, Will", but I decided to let it go. To begin with, Beth was a problem to be dealt with. Then, she was a strange phenomenon to be handled and now, well, now she was something to be scared of and I couldn't blame Mum for silently wishing that she wasn't in our lives at that moment.

'I know, Mum,' I said, 'And maybe we'll still get a chance but just not right now. Right now, Beth needs as much stability as I can give her, particularly after today.'

'Stability,' Mum said in a flat voice, 'Living in a hotel, giving press conferences and being shot at by nutters.' I sighed, I was well aware of the situation and certainly didn't need any reminders - as fast as the press had dispersed when Georgina Hamilton had begun her target practice, they had returned just as quickly and, as I pulled the curtain aside and peered quickly through the window, I saw that there were now almost as many of them as before although I did notice that one guy at the front was wearing what looked like a bullet-proof vest; no doubt imagining himself on the evening news - intrepid reporter coming to you live, not from the front lines in Afghanistan but from the mean cobbles of Park Lane.

'I know, Mum, give it a rest will you,' I said as I let the curtain drop closed again, 'I'm doing my best, alright?' A long sigh made its way down the phone line and then,

'I know you are, Will, I just…', she sighed yet again, 'I just wish we knew when all this would be over and,' there was a pause, 'Has it occurred to you, Will, that there are no parents to be found like we first thought. I mean, before we knew what Beth is. Do you realise that she's yours now, Will?' Had it occurred to me? I'd thought of very little else for what seemed like months although it had only really been about a week and, yes, it had occurred to me that this was no longer just a temporary solution until the real parents swooped in. That Beth would be with me forever. If I'd known then just how short "forever" would turn out to be then maybe I would have let Mum have her way and

I would have grabbed Beth and jumped on the first plane heading out to Spain that night but, I didn't. Instead, I flicked through the emails that had been piling up in my inbox - most of which were either trying to sell me something or offering me loans and it suddenly struck me with a jolt that, of all the things I may need to worry about in the coming months, for once in my life, money wouldn't be one of them and I couldn't help but wonder how that was going to feel. When Beth woke up, I went through the now all-too familiar routine of ordering dinner (which, when it arrived, was virtually cold by the time it had been examined and x-rayed by the security guys outside) and then we, once again, settled in for the long evening ahead. At the start of the evening, Beth was unusually quiet but I didn't know if this was down to what had happened on the balcony or just general boredom of being cooped up in the suite for so long. Every now and then she would pick up a toy or game and listlessly play with it for a few moments before putting it down again and picking up another. We had an assortment of movie channels at our disposal and I first tried Frozen and then Kung Fu Panda but neither seemed to hold her interest for long. As for me, I was nervy and uncomfortable, jumping at every sound within the hotel as I imagined various members of staff - even at one point the security guys - turning rogue and bursting into the room intent on finishing what Georgina Hamilton had started. As I sat staring at Princess Elsa warbling her way through "Let It Go", I craved a beer - badly - but worried that one would never be enough on a night like this and I needed to keep my head clear, so, instead, I opened a bottle of sparkling water from the fridge, making Beth laugh as I opened it too quickly and sprayed us both with about three quid's worth of fizz. As I flicked through my laptop every few minutes, I saw that the interest from the press and the public had now become a kind of hysteria - there was even a Facebook page set up by people who wanted reinstation of the death penalty for the woman who had dared to try to harm the Miracle Of Bethnal Green and it was about then that Spencer called again. After running through the usual pleasantries, he finally got to the point which was that, although This Morning were still consulting their moral compass regarding their policy on having a child as a guest, it seemed that their main competitor, Talking With Tiffany had no such qualms and they had requested that we guest on their show the following morning.

'Is that obligatory?' I asked wearily and I could hear the steel in Spencer's voice, although his words were innocuous enough as he replied,

'I believe it would be a prudent move - the more answers we give on National television, the less questions the press can find to bombard us with.' I closed my eyes as though I could will him away but, after a few seconds he was still there and sounding impatient as he asked,

'Can I get a hard tick on that Will? If we're going for it then we're going to need to meet beforehand so, what say I come to the hotel for about six and we can run through our game plan before the driver takes us to the studios'. Six o'clock in the morning. Hard tick. Game plan. I let these words wash over me for a moment and then, surprising even myself, I took a deep breath and then said it, just one word,

'No'. The silence that followed went on so long that I began to wonder if we had been disconnected and then I heard Spencer take a sip of his vitamin water or three hundred year old whiskey or whatever the hell it is that his sort drink. I had the impression that he was choosing his words carefully and I took the opportunity to jump in before he had a chance to start on his persuasion tactics.

'Look, Spencer, I've seen the woman's show and I know all about the scandal last year with that African couple. She's hard-faced and she's ambitious and I don't think she's the right sort of person to get the best from Beth.' It sounded crap even to myself but, surprisingly, Spencer seemed to buy it as he made a noncommittal humming noise before conceding that,

'You do have a point there, Will. Maybe another show would be better.'

'Thanks Spencer,' I said quietly and he cleared his throat,

'No problem Will. Look, I realise that all of this has been terribly difficult and that being paraded in front of the media is probably the last thing you feel like doing so, I apologise if sometimes I'm a little single-minded.' To be honest, he was a little single-minded in the same way that politicians are a little bit dishonest but I kept this to myself in the interests of not gloating over my tiny victory. A few minutes later, Spencer hung up with the promise that he would call in the morning with a new plan and, having now seen him at work for a few days, I had no doubt that he would and, having successfully dodged an appearance on Talking With Tiffany, I knew that I would end up agreeing to whatever he came up with next, whether I liked it or not. After putting Beth to bed, I wasted another couple of hours flicking between mindless TV and my laptop before finally turning in myself and, it was just as I was about to, finally, drop off that a thought that had been nagging me since the day before finally broke through to the surface and I bolted upright, heart racing, as I remembered finding Beth talking to herself in the bedroom and her telling me that she was talking to the lady from the steps.

CHAPTER 39

For the second time in only a few hours, I defied the rules imposed on me by security and by the contract that I'd entered into with Hall & Oakes. This time it was a breach of the whole "don't leave the room" rule but, by that point, I honestly couldn't have cared less about the consequences. Once the thought was in my head, it wouldn't go away and I tossed and turned for maybe another half hour before finally getting up and calling security to ask if they would go down and check on Grandma Shelly. I then waited another twenty minutes or so and, when there was no immediate call to say that everything was fine, I opened the door to the suite, instructed the remaining security guy to watch Beth and then jogged off toward the stairs, ignoring the guy who, torn between letting me go and leaving Beth on her own, was urging me to come back and I could still hear his voice halfway down the wide staircase. Once downstairs, it was easy to find Grandma Shelly's room - it was the one with the door wide open and the hotel manager standing outside looking like he was about to have a heart attack and he protested only weakly as I barged past him in the narrow hallway. As it turned out, the emergency services had been called but, this being Central London, they had not yet arrived which was why I was able to march straight into the room. Once inside, my path was blocked at first by Jack, one of the security guards who looked ridiculously huge inside the small tight space of the entrance. I knew that trying to barge past him as I had done with the Manager would be ludicrous as he was about a foot taller than me and seemed to be constructed entirely of muscle so I simply, quietly, asked him to move aside. For a long moment, he just looked at me and then, with a resigned nod, stood aside as he barked, 'Don't touch anything Sir.' Stepping past him, I surveyed the room with a dull lack of surprise. It was a room, rather than a suite like ours but still grandly furnished with a discreet bathroom leading off the main room. In one corner was a neat, old fashioned suitcase which was open and empty and, in the adjacent corner, Grandma Shelly was hanging from a curtain rail, swaying slightly in the breeze caused by my bursting into the room. I stared into her face which was much older than when I had last seen it but still instantly recognisable despite the grey skin and unseeing eyes.

'I'm very sorry Sir,' I heard a voice beside me say and I nodded without looking round, entirely focused as I was on just one item. As I stood there with the security bloke hovering awkwardly beside me, I could hear the clattering of footsteps outside the room signalling the arrival of the emergency services, the voices of the men and women who would soon herd us out of the room as they took control and I knew that I didn't have much time. Under the watchful eye of the guard, I stepped forward slightly, head bowed as though in prayer and began muttering nonsense words under my breath. Although he didn't move, the guard did, as I had hoped, look away slightly, either out of embarrassment or respect and it was then that I made my move, lunging forward fast before the man had time to make a grab for me.

'Hey, you can't.......' he began but it was too late and he didn't bother to finish his sentence as he saw that the evidence was already tampered with and that, to snatch it off me would mean contaminating it further with his own prints.

'Sorry man,' I said, stepping away from both him and the shell that was once a lady who tripped on the steps of Bethnal Green station and was changed forever. Once again, ignoring the protests of one of the men who was there to protect me and Beth, I strode out of the room, reaching the lift at about the same time as I heard the emergency guys reach that floor and head into Shelly's room. It was really simple, I thought as I rode the lift back up to my own floor and made my way back to the suite; either the security bloke would keep quiet and all, as they say, would be well, or he would spill his guts and I would shortly have the police rapping on my door. Either way was fine with me as I had only taken what was mine after all. When I reached the room there was, for once, nobody standing outside and when I got inside I found Hired Muscle Number Two playing Snap with Beth who looked wide awake and was shrieking with delight as she yelled "Snap" for what I guessed was far from the first time in the short time that I'd been away from the room. After checking that the guy was happy to continue playing with Beth a little longer, I helped myself to a couple of miniature whiskies from the mini bar and then moved into the bedroom for a little privacy. For a moment or two I sat on the edge of the bed; not moving, just enjoying the quiet and alone-ness of it and realising just how much I'd missed it and then, with a sigh, I reached into my pocket and took out the envelope that I'd taken from Shelly's room. The one with my name written on the front of it.

CHAPTER 40

It was my first (and I sincerely hope, my last) suicide note and I opened it with trembling fingers, my expectations formed by countless books and films and I frowned as I scanned the single piece of paper which, instead of the expected "I'm sorrys" and "don't blame yourselfs" contained just two lines. As I've said, I hadn't seen Shelly for years and I certainly wasn't expecting any long missive about how much I'd meant to her but, even so, I was surprised by the curtness of the note which felt like it had been written in a hurry as though, once the decision had been made, she couldn't wait to follow it through. I took a long sip of whiskey and then read it through again;

"End this, Will," it read, "For me and for Nancy. Find grace and leave me to my peace."

Well, that clears that up, I thought as I downed the rest of my drink and found my gaze shift longingly toward the mini bar as I pondered on how one could find any grace in such a sad and hopeless situation. For a brief moment, I felt a surge of anger as I wondered why the hell Shelly couldn't have just spoken to me - if she had needed me, I would have found a way, regardless of Spencer and his team of rent-a-goons. She had lived with these demons for over seventy years, what difference would a few more hours have made? Now all I was left with was this cryptic note and the unpleasant responsibility of having to break this horrible news to my family. Not though, I thought as I looked at the clock, for another few hours as it was now two o'clock in the morning and I had a feeling that my night wasn't over yet. As if to confirm this thought, I heard a knock at the door of the suite and, striding through the main room, I opened it to find two police officers standing on the other side.

'Mr Thorn?' One of them with a strong Irish accent asked, 'I'm very sorry for your loss - and sorry to bother you at a time like this but may we have a couple of minutes of your time?' I gestured them into the room and, indicating Beth who was still playing cards with the guard, asked if they minded coming through to the bedroom which the Irish one immediately did, although his colleague lingered for a moment, staring at Beth until his friend dragged him away. Once inside the bedroom, both of them tried hard not to look impressed with their surroundings as they asked what had made me think to ask security to check on Shelly at such a time of night, when I had arrived at her room and what I had seen there. The first question was the tricky one and I pretended to be still overcome with grief in order to give myself a little bit of thinking time. With everything that had already been in the press, I could have easily told the truth and told them that I'd found Beth talking to my dead Nan and that's what had alerted me to her death but I knew that there was a good chance of anything I said ending up in the papers - on the subject of Beth, people just didn't seem to be able to help themselves, however professional they might be - and I was reluctant to expose her to more scrutiny than was necessary. And so, of course, I lied. I told them that it was just a hunch; that Shelly was a very old lady who was unaccustomed to being anywhere other than her own home and that I had worried that it may all be too much for her. To my surprise, neither of them mentioned the note and I silently sent thanks to Mr Muscle Number One for his discretion although, rather than feeling like I'd got away with something, I felt like I'd only dug myself deeper into what appeared to be a bottomless hole. After a few more questions, the two officers stood, thanked me for my time and told me that they'd would leave me to get some sleep and I almost laughed out loud at the absurdity of the idea. Having seen the officers out, I relieved the guard from his Snap duties and ushered a very reluctant Beth back into bed, tucking the covers securely around her and gently refusing her request for a second story of the night.
'You're sad,' she said as she peeked up at me from the pillow and, as it was a statement rather than a question so I nodded.
'It's better now,' she frowned, as though puzzled by my sadness, 'Now that she's back with us on the steps. Where she always belonged.'
'Don't say things like that, Beth,' I snapped and then immediately regretted my tone but Beth just looked at me, that little smile playing around her lips and, for the first time, I just wanted to be away from her. 'Go to sleep, it's late,' I said softly and left the room, giving in this time as my eye returned to the mini bar and its promise of temporary oblivion.

When I woke it was not with a hangover but that slow, blurry feeling that tells you that you could probably have lived without those last two or three drinks and I grabbed a carton of juice from the mini bar, downing it quickly before washing my face, not wanting

Beth to see me bleary and unprepared for the day. As it happened, I needn't have worried as it was another half hour before I heard a stirring from the bedroom and then Beth padded out in her bare feet and gave me a smile that made me feel small and ashamed for snapping at her the night before. Although it was only seven o'clock, I ordered breakfast, wanting to fortify myself before speaking to Mum but, wanting to call her before she woke up and saw the latest shit-storm to hit the news. The police had done an admirable job of putting out as little information as possible but the press outside the hotel had seen an ambulance and police arrive in the early hours and had been swarming ever since, determined to fill in the blanks of the police's statement that "A person as yet to be unidentified had been found dead at the same hotel that the miracle of Bethnal Green was staying at." There are no suspicious circumstances and both Beth Green and Will Thorn were unharmed." I had barely put down the phone to room service when my mobile rang and I knew, even before I looked at it, that it was Spencer and I felt almost sorry for him as I realised that this was yet another aspect of the story for him to spin. I thought about the press, whose job it was to prod and pry into other people's lives and about Spencer whose job it was to handle what they printed. Then I thought about my job; the one I used to have about a thousand years ago; the one where I helped other people to get where they were going. A job that seemed almost noble when I compared it to the others I just mentioned. When I took the call, Spencer just sounded weary as he offered me his condolences and asked how I was. Although I was a little uncomfortable accepting the condolences on account of the fact that, really, I barely knew Shelly, I had no qualms at using it as leverage - particularly if a day or two of mourning, on top of the ordeal of the day before, would net me - and Beth - a couple of days off the media party. I thanked him, glancing at Beth who was, again, lurking by the curtains to the balcony, seemingly drawn by the noise outside and then cleared my throat,

'I appreciate that, Spencer. I'm sure I don't have to tell you that it's been a rough couple of days for us both.'

'Of course,' he replied immediately but sounding distracted, 'And, needless to say, if there's anything you need….' he let the sentence trail off and I frowned at the phone. I hadn't known him well or for long but, what I did know was that Spencer Hall was all about the job and didn't have a tendency to do distracted or vague.

'Thanks,' I said again and, then, 'So, with all of this going on - and the fact that, sooner rather than later, the press are going to find out about Grandma Shelly's passing, I was just thinking,' I paused, reluctant to annoy or inconvenience him when he clearly had things on his mind but then I looked again at Beth and gathered my reserve,

'I was thinking that, maybe, we could put things off for a couple of days, the television and that kind of thing, just while I get my head together and Beth has a chance to get over what happened yesterday.' There was no response and, although I knew that I was now rambling, I couldn't seem to help myself as I added needlessly, 'It's been, you know, quite stressful for us the last couple of days.' When there was still no response, I finally shut up and, the short pocket of quiet that followed finally alerted me to the fact that something was very wrong. I finally realised that Spencer's uncharacteristic hesitance was not, in fact, borne of respect for my loss or, for what Beth had been through when some mad woman had shot at her the day before and my mind span as it presented one disastrous scenario after another for my consideration, anything from Mum and Dad having an accident in Loret De Mar to some devastating and previously undisclosed news about Shelly. Still, even with all these possible catastrophes running through my head, I was completely and totally unprepared when Spencer finally replied, 'Forget the TV, Will, I don't think we need to worry about that anymore. I suggest that you take a look at today's papers and my office will be in touch in due course.'

CHAPTER 41

I felt like I had been shot at again. After Spencer hung up, I decided to grab a quick shower but, first I called down to ask for a couple of newspapers to be sent up, slightly curious but, at that time, not unduly concerned as I figured that, whatever it was that the press had printed this time, we'd ride it out just like we had before. Towelling myself off, I had just walked back into the main room of the suite when the first headline hit me like a blast of cold water and I froze in the act of drying my hair, confused by the headline and, more so, by the fact that somebody had entered the suite to deliver the newspapers without going through the tedious but expected identification routine. I opened the door a crack to confirm to myself that the security guy was still outside, which he was, and he bade me a curt good morning before turning away and I closed the door and padded back into the suite. The short trip to the door and back had changed nothing. As I returned to the main room, the newspaper on top of the pile still screamed "Phenomenon Or Phony?" I picked up the paper and was immediately assaulted by a headline below it pronouncing "The Scammer Of Bethnal Green" and I didn't bother to pick that one up to see what came next. Grabbing a coffee from the breakfast trolley, I fixed Beth some pastries and juice and then snagged the first paper from the pile and sat down heavily in the chair that would very soon relinquish the title of "my armchair". It only took a few seconds of scanning to get the gist of the article and, in disbelief, I read and then re-read the account of somebody called Tiernan Hobbes who was, apparently, a historian and who claimed that he had uncovered a number of discrepancies in Beth's story. Even before continuing, I bristled at this - Beth didn't have a 'story', she had simply answered questions that had been asked of her but, it seemed, such semantics were irrelevant to the likes of Tiernan Hobbes who went on to point out that there was a well known boxer in Bethnal Green in 1943 but his name had been Dickie Corbett, not Bobby and that his name was there for all to see on the recently erected memorial. Hobbes also claimed that Beth had repeatedly referred to "Bethnal Green Station," but in 1943, the station had actually been known as Bethnal Green Junction station. Despite the fact that Hobbes' revelations could be described at best as pedantic, this particular tabloid appeared to have decided to take the ball and run with it and the article, starting with the front page and its lurid headline, ran to four pages in total, all based on a couple of observations by some man I'd never heard of. I threw the paper into the waste bin and picked up the next, in which only one page had been dedicated to the story and which contained very little information other than the fact that there were suggestions that Beth may not be who she claimed to be. It seemed that Mr Hobbes had bagged an exclusive with the first paper, no doubt bagging an eye-watering payday in the process, and I really hoped that he would think it was worth it after Spencer had torn him to pieces in response. The brief moment of savage joy I felt at that prospect vanished abruptly as I replayed that morning's conversation with Spencer in my head, in particular the part where he told me that his "office would be in touch," and I felt the first cold finger of fear as I contemplated what that might mean. Refusing to waste time and energy on speculation, I picked up my phone and hit the speed dial which would connect me to the mobile that Spencer was so completely attached to that it was hard to believe that he didn't sleep with the head-set on but, for the first time since I'd known him, his phone rang and rang before finally kicking me over to his voicemail. Ignoring the growing sense of unease, I left a short message asking him to call me as soon as he got a chance. Without bothering to read them, I picked up the rest of the newspapers and dumped them into the bin. I know I shouldn't really have been surprised - I've followed enough news stories to know that the tabloids delight in building somebody up to mythical proportions only to then knock them down again with some piece of salacious gossip. But, Beth was a child and this felt sordid and petty and I was only glad that she wasn't able to read this rubbish as she nibbled on a cinnamon pastry and stared at an episode of Top Cat that was running on one of the endless repeat channels. As though to contradict the thoughts that I hadn't voiced, she turned to me and said,

'Don't worry. I'll be gone soon; it's nearly finished.'

'Beth, what......?' I started and she gave me a stern look, bits of pastry littering her nightie as she said

'Don't ask. Find grace, Will.' I stared at her as I realised that these were the exact words from Shelly's note and I slammed my coffee cup onto the table, my voice louder than I intended as I shouted,

'I don't know what that means! What is it that you want from me?'

'Everything alright in here?' I turned to see that the security guy, alerted by my raised voice had stepped into the room and I nodded,

'Fine. We're fine, sorry.' He nodded and disappeared back to his post and I let out a shaky breath as I sat back down. I've always hated losing my temper, ever since I was a kid; it always leaves me feeling ashamed and insecure, certain that forgiveness will be denied no matter how much I regret the outburst and, these feelings were magnified ten fold at having shouted at Beth who was, after all, just a kid.

'I'm sorry, Beth,' I said quietly, 'there are some things going on that I need to deal with - to think about - some people are saying some bad things about us.' Beth shrugged as though this were simply par for the course and I couldn't help smiling at the earnest look on her face as she said,

'But it's alright Will, they can't hurt me.' As I glanced toward the binned newspapers I wished dearly that I could say the same but I couldn't help the fact that the things they said - the things they implied - burned me on my own behalf as well as Beth's and I got angry again as I glanced at my phone which, for the moment, remained silent. Having been lurking since my shower in just a pair of jogging bottoms, I decided that it was time that I got dressed and I headed for the bedroom which was, of course, the exact moment that my phone decided to ring. I jogged back into the main room, ready for Spencer to tell me how we were going to deal with all this but, instead of "SpencHall", the screen of my phone was flashing "MumMob" and I fought the urge to ignore it as I picked it up and hit Receive.

'Will, what's going on? Are you alright? They said on the news that there was an ambulance last night and, now, the papers are saying all sorts of stuff.'

'Mum, slow down,' I said more calmly than I felt, 'Firstly, we're fine - me and Beth are fine but Mum, there was an ambulance and, there's something I need to tell you.' I'm not exactly sure what kind of reaction I was expecting but Mum was surprisingly unfazed as I outlined for her the events of the night before, starting with what I remembered Beth saying and ending with Grandma Shelly's remains being taken from the hotel in the dead of night. Although clearly hurt that I hadn't told her that Shelly was here - or that we had been in touch prior to that, she seemed entirely unaffected by the news of her death. What she wanted to talk about was what she had seen in that morning's papers and I became impatient as I tried to explain that, on that count, I knew just as much as she did and, that I was tied up talking to her about all the things that I didn't know whilst possibly missing a call from the one man who could sort all of this out. Having been singularly unimpressed with Spencer from the start ("He looks shifty - his eyes are too close together") Mum kept me on the phone for another five minutes before finally releasing me with strict instructions to call her later in the day to let her know what was going on and issuing, once again, an offer to fly back to be with us, something that I now wanted badly but wouldn't allow. After hanging up, a glance at my phone confirmed that Spencer still hadn't called and I sighed with frustration, wondering what we would do with the rest of the morning while we waited. As it happened, that was one question that I got an answer to quite quickly as, only a few minutes later, there was a knock at the door and, when I answered it, the security guy outside was now accompanied by the hotel manager who handed me a crisp white envelope and then retreated with a hasty,

'Do let us know if you need any help with arrangements Mr Thorn.' Puzzled, I mumbled something to the effect that he had already been extremely helpful and I quickly tore the top off the envelope as I strode back into the suite. The first thing that I pulled out of the envelope was a cheque for a really quite large sum of money, attached to a Hall & Oakes compliment slip. The second thing was a letter on paper sporting the same logo and company name and signed by Spencer. In very formal and curt terms, the letter stated that, due to recent information that had been brought to light, I had, in effect, breached the terms of the contract that I had signed with the firm and the letter was to inform me that the contract had now been dissolved and that the enclosed cheque was a courtesy payment for work undertaken while the contract was still valid. My first instinct was to pick up my phone but I stopped myself - Spencer hadn't failed to return my calls because he was busy or because he'd mislaid his phone; he'd deliberately avoided me in order to sever our relationship as quickly and as completely as possible. The old me would have laughed at just how betrayed and victimised I felt but the new me didn't care. As I re-read the letter which didn't even fill half a page, I just felt completely and utterly alone.

'What's wrong, Will?' I was startled to realise that I'd almost forgotten about Beth, despite the fact that she was, unwittingly, the reason for everything that had happened and was still happening and, as I stared into her impossibly clear eyes, I struggled to find the words to explain our latest predicament. The urge was there to tell her that everything was fine and then to occupy her with something while I figured out our next move but, this plan was flawed in the fact that, to begin with, she was unlikely to believe me and, secondly, a selfish part of me didn't want to deal with it alone, even if it meant burdening a child. So, I decided to tell her the truth but, as we all know, there are always degrees of the truth and I quickly calculated just how much Beth really needed to know.

'You remember Spencer?' I asked and she nodded

'The posh one.'

'That's him,' I confirmed and then sighed, 'Well, the thing is that Spencer has decided that he doesn't want to spend time with us anymore so we won't be seeing him again I don't think.' Beth frowned as she took this in and a few seconds passed before she asked the obvious next question,

'But why?' That was the part at which I decided that my truth and Beth's would part company and I smiled at her as I explained,

'He's just very very busy, that's all. He came to meet us because we needed his help and now he needs to help other people.'

'But what if we still need his help?' She asked and I paused - after all, wasn't that currently the million dollar question?

'Well,' I shrugged, 'We'll just have to manage without him - me and you and Mum when she gets back from Spain.'

'Spain, Spain, on the aeroplane!' Beth chanted and I grinned,

'You got it! Now,' I lifted the curtain slightly and glanced out of the window where, although I wouldn't have thought it possible, the number of reporters seem to have grown within the last hour, 'Those silly journalists are still outside so we're just going to stay here for a while longer.' Beth pouted but said nothing as she pulled a game out of the pile neatly stacked in the corner and began to play with it without much interest. I knew how she felt; with every hour that passed, I had begun more and more to resent our current situation and I craved just a simple walk to the shops or even just around the block. Christmas was on its way and, every time I looked out of the window towards the park, I saw people heading into Winter Wonderland, the annual over-priced Christmas fair that's held there every year and I yearned for just a quick walk around with a hot chocolate for Beth and maybe a mulled cider for myself. Still, I tried not to think about it too much as, at that moment, Winter Wonderland might as well have been on the moon rather than just across the road. Afterwards, I would laugh, but without much humour, at my despair at being trapped in a luxury hotel for yet another day as it was only about an hour later that there was a knock on the door and the security guy announced that the hotel manager was here to see me.

CHAPTER 42

I'm back in my room in a little terrace off a park in Carnforth having settled Mum and Dad into their hotel room. We have plans for dinner at a place called L'Enclume in nearby Cartmel that Mum read about on TripAdvisor and even the thought of it exhausts me - First the necessary small talk and then the weightier issues of what I'm doing here, why I look like I do and when I'm coming back to London. None of which I'll be able to answer to their satisfaction and so I'll end up sitting there, probably drinking a bit too much, as I watch the lines of worry on their faces grow deeper. Recently, I've been thinking of trying to get a job on the trains, swapping the grime and chaos of Bethnal Green station for the Cumbria Coastline and I wonder idly if this idea will cheer Mum and Dad up or distress them more. They came back from Spain just a few days after I got Spencer's letter and, by that time, it was all over and so, even though they think they know what it was like - what I went through - they don't. They can't; after all, Dad didn't even meet Beth so how could he possibly have any idea what this has been like for me?

After getting Spencer's letter, I had thought, briefly, of trying to secure the services of another PR Agency but I had no idea how to go about such a thing and, also, I had a pretty good idea that the speed at which Spencer had dumped us meant that such an endeavour would end up being fruitless, taking up a lot of time and energy for nothing and, by that time, I was starting to get the uneasy feeling that time was running short. At least now I can say that I've finally been inside The Grange Hotel proper and, after seeing Mum and Dad's room, can confirm that it has a comfortable old-fashioned feel that I knew Mum and Dad would enjoy, even if they didn't enjoy any other aspect of their visit. Luckily, I have a smart shirt that I bought a couple of months ago for a colleague's birthday do that I only spent half an hour at before the people and noise sent me fleeing so, I suppose it's good that it's getting a second wearing anyway. It's now almost a year since I last wore a TFL uniform and, since then, I've more or less lived in jeans, T.shirts and hoodies so it'll be strange to go through the motions of dressing up again. The day that I fled London, I left my flat in the morning with two bags, one containing a minimal amount of clothes and toiletries to see myself through a few days and the other, heavier, one containing Beth's clothes and toys which I dropped off at a charity shop before jumping onto a tube to Euston station. Barely used as they were, I hoped that at least some kid would benefit from her stuff. I'm not going all hippy or anything but life really is a lot simpler without a load of things cluttering it up and, these days, I tend to buy something only when it's predecessor has been exhausted. According to the wheezy old clock on the wall, I've got about thirty five minutes before I have to meet Mum and Dad in order for us to make the eighteen fifty four train to Cark and I need to shower again although I don't bother shaving these days so I don't need much time. It took a while but, once I was no longer around, the press finally started to leave Mum and Dad alone and they didn't have to move away as they once thought they would so, thankfully, their lives seem to be pretty much back to normal these days, although Mum said that somebody spat at her when she visited the memorial a few weeks back. People will forget though, eventually, because that's what people do - you think of all the major news stories that you see every year and then think about how many of them ever even cross your mind afterward and you'll see what I mean. Once again, I've let my thoughts run away with me, something that happens now and again if I let it, and it's nearly time to go. If I'm lucky, the evening will be over quickly and painlessly and I'll convince Mum and Dad that there's nothing to worry about, because there isn't. Not really.

CHAPTER 43

I suppose the biggest surprise was that I was actually surprised. As I opened the door, I had no idea what the Manager wanted to see me about but, as he'd always been friendly and respectful towards us, I wasn't unduly worried and I greeted him with a smile and a stupid joke about having seen him so recently. Responding to my greeting with only a weak smile, he was actually wringing his hands (something I'm not sure I'd ever seen anybody actually do before) as he cleared his throat and said,

'Yes, quite. Mr Thorn, I'm afraid this is a little awkward but I've just been informed by Hall and Oakes that they will no longer be covering your stay with us.' At the look of (I'm sure) obvious shock on my face, he quickly added, 'Everything up until this morning is, of course, taken care of by them as an, ah, courtesy but they are no longer able to continue with the arrangement.' For a moment, I could only stare at him as I got my head around the fact that what I was hearing was that, essentially, Beth and I were being turfed out of the Dorchester and left, unceremoniously, to our own devices. When I didn't reply, he ploughed on,

'You do, of course, have the option of continuing your stay at your own expense and I can........'

'No,' I interrupted, having already balked at the price of the room even when somebody else was paying,' 'We'll be leaving.' He nodded,

'Very well, I shall alert house-keeping.' This did, of course, raise a number of questions as the manager and the security guy both stood awkwardly in front of me, the first and most pressing of which was the one that dealt with how we were supposed to leave the hotel and get to the safety of my flat without being mobbed by London's entire press pool. As though reading my mind the manager, Mr Bennet, cleared his throat again and said, 'You don't have to leave immediately, of course but we will need the room back by early evening. I realise that your situation is a little, ah, delicate and so do let me know what time you will be ready and I will arrange for a car to collect you and your luggage from the back entrance.'

'Thank you,' I managed and forced a smile - after all, none of this was his fault and I could see that he already felt uncomfortable enough, 'We'll be ready to go at three o'clock.'

'Very good,' he replied and, as he turned away, I stopped him,

'Oh, would it be possible to have some coffee sent up and some juice for the girl, I'll pay for........'

'No need, Mr Thorn,' he said kindly, 'On the house and I'll make sure that they're sent up straight away.' He disappeared down the hallway and, as he left, the security guy, deciding that there was no time like the present, patted my shoulder and said,

'Mr Thorn. I'm sorry to add to your troubles but I've also been told that my services - and those of my colleagues - will no longer be covered.' He coughed self-consciously, avoiding eye contact as he added, 'I was told to leave earlier this morning but I, you know, just wanted to make sure you and the little girl would be OK.' I stared at him, touched that he had stayed at his post without pay and I swallowed loudly before I said,

'Thank you, Guy, I really appreciate it. We'll be fine.' And we would, I thought as I closed the door behind me, because we'd have to be - I had the cheque from Spencer that would keep Beth and I going for a while but that wouldn't last too long if I was paying for things like security, not to mention eye-wateringly expensive hotel suites. No, I thought as I started to pack up our things, we would manage somehow. True to his word, Mr Bennet sent up our drinks and, when I opened the door to receive them, I saw that Guy had quietly slipped away and I found myself hoping that his next job would be a bit less stressful. With all of our stuff packed and waiting neatly by the door, there was really nothing to do but wait and so we did that, Beth playing on the one game that I had allowed her to keep hold of and me avoiding the urge to check what the media were now saying. Eventually, three o'clock arrived and a porter appeared to take our luggage and escort us, for the last time, through the kitchens and out the back door into the car that was waiting for us. Having gotten wise to this manoeuvre some time since, the press were waiting for us as the gate opened but our driver didn't stop or even hesitate as he eased the car onto Brannocks Road and then sped up as we joined Park Lane. Confident that we'd lost the press, if only momentarily, I got the driver to stop briefly in Highbury so that I could deposit Spencer's cheque and pick up a couple of bags of groceries and then we were on our way again, pulling up only minutes later outside my flat. Although it had, in reality, only been a few days, it seemed like months since I had last seen it and it would have been a welcome sight, as home usually is, if it hadn't been for the four or five reporters still hanging around outside.

Throughout the journey, Beth had been quiet and still and I wondered how much she knew about what was going on - although I had taken care to tell her only the bare minimum, she had this way of intuiting the stuff that wasn't said and I tried a couple of times to draw her out but she had simply shrugged and said that she was fine. After getting out of the car (which, as it turned out, Spencer had also paid for; he was all heart, that guy), I picked up Beth while the driver grabbed our bags and, together, we walked quickly down the path and into the flat, the driver giving me the impression that he was some kind of veteran at this as he deposited our bags in the hallway and then left, closing the door behind him without the press managing to get a glimpse, let alone a foot inside the door. Then we were alone again. This time, in the privacy of my own home, I did turn on the TV and there was almost a degree of comfort in discovering that it was just as bad as I had expected. The first channel that I hopped onto showed a large group of people surrounding the memorial in Bethnal Green Gardens. As the camera panned the scene, I saw that many of the people were holding signs and banners, all of which said things like 'Fraudster', 'Scammer' and even 'Monster.' As I watched, the camera jumped to a woman who looked to be in her sixties and who was standing at the stairway end of the memorial. As the camera zoomed in on her, the sound kicked in and she said in an accent that could only come from Bethnal Green,

'Well, it's the disrespect isn't it? It's making a mockery of all those poor souls what died here that day - my uncle were one of them.' The shot panned away again and now, in the calm quiet of a TV studio, a talking head was informing those of us who had just tuned in that the day's main story was the news that the so-called Miracle Of Bethnal Green was, in fact, a hoax. Within minutes, I discovered that what was being said on the television was kind compared to the uncensored venom that was quickly doing the rounds on the internet and I hurriedly logged off before Beth could look over my shoulder and get the gist of it but the screaming headlines would be hard to forget. For the next few hours as I unpacked our things, cooked some macaroni cheese and, generally, tried to create some kind of semblance of normality, I found that I couldn't stop myself from sporadically checking both the TV and the internet for any new developments. As it would turn out, those few hours would be remembered fondly as a kind of golden age before the death threats and lawsuits began but, at the time, it was terrifying, confusing and made me more angry than I can explain in that all of these things were being said without my even being given the chance to respond. As I no longer had the use of Spencer and his agency, I called a few TV and radio stations in the hope of being given a chance to explain my side of things but hit a brick wall each time; It seemed that, without representation, you didn't get past even the minions' minions and it soon became very clear that the very same people who, the day before, would have bitten my hand off for an exclusive, were now determined to keep me at arm's length. Suddenly, as far as the world was concerned, Beth and I were poison. The thing about poison is that people avoid it vigorously because they're scared of it and I knew that I should be using that to my benefit but, without even the benefit of the doubt from the people that I needed to get through to, it seemed that the only avenue open to me was to vent on social media and, for the moment, that was something that I just couldn't bring myself to do. The biggest joke was that I had plenty of media representatives right on my doorstep - every time I opened the living room door I could hear them out there - but these were not serious journalists interested in finding out the truth, just hacks who wanted pictures of me and Beth looking guilty and rough and, if possible, as a bonus, wanted to goad me into yelling something incriminating or, even better, taking a swing at one of them because, after all, that's the stuff that shifts tabloids. Although I knew that we couldn't hide in the flat forever, I had no intention of us showing our faces that night and so we settled in for an evening in the flat which, although not as luxurious as the Dorchester, was nonetheless comfortable with the major bonus that a cup of tea didn't cost a fiver. After watching a few hours of rubbish telly, it was just about time to put Beth to bed and I heaved myself out of my chair and into the bedroom to put the heater on for a minute before bringing Beth through. I'd just flicked on the space heater and turned down the bed when I heard the crash and, a second or two later, the shrill sound of Beth screaming and I ran from the room, jabbing my toe painfully on the bed post as I went although I wouldn't even notice that until much later. As always, I'd left the door between the kitchen and the living room open and so, from where I stood, I could see the shards of glass littered across the kitchen floor and I pulled on a pair of trainers, urging Beth to stay where she was in the relative safety of the far corner of the living room. As I walked gingerly into the kitchen, I immediately saw the brick which, on its journey through the window had also managed to decimate my cafetiere which now lay in several chunks of glass, metal and plastic on the counter and in the sink. At first I hesitated, some dim idea of not touching evidence and all that stopping me from touching anything but then I reached forward, carefully brushing a few bits of glass off the brick before tweezing the elastic band off it in order to retrieve the note that had been attached to it. As I stared at the note, I was vaguely aware of a commotion outside but it seemed to come from a long way away as I unfolded the note and read,

"Bethnal Green sentences you to death - a sentence that still existed in 1943!!" For a moment, I just stared at it, not quite able to believe what I was seeing but then I flung it back down on the counter, partly for the evidence reasons that I just mentioned and partly because it was vile and I didn't want to be touching any part of it. Grabbing a dustpan and brush from underneath the sink, I started to sweep up the pieces of window and coffee jug glass and poured them first into a used jiffy bag and then popped the jiffy into a carrier and it was then that I finally, properly, registered the noise from outside. Hesitantly, I opened the kitchen door which backs onto an alley running between my building and the house next door and called out,

'What's going on?' It took my eyes a few seconds to adjust to the darkness after my brightly lit kitchen and so, at first, I couldn't figure out what it was I was seeing but then, as my sight, adjusted, I realised that it was three or four blokes, one of whom appeared to have been pushed to the ground and was being held there by one of the others.

'You both alright in there?' One of the guys who were still standing called and I nodded, 'We're fine.'

'Lying Scum!' the bloke on the ground screamed and the one holding him down gave him a warning kick to the ribs,

'The police are on their way mate, maybe you'd best save your breath for when they get here.'

'Is that....?' I shook my head and moved closer to peer at the man who was squirming on the dirty tarmac, 'Is he the one that threw the brick?' The bloke whose foot had just connected with the other guy's ribs nodded and I moved closer still so that I could see his face.

'There's a kid in there, you fucking troll,' I yelled as I looked down at him, 'Do you realise that?' Of course, that was a stupid question as, of course he realised that - it was, after all, why he was there in the first place and I moved away again to prevent myself from giving in to the urge to give the idiot another boot, but this time somewhere a bit more sensitive than his ribs. I moved back inside to check on Beth and, as I did, I heard the brief bloop of a siren outside and I strode down the hall to open the door to the two officers who introduced themselves as PCs Sam Roberts and Gita Patel. As I led Starsky and Hutch through the living room to the kitchen, I noticed them both slow as they clocked Beth and I suppressed a sigh, reminding myself that I would probably have done the same in their shoes which looked to be sensible, sturdy and left a slightly mucky stain on my living room carpet. As we reached the alley, the bloke on the ground was still struggling and swearing but it seemed light work for the officers to haul him to his feet and handcuff him before dragging him back through the flat and out to the police car where he was locked in securely before the officers returned to take our statements. As they needed to speak to the reporters as well, I had no choice but to invite everybody inside and so, after putting Beth to bed, I found myself in the bizarre situation of making tea for two police officers and three reporters, all of whom were squeezed into my small living room. The facts being as plain as they were, and the fact that the brick thrower was still yelling about how I deserved to die meant that it didn't take the officers too long to get the gist of what happened. Although they clearly knew who I was, they maintained a friendly and professional air and even gave me a number to call should I decide that Beth and I needed some official kind of protection. By the time everybody got up to leave, it was late - about eleven and, as I showed them to the door, I thanked the officers and, more profusely, the reporters, Rick, Harry and Steve for apprehending the guy in the first place. As I closed the door behind them, the flat seemed suddenly quiet, even the thudding of the bloke upstairs stereo seeming muted and distant. I thought about making another cup of tea and then changed my mind, deciding instead to hit the sack after what had been an eventful day to say the least. Although, by the end of the evening, I hadn't considered myself and the reporters to be friends, I had thought that we had reached a kind of understanding and so, despite my newly heightened immunity to surprise, I was still shocked when I woke in the morning to a bunch of headlines along the lines of "Sun reporter saves fraudster from would be assassin" and "Brick drama for con-man." If I'd expected the sympathy to be with me and Beth, I would be sorely disappointed as it seemed that the general feeling of both the press and public was that a low life like myself should expect nothing else and that we should all stop and take a moment to honour the brave journalists who jumped in to protect myself and Beth despite our transgressions. None of the articles mentioned, of course, the fact that the only reason that the press were out there in the first place was to harass and and stalk us in the hopes of goading me into an outburst. With all of the accusations of fraud and scamming, I'd almost hoped that the traumatic events of the evening would prompt Beth to pull one of her stunts - maybe the horror face one from the magazine studio or the disappearing trick - but she remained quiet and passive throughout the whole ordeal, not even emerging from the bedroom until the police and reporters had left and, then, just to ask for a glass of water. That morning, exhausted, I decided that Beth and I would sit and have breakfast properly before even thinking of looking at anything on the TV or the internet and so it was about ten o'clock when I finally clicked the remote to switch on the television and, immediately, discovered two things. First, that Beth and I were still the main topic of conversation on most of the news channels and, secondly, it was Christmas Eve.

CHAPTER 44

One thing I knew for sure was that we wouldn't be going out carol singing but, still, I felt that I should be doing something. I still had the nagging feeling that time was, somehow, running out and I wanted to do something to mark the occasion. I didn't fancy doing anything that would leave the two of us exposed for any length of time so things like WInter Wonderland were out but I thought that maybe I could manage a quick trip to the shops in order to muddle together some kind of Christmas for us both. I knew from half-listening to Mum for more Christmases than I could remember that there was unlikely to be much left on the shelves by now (and you can forget a Marks & Spencers turkey if you leave it any later than early December) but I thought that we might at least be able to scavenge some mince pies and maybe some toys and tinsel. Taking a quick look through the glass of the front door I saw that the media's number had dwindled to five (and even they would be gone by the end of the day - apparently even reporters have loved ones that they want to spend Christmas with) - and so I quickly got us both ready and, less than an hour later, we were out the front door, heads down and moving quickly as the press hurled questions and taunts at us. I couldn't face the hassle of Stratford and so we headed for the Kingsland shopping centre in Dalston, dodging our way past pubs filled with office workers celebrating their temporary release from the workaday world and I imagined that the area would be pure carnage by late afternoon. Depending on our shifts, Christmas Eve would normally be myself, Andy and the girls with a few beers in the Salmon & Ball and maybe a chinese and I felt a brief pang at the memories of the ghosts of Christmas past. Still, I thought, as I smiled down at the ghost of Christmas past and present as we crossed the road toward the shopping centre, we would do our best to make the most of it and, I was sure, a bunch of goodies from M&S or Waitrose would go a long way toward achieving that. Our first stop was Matalan where I instructed Beth to pick out a few things for herself (I know I had Spencer's cheque burning a hole in my bank account but it wasn't yet cleared and I was still being cautious, convinced that he would, for some reason, change his mind and cancel it) and then we popped to Fed for a pizza which, let's just say, did not impress Beth in the slightest but the opposite was very much the case for the chocolate fudge cake. Fully refreshed, we then hit Sainsburys and M&S and bagged decorations, mince pies, pigs in blankets and a whole load of other stuff that will make you put on a stone just by looking at it. Although we'd got the bus there, by the time we left I was laden down with bags and so I decided to treat us to a taxi home. Our couple of hours of near-normality had put me in a mood that, although maybe not quite festive, was certainly more optimistic than it had been and there was a spring in my step as we walked to Dalston Lane in order to flag down a cab. The walk was a little slow-going due to the fact that Beth had insisted on wearing the new ludicrously pink shoes that she had picked out in Matalan and which, despite being almost a size too big,were, apparently, the only ones which would do.

'Well, I suppose you'll grow into them,' I said at the time and she smiled but didn't reply and I felt, again, that tug of time moving too quickly. Within a couple of minutes, a black cab rounded the corner toward us and then slowed at the sight of my out-stretched hand. I had just reached out to grab the door handle when the driver, a white fifty-something with a shaved head and tattoos, took a good at me, cursed and then put his foot down and sped away. And I wasn't even going to ask him to go South of the river. Thankfully, the next cab that approached, only five or six minutes later, stopped by the curb long enough for us to climb inside and, if he knew who we were, he kept it to himself for the duration of the journey. With traffic just after lunchtime being reasonably light, we were home in less than fifteen minutes and I heaved our shopping past the remaining reporters who were starting to look cold, tired and fed-up and I felt like telling them that they might as well go home as we wouldn't be coming out again this side of Baby Jesus' birthday but I didn't, maintaining instead a dignified silence as I struggled to unlock the front door with my arms full. Once inside, I saw that there were two envelopes on the mat and, figuring that they weren't Christmas cards, I picked them up and stuffed them into my jacket for consideration at a later date. Leaving Beth in the living room to examine her booty, I headed into the kitchen to put away the shopping. The piece of chipboard that I'd used to block the hole in the window was still in place but I made a mental note to call the glazer as soon as I'd got the shopping squared away, the idea of just a thin and hastily placed piece of wood separating me and Beth from the outside world making me feel less than secure considering our current situation. Once I was finished in the kitchen, I returned to the living room intending to make that phone call but was stopped dead as I realised that, once again, Beth had vanished although, this time, there was no deafening voice bouncing off the walls. A quick look through the bathroom door showed that she wasn't in there and I moved through to the bedroom, wondering if she'd decided to take a nap. At first glance, it looked like the bedroom was empty and I was about to retreat when a tiny sound brought me back. It was the kind of sound that I would have missed had Graham in the flat upstairs had his TV on but he didn't and I so I didn't. Moving into the room, I had an attack of deja vu as I remembered the time, not too long ago, when a tiny sound like this one had sent me clambering into a tube tunnel and, through association, my heart was in my mouth as I moved until I was standing in the middle of the room.

'Beth?' I called softly and then, when there was no reply, 'Where are you hon?' Not moving from my spot in the middle of the room, I spun around slowly, taking in the whole of the room which was small and contained a limited number of hiding places. Moving quietly, I opened the wardrobe door but there was nothing inside other than my modest collection of clothes and slightly more extensive range belonging to Beth. Closing the door, I looked around again and then moved to the window to pull aside the long heavy curtain (essential for when you work shifts and you sometimes need to attempt sleep with mid summer sunshine outside). I'd just let go of the curtain on the right hand side when I heard a yell from beside me and Beth jumped out from where she had been hiding behind the left hand curtain, grinning up at me as my heart-beat attempted to recreate something heard at a rave club.

'Jesus, Fu....' I yelled but managed to stop myself before the expletive escaped. As is the case when scared, my first impulse was to snap at her for making me jump but her grin was infectious and I felt a bubble of childish laughter building in my chest as I looked down at her.

'You got me!' I laughed and her grin widened.......and then carried on widening, first the manic grin of the Joker in the Batman films and then, just for a second, something even more grotesque and then it was gone and, once more, it was just the delighted grin of a little girl who has successfully scared the living bejeezus out of someone.

'Come on' I said, holding out my hand, 'Come and help me figure out where to put our tinsel and stuff.' Although she came with me readily enough, I wasn't getting much enthusiasm from her when it came to the Christmas decorating, in fact, I felt that she was largely humouring me as I pretended to be stumped by the project and she pointed first to the top of the window frame and then to the door frame and I dutifully draped the tinsel where instructed. Once we'd finished, although not exactly festive, the living room was now at least giving a nod to the fact that it was nearly Christmas and I set about putting together some dinner from the goodies we'd bought, thinking that we'd then find something suitably Christmassy to watch until Beth's bedtime. Although Beth had already been playing with and wearing the things that she'd chosen for herself, I had picked out another item while she wasn't looking and planned to wrap it for her once she was asleep, figuring that every kid should have at least one thing to unwrap on Christmas morning. I arranged our Christmas Eve picnic on a tray and then brought it through to the living room with a glass of milk for Beth and a glass of Cabernet for myself and, turning on the TV and flicking quickly away from the news channels, I was happy to find that The Polar Express had just begun on one of the kids channels. Leaving Beth in front of Hero Boy and his adventures in the North Pole for a moment, I remembered the two envelopes that I'd picked up from the doormat and hastily grabbed them from my jacket pocket that was hanging up in the hallway and ripping one of them open as I walked back into the living room. Reading through the letter inside, I sat down heavily in my armchair and then read it again, unsure if this was some kind of joke or prank. "Dear Mr Thorn," the letter, whose letterhead announced that it was from the desk of a firm of solicitors called Stunt Palmer and Robinson in Bethnal Green, read, "We are acting on behalf of one Mrs Mary Bledsoe of 4 Gosset Street, Bethnal Green." The first time I reached that part, I frowned, certain that I knew nobody by that name but, as I read further, it was made more than clear. Essentially, the letter was telling me that this Mary Bledsoe of 4 Gosset Street, Bethnal Green, was suing me for emotional distress and disrespect with respect to my recent claims in the media. It turned out that Mary Bledsoe (of 4 Gosset Street etc), was the niece of a gentleman who died during the tragedy at Bethnal Green and that, apparently, reading about Beth in the papers had distressed her so violently that she felt the need to sue for large amounts of money in order for amends to be made. Ripping open the other envelope, it was no surprise that it was almost exactly the same except that this time the solicitor was a lone wolf called Ethan Gale and the complainant this time was a Mr Albert Shaw of 7 Pollard Row, Bethnal Green. Merry sodding Christmas. I realised that what I really needed to do, and fast, was to follow in the footsteps of Mary Bledsoe and Albert Shaw and get myself a solicitor but it was seven o'clock on Christmas Eve and I was pretty sure that no such professional would appreciate my calling their emergency numbers at that time so I put the letters aside, confident that there would be more where they came from before this thing was out and that nothing could be done about it for at least a couple of days. Of course, the legal and financial aspects worried me but, more than that, the idea that I would make all of this up, distressing elderly people in the process, for some kind of personal gain, wounded me more than I would care to admit. Deflecting Beth's questions about what was in the letters, I settled down again to watch The Polar Express but my heart was no longer in it and, rather than the magical experience that it should have been, I now just found Hero Boy and his pals' voices grating and annoying. After what seemed like an eternity, the film finally ended and it was Beth's bed-time. Having gone through the usual rigmarole of teeth cleaning, toilet and into bed, I offered a story but she just shook her head, eyes already closing.

'Well, alright,' I said, 'Sweet dreams and, remember, what you wake up, it'll be Christmas!'. Settling back in front of the television, I vowed that I would have just one more glass of wine, as it was Christmas, but, in reality, I knew that I would be finishing the bottle and, so it was that, within what was really quite short a time, I was rinsing out the empty bottle and gently placing it into the recycling bin to avoid clinking. Before turning in myself, I wandered down the hallway to the front door, just for the novelty of being able to look through the window in the door and not see the shadowy figures of

London's press. As I reached the doormat I saw, again, a flash of white on it but this time, rather than an envelope, it was just a piece of paper, stark white with just three words printed in red block capitals. I hesitated at first, aware that blindly obeying the instruction on this anonymous missive would most likely turn out to be a really bad idea but after a minute or so of indecision, I finally decided to do as the note said. I opened the door. Outside, it was full dark, the widely spaced street lights barely making a dent in the blackness but the light spilling from the hallways was enough to see what was directly in front of me. Staring at the other side of the front door, I wondered briefly what would have happened if Graham from upstairs had discovered this before I did and then, hot on the heels of that thought, I remembered that Graham goes home to his family in Leicester for Christmas and probably wouldn't be back until the day after Boxing Day. Maybe it was the wine but I didn't feel angry or even upset, just very very weary as I walked quietly through the flat to the kitchen to grab a brillo pad and a bucket of hot water and then back through to the front door. Back on the front doorstep, I began to methodically scrub the red words off the front door, first "We will", then "bury" then "You Both". To be honest, the threat didn't particularly bother me - people who intend harm don't tend to threaten you first; I learned that much from my time working the pub-closing shift at Bethnal Green tube station. No, what annoyed me that night, and continued to annoy me long after, was that someone was able to come to my home and make threats and accusations without allowing me even the decency of responding to them. After my exertions, I briefly considered jogging down to the convenience store down the road for another bottle of wine; it would be open for about another ten minutes and I could have made it if I hustled but then I realised that it would mean either waking Beth or leaving her on her own for the best part of half an hour and so I abandoned the idea which was probably a wise move on all fronts. Instead, I quickly drank a glass of water then padded through to the bathroom to brush my teeth, brooding on the fact that a day which started reasonably well had gone downhill so bloody quickly. As I gratefully climbed into bed, I resolved that, although, in a few days time, I would need to deal with things like solicitors and, following the threats, probably the police, the following day - Christmas Day - was going to be about nothing but games, good food and keeping the outside world firmly in its place. As it would turn out, in all of this mess, and although it didn't go entirely to plan, it was the best decision I ever made as, the following day, Beth would be gone.

CHAPTER 45

The following morning I was very deliberately up before the birds and, more importantly, Beth, in order to wrap Beth's extra gift which I'd forgotten to do the night before and, more to the point, check the flat to make sure that no more tidings of comfort and joy had been left for us while we slept. Thankfully, all was quiet and un-defaced and so I quickly wrapped the present and then set about putting some breakfast stuff together from the haul bought the day before, which included special Christmas coffee for me and cranberry spice muffins for us both although I realised that, Beth-wise, this was ambitious and that I would no doubt end up making her some toast and jam. I had always been under the impression that kids got so excited about Christmas that they got up in the early hours of the morning if allowed but, on that particular Christmas morning, I ended up going in to wake Beth about nine o'clock, leaving her until then on the assumption that she was exhausted and needed the sleep. When I walked into the bedroom, she was wide awake and sitting on the bed facing a blank wall and, although she looked up when I entered the room, it was only a brief glance before she resumed gazing at what appeared to be absolutely nothing. I hovered for a second, unsure what to do - I had the vague thought that she might be sleep-walking, or rather, sleep-sitting and I remembered hearing something about how you should never wake somebody in that situation as it can be dangerous but she didn't look like she was asleep, in fact, she seemed completely alert and aware of her surroundings - even if she did seem unusually fascinated by a blank picture-less and window-less wall. Still half-attached to my sleep-walking theory, I moved forward very slowly and very quietly, determined not to startle her and, it was as I got closer that I noticed that she was holding something although, at that moment, she was holding it so tightly in her fist that I couldn't make out what it was, just a tiny flash of red cupped in her tiny pink hand.

'You alright Beth,' I asked quietly and, although a small frown appeared and then smoothed out, there was still no response.

'It's Christmas!' I said in a jolly voice that seemed to fall flat as it entered the room which, all of a sudden, felt airless and dark. For a moment, I stood un-moving, trying to figure my next move and, it was then that Beth finally turned to face me, shifting slowly on the bed until she was looking directly at me and, once we were facing each other, she opened her hands and said

'There's no more time, Will. She's waiting.' As I watched, the thing that she was holding in her hands and which, at first, looked like a small red ball, started to open and spread like a flower until it filled first one hand and then the other. Without looking down, she pulled her hands apart and the red thing, no longer a ball or a flower, oozed from her hands and slid to the floor, growing all the while until it settled like a rug on the carpet measuring about two feet square.

'Who's waiting, Beth....?' I began and she put a finger to her lips, silently pointing down at my new red rug which rippled and then rapidly started to change colour, moving through every spectrum of the rainbow before clearing to nothing and then, slowly, an image began to form. At first, the image was fuzzy and I couldn't really make out what I was seeing but then it began to clarify and, within a few seconds, I could see that it was a door - a drab grey door that you tend to find in tower blocks; doors that have super-strength locks on the inside to protect the occupants and their belongings from the meth heads and petty criminals that they share a communal entrance with. Although I'd never been there, I knew instantly whose flat this was and I found that I didn't want to look at it, didn't want to think about what those years must have been like but it was as though I was unable to turn away. Of course I knew where it was; it was a tower block in Surrey that stood like a sentinel at the end of a grey and down-trodden street of terraced houses and cut price off licenses and mini marts. I'd heard about it over the years and it was strange to see it now, like talking to somebody on the phone for years and then finally getting to see what they look like. Without warning, the image - and the rug - suddenly disappeared and there was nothing left but a blinking red dot, like the light on a DVD player or laptop and my mind reeled at the association; was that what this was, some kind of electrical projection? I looked at Beth who was sitting quietly on the bed, staring at the blinking red dot as though waiting for it to do something else (waiting for somebody to push a button on the remote control to start the next scene, my mind whispered) and I shook my head to clear it.

'Come on Beth, I'm making breakfast.' Having said it out loud, I suddenly panicked, realising that I had been scrambling eggs and that they must, by now, be burnt to a congealed mess but, looking at my watch, I saw that, impossibly, less than two minutes had passed since I walked into the bedroom. When she didn't move, or even react, I sighed and left the room, suddenly annoyed. I'd woken up feeling reasonably optimistic that, despite everything, we would just have a nice, quiet, drama-free Christmas day. It was, I thought petulantly, the least that we deserved - that I deserved - after all the shit that had been thrown at us over the past week and, whatever this latest revelation was, I couldn't help wishing that Beth could have kept it to herself for just one day. I went back into the kitchen, not caring for the moment, whether Beth followed or not - for the time being, I was done and so, in fact, were the eggs so Beth could join me or not, as she pleased, but I wasn't going to let them go to waste. As I transferred the eggs to a bowl and dumped the pan into a sink of soapy water, I heard Beth's faint footsteps padding into the living room and I smiled as I placed everything on a tray and carried it through; maybe the day would be salvaged after all. As I walked into the room I saw that Beth was sitting on the floor next to the coffee table which was the only dining option that I had apart from a tray on the lap on the sofa and smiled as I put her plate and glass in front of her and then arranged my own food and coffee. I found something mind-numbing on the television and we watched and ate in a comfortable silence for the most part with Beth, to my surprise eating everything in front of her without comment or complaint. Although it felt like a betrayal, I couldn't stop my mind from wandering, from reviewing, incident by weird incident, everything that had happened since Beth came into my life. She knew things that she couldn't possibly know, they said, she talked about things as though she were there, it was what made her the Miracle Of Bethnal Green in the first place but, did it have to be a miracle? I glanced at Beth who was absorbed in her muffin and whatever was on TV and I briefly closed my eyes. There were still a few people around who survived Bethnal Green; was it possible that one of them could have groomed her - teaching her day after day until she knew the facts as well as she knew her own name - and then, if it were possible, to what end? Whatever programme was showing on TV ended and was replaced by a couple of popular evening presenters pretending to be best buds as they wished everybody a merry Christmas and promised an imminent performance by Fifth Harmony, whoever they were. I cleared away our tray and quickly washed the dishes, leaving the pan to soak for a bit longer, not wanting to leave Beth alone for the time it would take me to scrape and scrub all the egg traces from it. When I returned, Beth looked up at me from her place on the floor and said,

'It's time Will.' That again, I thought and sighed, it seemed that playtime was over.

'Look, Beth, I don't know what it is you want me to do but.....'

'It's time,' she repeated then, 'You know where to go. I showed you.' I shook my head, 'It's Christmas Day Beth and, it's a long way - too far for us to go today, there's no transport or anything running.'

'It's time,' she insisted, this time louder and with a sense of urgency that gave me pause. I looked at her face with its clear, unblemished skin and thought of her face that day in the studio, crushed and bruised; that had to be real didn't it? *She was sat in front of a make-up artist*, my mind whispered, *a stage make-up artist!*

'Well, what is it?' I asked impatiently, 'What's so important that we have to go there today, it'll still be there tomorrow won't it?' Her only response was the steady gaze that I'd grown to know so well and I sighed, not yet ready to admit to myself that I was about to pay for a taxi - a Christmas Day double time taxi - to Surrey without even knowing what the hell it was that I was doing it for. I was giving in to the whim of a child for no real reason other than the fact that she was insisting and I knew how ridiculous that was. I also knew that my resistance was only delaying the inevitable.

'You need to get dressed first,' I said curtly, heading for the bedroom without checking to see if she was following. Once there I pulled jeans, a pink jumper, socks and sneakers from the wardrobe and Beth stood silently as I dressed her. It briefly occurred to me that, had we been on better terms, I could have phoned Andy and asked him to take us but I dismissed that idea before it had even formed - Andy would be hungover, probably only just up and getting ready to go to lunch at his Mum's and he certainly would not have welcomed a one hour plus drive, even under better circumstances. Picking up the phone, I dialled the number of my local cab office, wondering if they'd even be there - and wondering if I wanted them to be but, after only two rings, the call was answered and the guy on the other end, sounding less than delighted, said that somebody would be with us in twenty minutes. I got us both into our coats and then we waited, mostly in silence, for the cab to arrive. Eventually, the car arrived, driven by an exhausted looking Polish guy who didn't seem thrilled to be making the journey and, less so, when he realised that I had a kid with me but Beth was quiet through the whole trip, staring straight ahead the whole time as though willing us to get there faster. The roads were Christmas Day quiet and, between my flat and the Marylebone Road we encountered only a handful of other cars, most packed to the rafters with wrapped presents to be taken to family or friends. Once within a breath of Central London, there was more but then when we got onto the A40 we had a clear shot through and, in less than fifty minutes, the driver was nosing the car around the perimeter of Richmond Park then shooting off toward Kingston and the Madingley tower block which had been Grandma Shelly's last home. As the driver pulled up outside the block of flats, I remembered that there had been a fire there a while back and, as I climbed out of the car, I couldn't help thinking that anything, even a fire, could probably only improve the building which was drab and depressing in the harsh December light. There wasn't a great deal around and certainly not much that would be open and so I paid the driver and then persuaded him to go off and find a garage or something and get himself a coffee then pick us up again in an hour's time. I figured that, if that wasn't long enough for whatever the hell this was then that was just too bad as I had no intention of wasting any more of this day than was absolutely unavoidable. The block was served by one main entrance and, although there were buzzers beside the door, the door had been wedged open and the electronic entry system looked like it probably last worked when Margaret Thatcher was in power. I was about to complain that we didn't even know which flat it was but, before the words formed, I realised that that wasn't true as Beth's little rug vision had showed us that it was flat number thirty three. A quick look at a faded and yellowed map just inside the entrance showed us that we were after the third floor and because, of course, the lift wasn't working, we set off up the stairs which smelled of urine and something even less pleasant. Thankfully, there weren't too many stairs (an indication, I suppose, of how small the flats were) and, soon, we were standing outside number thirty three which, although as dowdy as the rest, was clean and had a newish looking floral welcome mat on the floor outside. The next whinge that I had prepared was that we had no way of getting into the flat but, as we stood there and, despite neither of us touching it, the door swung inwards, only the absence of a creaking sound stopping it from being like something out of a horror film. Putting out a hand to stop Beth from just marching into the flat I tentatively reached out and pushed the door all the way open, feeling a little silly already as I gently called out,

'Hello, is anybody in there?' When there was, unsurprisingly, no reply, I grabbed Beth's hand, pulling her behind me as I walked into the flat, through a short, narrow corridor and then into a living room. Glancing around, I saw that the room was neat and clean

but sparse in terms of decoration and nick nacks. The sofa and chair were serviceable but brightened a little by floral cushions that looked home-made and were matched by curtains in the same brown and green pattern. Telling Beth to stay put, I did a quick walk through of the rest of the place which, like the living room, was clean but sparsely furnished; in the kitchen, the surfaces were scrubbed and just one plate and one cup, now both bone dry, sat on a dish drainer next to the sink. In the bedroom, which had a delightful view of a dilapidated kids playing area, the single bed was neatly made with ironed sheets and an old fashioned eiderdown and there was a cheap looking dressing table with nothing but a hairbrush sat on top of it. I thought of Mum's dressing table, cluttered with all her pots and potions and perfume bottles and felt a lump form in my throat at seeing how Shelly had lived and I wondered how often she had even left this flat in the last few months. Having established that Beth and I were alone in the flat, I took a moment to have a look through her fridge and cupboards - not out of nosiness but in order to bin anything that would go off and stink the place out but there was nothing; there were a few tins in the cupboard which I left alone and, in the fridge which, again was old but clean, there was nothing but a brand new jar of piccalilli (does anybody actually still eat that stuff ??) and a surgical looking band that looked like the sort of thing you would put on your forehead to get rid of a headache. As I returned to the living room, I heard a sound like somebody clearing their throat from the direction of the front door then as I grabbed Beth, startled, I heard a female voice call,
'Hello? Is there somebody here?' Relaxing my grip on Beth's arm, I took a step toward the door of the living room and was about to take another when I saw a peroxide blonde head poke itself around the door.
'Hello,' I said in what I hoped was a tone of authority and the head was joined by the rest of its owner.
'Who are you?' Although the question itself was brusque, the tone was more curiosity than fear or threat but then, before I could answer, her eyes widened as her gaze travelled from me to Beth. 'It's you!' She whispered, managing to look both fascinated and horrified at the same time and I took a moment to examine her. From what I could see, I put her at about fifty but a well-worn fifty. Her hair was indifferently cut to about shoulder length and was the kind of bleached blonde that looks yellow and her clothes, threadbare black leggings and a thick red jumper were inexpensive and unfussy.
'I'm Will,' I said quietly, 'Shelly was my Grandmother and,' I gestured needlessly as I added, 'this is Beth.'
'Yes,' the woman said quietly, 'I know about you both. Not just from the papers of course - Shelly told me about you. About her other life.'
'What's your name?' Beth asked as it appeared that no introduction was forthcoming and the blonde started slightly as though Beth had yelled at her.

'Sorry love,' she said after a moment, 'It's just you. Being here. It's all just a bit unexpected. I'm Grace.' So now we knew her name but that generally only covers a very small part of the whole "who are you" question. Perching on the edge of an armchair, I continued to study the woman who looked as though she were perfectly comfortable in Grandma Shelly's flat and, as though to confirm this, she strode toward the kitchen with a cheery,

'I'll put the kettle on, shall I, just let me pop back to my flat to get some teabags and milk.' As both the living room door and the front door were still wide open, I watched as she walked out of Shelly's flat and straight into one directly opposite, from which she emerged seconds later carrying a box of supermarket own brand tea-bags and one of those little one pint jugs of milk. I offered to help but she waved me away, busying herself in the kitchen for a few minutes before carrying a tray through to the living room with two cups of builders tea and a glass of milk for Beth.

'So, Grace' I said after thanking her for the tea, 'You're Shelly's neighbour. How long have you lived here?'

'Oh, pretty much my whole life,' she said and then, looking round the flat as though seeing it for the first time, 'It may not look like much but it's cheap and most are alright sorts around here apart from a few of the lads from the Cambridge estate who seem to be round here all the time these days.' She took a sip of her tea which must still have been scalding, 'I've been onto the police, like everybody else here, but they're not interested are they? But, I'll tell you one thing, they'll be interested enough once one of those little toe-rags stabs someone who doesn't come out of the hospital after.' Although I was nodding politely, I really didn't particularly care about the toe-rags from the Cambridge estate; particularly as I'd asked the taxi driver to come back for us and the clock was ticking. 'Course, I wasn't just her neighbour,' Grace said as though sensing that I was becoming impatient and I nodded,

'You were friends too,'

'Oh, a bit more than that,' she replied with a sly smile and I raised my eyebrows.

'You see,' she continued, it's all been a bit one sided as I know all about you - always have done but you've never even heard of me, have you?' I was getting more confused by the second and I wondered, briefly, if Grace was on something - to be honest, I probably wouldn't have blamed her if she was, I'd probably be on something too if I had to live in that place but, no, aside from the odd things that she was saying, there were no signs that this was the case. Although she'd been perfectly amiable, I couldn't shake the feeling that she was somehow toying with me and I was starting to lose patience. We hadn't even begun to look for whatever it was we were supposed to be finding here and a quick glance at the clock told me that we now had less than forty minutes before our chariot would re-appear.

'I bet you all thought that she was always on her own all these years, didn't you. Your family, I mean. All on our own but it didn't make any of you feel like reaching out to her did it?' She slurped back the last of her tea, 'She wasn't, though. On her own, I mean. She had me.' I sighed impatiently,

'Look, I've no idea what you know, or what you think you know about my family but , either way, it's really none of your business. I'm grateful that Shelly had you but I really don't want to hear another word about my family so spare me any lies or theories as I really don't have the time.'

'Lies?' She smirked, 'that's your department isn't it? I'm not the one that's been parading the "miracle of Bethnal Green" around the place,' she stared at Beth, 'Little Miracle are you love? Gonna come round my flat and turn water into wine?'

'Stop it,' I said, standing up, 'Thank you for the tea but I think it's best that you left now, we've got things to do.'

'That must be nice,' she sniffed, 'Going to your folks are you? Celebrating Christmas with your family?'

'No, nothing like that,' I said irritably, 'It's just that we're here for something - for a reason and it's private,' I gave her a sarcastic look, 'It's a *family* thing.' Grace laughed without humour and, although she set her cup back onto the table, made no move to leave,

'She your family now then?' she asked jutting her head in Beth's direction and I nodded, 'Yes, she is.' Grace's expression was hard to read as she simply contemplated me for a few moments as though I were some strange, exotic creature to be examined but then she smiled and there was a kindness to it as she said,

'She's not though, is she. Not really. But, I am, Will. I'm what you came here to find.'

CHAPTER 46

Grace. As I stood there, the world wavered for a moment as Grandma's Shelly's last words came back to me - not find grace but find Grace! Whatever it was I thought that we were there for, it wasn't that. It wasn't that jaded and faded woman who seemed as much a part of that tired tower block as the bricks themselves.

'Family,' I said flatly, 'I don't think so. What's this really about?' I stood and waved a hand in the direction of the door, 'If it's money you're after, you're a bit late jumping on the bandwagon as we're not exactly popular these days.'

'I've got money,' she said, her steady gaze still never leaving mine, 'Enough to get by anyway and, this flat is mine to do with as I please.' I froze, my arm still pointing toward the door as I processed what she had just said. I'll be honest, my first thought was that maybe she was one of those vultures who befriends vulnerable and older people only to con them out of their belongings and, as if reading my mind, she gave a short humourless bark of laughter, 'All above board and, I'll be happy to explain it all but, first you might want to get rid of that taxi that just pulled up outside and, then, you can put the kettle on again.' I walked over to the window to see that our Polish friend had, in fact, returned and I stood there for a minute, torn and, again, Grace laughed at me.

'You can leave the girl here with me - don't worry, I have absolutely no desire to abduct her.'

'Maybe not,' I replied, 'but as you may have heard, it's been quite a week for Beth, what with people shooting at her and all so you'll forgive me if I'm not feeling especially trusting at the moment.' She nodded and her face softened as she said,

'Understood. It'll only take you a few minutes and I promise that Annie will be safe with me.'

'How do you…..?' I began and she shook her head,

'In a minute and,' she smiled, 'When we're finished, I'll even let you use my phone to call another taxi.'

Needless to say, the driver wasn't too impressed with the new plan but I gave him an overly generous tip and he, eventually, begrudgingly, wished me a Merry Christmas and then was on his way. As I took a moment to collect my thoughts in the frigid air, a young lad, probably about six or seven, trundled past me on what was, no doubt, a new Christmas bike and I smiled at him as I said,

'Merry Christmas!'

'Fuck you, paedo!' he responded and pedalled off toward the play area. Yeah, that as well, I thought as I headed once more toward the entrance of the block of flats. By the time I got back upstairs and into Shelly's flat, Grace was making more tea and Beth was helping, arranging cups on a tray already holding a plate of biscuits that had been magicked up from somewhere.

'She was pregnant,' Grace said when we'd all taken our seats again in the living room and I stared at her blankly,

'I don't know what you're………'

'Shelly. She was pregnant when it happened. When Bethnal Green happened.'

'No,' I replied immediately, 'that's not true.'

'It is. She didn't know - not until a few weeks later and, by then she'd left, which is why your Granddad didn't know.' She picked up her cup but only held it in both hands without drinking it. 'By the time she found out, she was here and,' she reached into her handbag which was nestled on the armchair beside her and fished out a packet of cigarettes and a plastic lighter, shooting Beth an apologetic look as she lit up, 'About seven months later, I was born, just down the road at Kingston Hospital.'

'No,' I interrupted, 'you're lying. We saw her - when I was a kid at Granddad's funeral. She didn't have a kid.' Grace shrugged and tapped her ash into a short stout plant-pot on the table in front of her,

'I was with a neighbour that day. None of you knew about me because she didn't *want* you to know about me. Because she didn't want anything to do with that lot. Apart from you, of course.' She seemed to consider this for a moment then, 'I think she wanted me and you to meet - I mean, before now, but she knew your Mum and Dad would be against it.'

'They would,' I said faintly, still trying to take in the fact that everything I knew about Grandma Shelly had just been re-written in the space of ten minutes.

'Your Dad hated her,' she stated as though it were simply a fact and I shook my head,

'It's not that simple, she....' I opened my hands in a gesture of helplessness, 'She abandoned him. I know that she was grief-stricken after losing Nancy but she still had another kid - my Dad - and she walked out on him. Can you imagine how that made him feel?'

'No,' she said, 'and that's the truth but,' she finally took a sip of the tea she was holding, 'You need to understand where her head was at back then - she thought he'd be better off without her; she thought *everyone* would be better off.' I shrugged,

'Sure, I understand that, at first, but what about after? What about all those years that passed before she even got in touch?' She leaned forward and stubbed out her cigarette,

'I'm not here to justify anything or to ask your forgiveness, just to tell you the way it was. Now she's gone, I thought it might, you know, be important'.

'It's not,' I said and then regretted it - I was entitled to my outrage on behalf of Dad but I realised that, if Grace was telling the truth, then I was talking about the mother she'd just lost.

'Sorry, I just need a bit of time to get my head around all this.' She nodded,

'Course. I'll get you a taxi in a minute. The funeral won't be for a few weeks - unusual circumstances and all that - so I'll give you a call and we can talk again.' She got up from her chair and walked slowly toward the old fashioned telephone in the corner and I glanced over at Beth who hadn't said a word during the whole conversation but was, I knew, taking everything in as she sat silently watching us.

'He'll be here in five minutes,' Grace said as she hung up the phone and then, without another word, she walked out of the flat, into her own and I heard the door close behind her. Realising that my first visit with my newly found Aunt was over, I quickly washed up our cups and got myself and Beth into our coats before going back outside to wait for the taxi. As we waited, I was grateful for the freezing air which helped prevent my brain from over-heating with all the new data it had just been subjected to. The journey back was as uneventful as before and Beth was quiet, gazing out of the window as a few flakes of snow began to fall as though to remind us that it was Christmas.

'Been visiting family?' our driver asked as we pulled out of the street and I laughed out loud,

'Yeah, something like that.' For the rest of the journey, I sat back and let the driver's words wash over me as he told me about his family back in Slovakia and how they would be spending their special day. Finally, we were pulling up outside the flat and, with an empty wallet and a head full of questions, I gratefully let us in and wandered through to the kitchen to fix something to eat (and myself a large drink) noticing that I hadn't gotten around to phoning somebody about the window. As I sat down with my drink I noticed that I had a missed call from Mum and chuckled softly to myself, wondering how the hell I was going to even begin to tell her and Dad about the afternoon that Beth and I had just had.

'It's nearly time, Will,' Beth suddenly said into the quiet of the room and I sighed inwardly, wanting nothing more than to have a couple of drinks and possibly fall asleep in front of "It's A Wonderful Life".

'Everything's fine, Beth,' I said feeling suddenly exhausted by the events of the day.

'Yes, but it's nearly time.' Although, this time, I registered that there was a sadness in her voice, it suddenly seemed to be coming from so far away that I nodded and heard myself tell her again that everything was going to be alright as I realised that my eyes were already closing and that I was powerless to stop them. When I opened them again, it felt like only seconds had passed but the room was dark and Beth was gone. Again.

CHAPTER 47

It's been a week since Mum and Dad left Grange to go back to London and, every day, I wonder what it would have been like if I'd gone with them - would people still remember and, if they did, would they still care? By "people" I do, of course, mainly mean the press; the so called professionals who incited the public to first worship Beth and then to vilify her, and me. The same people who paid Shandy for an exclusive on her "life with the Bethnal Green fraud" in which she detailed what a monster I was and how badly I treated her during our "romance". I suppose I can't blame her really - she was already mad with me and so I imagine the opportunity to not just slag me off but to also get paid a huge sum for the privilege was just too good to turn down. There had been one magazine - a monthly called "Our Times" who had contacted me shortly before I left London and, although I declined to be interviewed, they still went ahead with their article pointing out that I too had been duped by Beth and speculating on who may have been behind the little girl's deception. Although I appreciated even just one publication being on my side, I was in no fit state to participate and I left before the magazine hit the shelves, hiding away while imagining the press still hanging around the driveway of the flat I left behind. Surprisingly, that night at L'Enclume, although sad that I had no plans to return, Mum had been quite enthusiastic about my idea about a job on the local train line here and even offered to buy me a suit to wear for an interview which made me smile as I still have a fair bit of Spencer's cash stashed away in my account - that sort of wad goes a surprisingly long way when you rent a small room and don't spend money on anything much apart from food, books and the odd six pack of lager. But, of course, that conversation with Mum then,inevitably, led onto the other thing.

'Have you ever, you know, thought about doing something about it?' Mum had asked. We were on dessert by that point (some poncy citrus thing made with foam and burnt sugar) and I'd laughed,

'I was wondering when you were going to ask, Mum,' I said, 'but no, I haven't as I think it'd make me look like a bit of a prat.'

'Oh, I don't know....' Mum began as she sipped her coffee but I could tell that she knew that I was right. You see, I know I've mentioned a couple of times that, during the whole Beth thing, I was overdue a haircut and I have had one since - several in fact as I now tend to keep it military short and get irritated at even a couple of weeks worth of growth. You see, that day - that last day - changed me; changed everything really and, when I woke up the next day, my hair had turned completely white.

CHAPTER 48

When I woke up to an empty room I wasn't unduly alarmed. Although I didn't feel like I had slept exactly, I had the woozy, disoriented feeling of having nodded off unexpectedly and I rubbed my eyes and sat up. I figured that Beth had just fancied some time to herself and, God knows, I could understand that after the last few days. I glanced at the clock on the wall opposite and saw that it had just gone six and I blinked at it; if I hadn't been asleep then I'd somehow zoned out for about an hour and a half and I bolted upright as I called Beth's name. A quick check of the the bedroom and bathroom confirmed that she wasn't there and I ran to the hallway which was also empty but I saw with a sinking feeling that the front door was wide open. Although I had warned Beth, repeatedly, about opening the front door, there was really no explanation other than Beth had wandered outside; Graham wouldn't be back from his folks place yet and I was pretty sure I hadn't opened it while I was zonked out. Quickly grabbing a fleece and my keys, I ran down the hallway and outside, slamming the door behind me as I ran out onto the pavement. At first I saw nothing; literally, it was six o'clock on Christmas evening and I was guessing that, behind all the doors in my street, people were either in a stupor from too much booze or sleeping off an indulgent lunch but then I saw her. To begin with, I wondered how I could possibly have missed her, standing as she was, right in the middle of the road at the top of the street but then I realised that I hadn't missed her, she simply hadn't been there until that moment. So far away, I only recognised her from the blonde hair and the bright red pop of her coat but, even from where I was standing, I could see that she was standing perfectly still in the middle of the road at the junction of Queensbridge Road and I was just thankful that the festive holiday meant that there were no cars on the road that I could see at that time. I called her name again and she didn't respond, turn her head or, in fact, give any indication that she could hear me, just continued to stare straight ahead and I set off at a jog toward where she was standing. Like in a dream - or nightmare - no matter how far I ran, Beth only seemed to get further away and I picked up my pace until I was at a full on sprint but still she seemed to just keep slipping further away. I called out again as I felt sweat start to stream down my back (I wasn't, and am not, exactly what you'd call a gym bunny) and I longed to rip off the fleece which felt like it was suffocating me. I was just about to yell her name again (or drop dead with a coronary) when, suddenly, she was right in front of me, standing stock still with that semi-smile of hers and I took a minute to catch my breath and take off my jumper. As I pulled the fleece off the top of my head, emerging from its stuffy woolly depths back into the freezing air, I realised that we were no longer standing at the end of my road but directly outside Bethnal Green Station. The station was, of course, closed (and would be running only a limited service the following day, Boxing Day) with the metal grills pulled across both the street entrance and the entrance to the steps. Across the road, I could just see the upper part of the memorial above the park fence, the top of the stairway sparkling with the frost that had settled on it during the day and I imagined that, untouched, it probably covered the whole memorial, finding it unlikely that anybody would be visiting to pay their respects on Christmas Day. Just up the road, toward the City View, I could see a homeless bloke wrapped in a sleeping bag in a shop doorway but, otherwise, it seemed that the street, maybe even the whole of the East End, was deserted, the litter of Christmas Eve's festivities still lining the street where it would stay until the day after Boxing Day when the East End would start to crank back up to its usual routines.

'What are we doing here, Beth?' I asked softly and she turned to face me, specks of snow dotting her red coat as it began to fall again and she smiled sadly as she said,

'They said I couldn't bring my doll.'

'Who said, Beth?' I asked but it was as though she didn't hear me as she repeated,

'They said I couldn't bring Flossy.' then, 'She doesn't belong there.' As her gaze returned to the steps, a fear gripped me and I grabbed for her hand, afraid that she might vanish again.

'You don't belong there either,' I shouted, my voice loud in the empty street and I lowered it as I added,

'Come on. Let's go home and get Flossy, shall we?' Her only response was another sad smile and her hand slipped out of the tight grip of mine like water.as she turned and began to cross the road toward the park, her steps so light that they didn't even disturb the two pigeons that were fighting over the remains of someone's Christmas Eve kebab and I hurried after her, grateful once again that there was no traffic. Once across the road, I followed Beth into Bethnal Green Gardens which looked as though they had been part of the same Christmas Eve party as the street that ran alongside it. Beth was standing in front of the memorial which, having benefited from some serious fundraising that year, was almost complete and, as I stood beside her, the names on the stairway part seemed to glow in the early evening darkness, all seventy three of them but there was one that shone brighter than the others, Annie Drinkwater, age five.

'We're all here,' Beth said quietly, 'And we'll still be here but somewhere else too. It's time.' I'd tried wheedling, using her doll as a lure, and that hadn't worked so now I decided to try another tack.

'Let's just stop this now, Beth, it's cold out here - and dark - and we should be at home. Let's go.' I reached again for her hand and she shook her head, a firm but forlorn gesture and then stepped forward to place a hand on the long flat part of the memorial that runs along the ground. As she ran her hand along one of the long thin etched metal plaques, I heard voices, silvery whispers that seemed to come from everywhere and then converged to echo around the memorial before disappearing.

'Don't forget me, Will,' she said and then stepped lightly onto the platform of the memorial, pirouetting to face me as though she were about to start to dance and then she grinned as she raised one hand and swept it over her head, producing a rainbow of light, inside which, images flashed. I stepped forward to get a closer look and the images slowed and I gasped as I realised what it was I was seeing. Transfixed, I stood and watched as Grandma Shelly walked down the aisle, glowing in a simple white shift dress, to meet my Grand-dad who was waiting for her, then as she cradled a new-born, proud and happy, and then another, a bit more tired but still radiant. Then there was a different Shelly. This one wore black and sat in the corner of a messy sitting room, staring into space as a toddler ran amok in the gloomy space, then she was in a bathroom, holding a bottle of pills as she stared blankly at her own expression in the tiny mirror above the sink. I got it, I didn't need to see more. As though I'd said this out loud, the picture suddenly changed and this time it was me but, a me many years from now and I was surrounded by people, Mum, Dad, a woman and little boy that I didn't recognise and there, smiling shyly to one side was Grace, looking older and frailer but happy. I wanted to linger on this one, fascinated by the pretty brunette and impish looking little boy by my side but they began to fade and, a second or two later, were replaced by, I suspect, what it was that Beth really wanted me to see. In this scene there was only one person, a woman and one that I recognised instantly, not from my lifetime but from another of Beth's "visions". I watched closely as Beth's mother first walked the streets of Bethnal Green, clothes in rags as she pounded the pavement calling for her daughter. Then the rapid decline into alcoholism and madness, rough men taking advantage when she was either unable to fight them off or just simply didn't care and then a body in a gutter like a bunch of old rags.

'She's waiting,' Beth said and then repeated, 'Don't forget me Will.' I had a million questions, not all of which were based on the Beth version of Christmas past and future that I'd just seen but I struggled to articulate them as she smiled at me from the slightly raised perspective of the plinth.

'I wouldn't ever, Beth, but there's no need; you can stay!' But of course, she couldn't, I knew that then - had known it since "She's waiting" and I forced a smile.

'I'll look after Flossy,' I said and she giggled,

'You better and Peppa!'

'Every day,' I smiled, 'But Beth........' I had no idea what it was that I was about to say and it didn't matter because she was gone. Somewhere between the first word and the second, Beth turned her back on me, walked toward the tall hooded staircase feature and vanished. This time for good.

CHAPTER 49

I don't know how long I stood there that day. Christmas Day. I know that it was long enough that my fingers turned to useless lumps of ice and my feet inside their cheap trainers felt so brittle with cold that I thought they would snap if I made any sudden movements. In the end, it wasn't the cold that forced me to reluctantly leave that place but simply the slow realisation that she wasn't coming back and eventually, in something like a state of shock, I shuffled out of the park, head down against the snow that was now falling harder and slowly made the long walk back to Hackney, constantly glancing down and to my left as I kept forgetting that she was no longer there. When I arrived back at my flat, a couple of the reporters were back and, spotting me, they immediately began raising their cameras and shouting questions, their eager pushiness turning to expressions of confusion as they saw that I was alone. I'm pretty sure that the expression I was sporting at the time was not dissimilar as I struggled to comprehend what had just happened and how it was going to impact on my life as I was beginning to know it. Ignoring the media's questions, I pushed past them and into the flat, gratefully pouring myself a large drink and turning the space heater on full blast. If I was thinking at all at that point, and I'm not sure that I was, it was about what I was going to tell people; how I was going to explain that Beth was here and then she wasn't. I knew that there was a possibility that I would be arrested and I examined this idea not with fear but a kind of idle curiosity - they would think that I'd done something to her, got rid of her in some evil way out of anger, calculation or madness and I was starting to think that the latter was probably the one they'd go for. Already, as I stood in front of the heater, I knew that the reporters outside would be firing at the ozone with their mobile phones, desperately trying to find out if I'd left Beth with family, friends or maybe dumped her back onto social services. I fired up my laptop to see that me and Beth were still the number one trending story, interspersed with a million people's phony hopes for a great Christmas for all their friends and family and, if possible, peace on Earth - at least until they've had a few more drinks and started feuding with the in-laws. The London Online site who were clearly the most on the ball, even on Christmas Day, had a few photos, taken from a distance of me running up my street like a madman and then, what appeared to be a few shots of me standing at the top of the road talking to myself. As I said, if it came to the law, I suspected that madness would be their obvious choice and I wondered if I ought to be pre-empting things by getting in touch with a solicitor although, it seemed that person would have their work cut out with first the lawsuits already received and now this. As much as I didn't want to, I knew that I had to call Mum and, having warmed up (a combination of a large whiskey and the heater) enough to take off my fleece, I reached for my mobile which I'd dumped onto the coffee table. I'd barely closed my hand around it when it began to ring and I saw with no real surprise that it was Mum, racking up her roaming charges from Spain, after all, with everything that had happened, would it really be so weird that she would already know? I hit receive and said hello but Mum was already speaking even as the call was connected, agitation and something else making her voice sound strained and urgent.

'Oh, Will, I don't believe it. It's just so awful!'

'I know Mum, but it'll be ok. I'll explain properly when I see you.' There was a pause that, knowing Mum as I did, was way longer than it should have been then, quietly,

'What do you mean, Will. How will it be OK? How can it?' I sighed,

'I know it's difficult to take in right now but Mum, it was true - it was all true and now she's gone. All I know is that It was her decision and it's for the best.' We had another of those pauses and, when Mum spoke again, the panic in her voice was gone but it had been replaced by a quiet cautious tone that I liked even less.

'We're coming home Will. They're going to blame you for this and we need to be there with you.' A shaky sigh made its way down the line and then she said,

'I'm sorry that she's dead, Will, I really am, but she brought it on herself didn't she?' For a moment, I said nothing as I tried to process what she had just said, running it back through my head to see if it made any sense a second time around but it didn't. I was about to ask what she was on about when I was struck by a sudden intuition and I grabbed the TV remote and turned it on, finding what I was looking for immediately as I flicked to the first news channel. Although I couldn't, initially, focus on the text that was shooting across the bottom of the screen, it wasn't hard to get the gist of the general story as the screen behind the perma-tanned newsreader was all but taken up by a large head and shoulders photograph and, below it, the word "Suicide" in a type so large that even the partially blind could read it. As though the news had filtered through that I'd finally got with the program, my landline began to ring at exactly the same time as I heard a pounding on the front door, both things no doubt reporters eager to get my comment on the latest crisis to hit my erstwhile dull and ordinary life.

'Will, are you still there?' In my shock, I'd almost forgotten that Mum was on the line and I quickly put the phone back to my ear, never taking my eyes off the television and JoJo's picture as I said,

'Yes, Mum. I think you should come home.'

CHAPTER 50

It was the guilt, she said in her note. The guilt of starting the chain of events that led to a nation believing for the first time in years in a genuine miracle, only then to have it snatched away from them within a matter of weeks. Josephine "JoJo's' mother was on every channel, tearfully telling the world that her daughter lived to help people and, having found out that she'd been duped, couldn't live with the shame of what she'd started. I watched all of the footage sympathetically, after all, guilt was something that I could relate to - the guilt of not being able to make Beth stay, guilt at what I'd put Mum and Dad through and, now, the guilt of knowing that if JoJo had known what I now knew about Beth, she'd still be with us, updating her Facebook page and moving on from the disciplinary action that followed her initial ill-advised posts about Beth. I had wanted to meet Mum and Dad at the airport but, always the voice of reason, Mum had argued that all I would be doing would be to bring the press to an open public space where they could photograph the three of us to their hearts content and so I stayed at home, brooding and pacing the small space while I waited for the call to tell me that they were home. The internet frenzy regarding JoJo was such that it wasn't until about three hours after the news had broken that the first hashtag - #whereisbethgreen? began to do the rounds, picking up momentum as it went until it inevitably topped the trending charts. It would be really nice, I thought as I waited for the call, when the day finally arrived when the top trending story was about some vacuous celebrity or a prayer for whatever country the latest atrocity had occurred in. Ah, the good old days. Mum and Dad's flight was, of course, delayed and so, by the time the call did arrive, I'd practically worn a groove in my carpet and it was a relief to stop pacing and call a cab to take me away from that flat and from the inside of my own head for a while. When I got there, Mum and Dad didn't seem to have unpacked anything apart from a large stuffed donkey wearing a sombrero which lay lopsided on one of the armchairs and jarred badly with their matching expressions of anxious confusion.

'Where's.......? What have you......?' Giving up on the attempt for a full sentence, Mum grabbed me while Dad waited his turn.

'Firstly,' I said, 'I didn't do anything to my hair, it just sort of happened. Secondly,' I tried for a grin which made it about half-way, 'On the "where's Beth" conversation, I'll tell you everything but, any chance of a cup of tea first?' I'd told myself that, once I'd told them everything, we'd all go to the police together - before they got wind of the whole thing themselves and decided to come calling, thus putting me immediately on the back foot but, one look at their tired, worried faces was enough to convince me that, whatever the end of this story was going to be, it was going to involve nobody but myself. We had the tea that I'd asked for and then Dad opened a bottle of the Rioja that they'd brought back with them, then another and, by the time that we'd done the second bottle, it was decided that I would stay the night. As it was, we had a really nice night - lots of talking and laughing and tentative discussions about the possibility of Mum and Dad joining the Hiddlestones in Spain for good and, although I wasn't admitting it to myself at the time, it was a kind of goodbye.

The following morning, I walked myself into Stoke Newington police station and told them I wanted to make a statement about a child known to me as Beth Green. I didn't, of course, tell them the complete truth - I wasn't quite that far gone yet - instead, sitting in a poky little room with the world's worst cup of coffee, I told a WPC Tanya Dawes that I had been at home with Beth the previous evening when a woman claiming to be Beth's mother, turned up on my doorstep and snatched Beth from my clutches. I told WCP Dawes that, although this was against my will, Beth had seemed happy to go and that I didn't believe that the woman posed a risk to the child. Once I had all that off my chest, a report was filed and I was given copies of various pieces of documentation along with phone numbers that I could call day and night for updates on the investigation. That done, I walked out of the police station and back to my flat, stopping only long enough to pack one bag with the bare essentials and another full of Beth's stuff, then I dumped the second bag outside a charity shop before jumping on a tube to Euston then a train to Grange Over Sands; somewhere that I'd been to only once before on an ill-planned stag weekend and which seemed suitably random and obscure for my purposes. It was in this place that I finally was able to breathe and, within a few days, I'd found a room to rent and even a job which, although not great, served its purpose in occupying my time and stopping me from thinking too much. Stopping thinking was always the main goal but first I knew I had to do this - write everything down and tell the story once and for all in the hope that, in doing so, the world would finally stop looking for me and I would finally be able to write "the end" both physically and metaphorically and so that's exactly what happened.

CHAPTER 51

Well, almost.

In the months after I moved away from London, the idea was to move on and, in order to do that, I had to try to consign everything that happened to the back of my mind but, something kept niggling at me, invading my thoughts at odd times in a surprisingly persistent way. I tell myself that it wasn't Beth putting these thoughts into my head as that's a bit new agey for my liking but, at the same time, I can't say with all honesty, that it wasn't. After waking at three o'clock in the morning for the second night running with the thought stuck in my head, I decided that the only way to exorcise it would be to investigate it so, the following morning, no longer having a computer of my own, I set off for the local library which sported a grand total of three terminals for customer use. In the end, I was there for my whole allotted two hours that day, and the day after, and the day after that. All in all, it took me just under two weeks and, when I finally found what I was looking for, and then did a few more checks just to be certain, I sat there blinking at the computer, not quite able to believe what I was seeing. I had set out to find out about Ellen and her black baby - the family event that Beth had been forbidden to talk about some decades before I was born and, after a few false starts and wrong turns, I had done just that. During my time-consuming and often frustrating research, I learned that after being made to leave the family home, Ellen Drinkwater, unmarried and without a job, had tried her hand, briefly, at her mother's profession but that career plan was aborted early on. From what I could gather, she and her son moved around a lot, staying with various friends and shady acquaintances until, around 1948, she met and married a carpenter from Camberwell and they raised her son together. From there it got a bit easier as the war was over and more records were available and I saw that Beth's sister, now Ellen Lawson, stayed in Camberwell until her husband's death in 1992 and her own in 1998. The surprises started when I saw that her son, Nathaniel, went to Oxford University on leaving school and, after a brief stint at teaching English back in the East End, wrote a book that most people I know have either read or have sitting on their book shelves at home. The book was called "Black Sheep Of The Family" and, having never read it myself, I went straight to the biography section of the library afterwards and took it out on loan; reading the whole thing in one sitting, reduced to tears of laughter at some of the descriptions of his childhood and then the other kind as he described how his mother, although generally a happy woman, spent her whole life consumed with grief at the death of her younger sister, Annie Drinkwater, at the age of five, on the steps of Bethnal Green station.

I briefly thought about contacting Nathaniel Lawson but dismissed the idea immediately; he would know who I was and what had been said about me and I had no illusions that I would be able to convince him that some of these things - most of these things - weren't true and so I left it alone. I carried on with my new life and resisted every time somebody, usually Mum, told me that it was time to come home - that the East End is part of who I am. I remembered that day in Bethnal Green Gardens, the woman from Manhattan at the memorial telling me that Bethnal Green was "a place, just like any other" and I've decided that she was right.

And so, I think that's it. I can't tell you where Beth is now or, whether I'll ever see her again, although the answer to the latter is that I hope so. Grandma Shelly once asked me why Beth was here and, at the time I wasn't able to answer but now I think I can. Now I know what happened to Beth, and why. I know what happened to those that she left behind and I know what happened to Ellen and her baby. I think that's it.

THE END 29/7/16

Just The Facts

On 3rd May 1943, an air-raid Civil Defence siren was heard in London at 8:17 pm, triggering a heavy but orderly flow of people down the blacked-out staircase of Bethnal Green station from the street.

A middle-aged woman and a child fell over, three steps up from the base and others fell around her, tangled in an immovable mass which grew, as they struggled, to nearly 300 people. Some managed to get free but 173, most of them women and children, were crushed and asphyxiated. Some 60 others were taken to hospital. News of the disaster was withheld for 36 hours and reporting of what had happened was censored, giving rise to allegations of a cover-up, although it was in line with existing wartime reporting restrictions.

Although parts of this novel are based on factual events, Beth Green is a work of fiction.

For more information on the Bethnal Green memorial, or to make a donation, go to:
https://www.facebook.com/bethnalgreenmemorial/

The Daily Express. 4th March 1943

Russians announce: "Rzhev captured after fierce battle"   *Hitler's capital has no light, gas, water*

AFTER RZHEV—OREL
New evacuation report

Berlin still burns, London gets brief reprisal

Express Raid Reporters

GOERING sent a small force of "reprisal" bombers to London last night as Berlin—without gas, water and electricity—still burned after its heaviest ever R.A.F. raid on Monday night.

AND IF SMOLENSK GOES TOO—

Express Military Reporter

THE German High Command keeping on the defensive of Rzhev last have drawn their...

'STALINGRAD' FEAR

GIVEN UP

Russians capture big booty: Germans burning villages

From E. D. MASTERMAN

STOCKHOLM, Wednesday Night.

A SPECIAL Moscow communiqué to-night says that the Red Army captured Rzhev, the German hedgehog fortress facing Moscow, after days of furious fighting, and that great booty was taken.

The Germans, anticipating the announcement by eight hours, said Rzhev was evacuated according to plan and to the complete surprise of the Russians.

Unofficial news from Moscow tonight is that the Germans are now evacuating Orel, and it is believed that Stanislaus that a great new Russian offensive is under way on this central front.

New thrust

100 MILES

IT WAS VITAL

BOY WITH A V.C.

THIRD OF PANZERS LOST IN TUNISIA

By MORLEY RICHARDS

GENERAL ANDERSON'S First Army and the American fighting in Central Tunisia have between them knocked out at least a third of the total tank strength of the Axis in North Africa.

First action

All repulsed

AIR RAID ON ONE STONE HUT

We hit Hitler's molybdenum

Express Air Reporter

MOSQUITOS bombed yesterday afternoon one of the weirdest targets of the war: a small concrete building on a molehill above a lake in Norway.

Next three months vital in Atlantic

By W. R. CROMLEY

The 1943 frigate

Commons lose all powers

Until new Speaker is chosen

By GUY EDEN

TODAY Britain has a Parliament without constitutional powers to make new laws.

Persecution conference

HOARE FLIES TO SPELLMAN

'Hitler is arms designer'

HE GOT FOUR

In 20 minutes

Spanish chief is home from Russia

THANKS—BY STALIN

THE BELLS

They may ring for sea invasion, too

4 A.M. LATEST

STALINGRAD HIT HITLER'S PLANS'
—Nazi General

Hanging by feet

Pioneers drop spades to grab rifles, and—

'OLD SWEATS' HOLD TUNISIA GAP

WITH THE FIRST ARMY IN TUNISIA, Wednesday.

'STICK THERE'

Beaten German general says

100 TO 1 AGAINST

Dachau bosses killed

EARLY SUMMER

Discontinued

Cardinal Hinsley

Finn Premier fails

Jap riot: Germans threaten reprisals

Swiss may lift ban

Bevin wants dockers to leave docks

By TREVOR EVANS

'R.A.F. is dropping railway tickets'

Printed in Great Britain
by Amazon